A BARGAIN
WITH THE
SHADOW
PRINCE

A BARGAIN WITH THE SHADOW PRINCE

USA TODAY BESTSELLING AUTHOR

GENEVIEVE JACK

A Bargain With the Shadow Prince: A Bargain With the Shadow Prince Book 1

ABOUT THIS BOOK

It takes a monster to stop a monster.
Light the candle.
Stand naked before the symbol.
Offer your blood.
The advocate will come.

I left my abusive crime boss husband expecting to start over from nothing. After all, the prenup I signed when I married him is ironclad. But when Tony uses a loophole in the law to go after my ancestral family home—the one I'm currently living in and my grandmother is dying in— I'm desperate to stop him.

My witch best friend Maeve offers a solution. She lends me a family spell to call a supernatural advocate to deal with Tony. After all, it takes a monster to stop a monster.

But when I follow her instructions, I'm not expecting the darkly handsome Damien to form from the shadows, or to learn that he's been a prisoner of Maeve's family for centuries. From the moment he accepts my bargain and drinks my blood, he awakens a passion in me, one charged with latent magic. Magic formidable enough to restore my true self. Magic that holds the promise of Damien's freedom.

I

SOULLESS

ELOISE

My attorney's nail polish is the same color as her hair, a shiny black called Soulless made by Skull and Thistle, a beauty brand that caters to a woman's inner goth. I know this because Maeve Gowdie, Esq. is also my best friend, and I saw the bottle of polish the night I was curled in the fetal position on her floor. At the time, I thought things couldn't get any worse than having to move in with my grandmother to escape my abusive husband.

I was wrong.

"Can you repeat that?" I heard her well enough but don't want to believe what she's saying.

"Tony wants the house, Eloise. *Your* house. Harcourt Manor."

My eyelashes flutter like dying butterflies against my cheeks, and a tiny muscle below my right eye starts to twitch. Has all the air left the room? My necklace is suffocating me. With trembling fingers, I slide the drop pearl back and forth along its chain, making room between it and my throat. "That *can't* be right. That house belongs to my grams."

"Not legally, it doesn't." From her leather chair behind an enormous walnut desk, Maeve retrieves some paperwork, the skeleton mermaid tattoo on her arm swimming with her movement. She turns a page toward me. "When your parents were killed, you were named beneficiary of the property, but you were under eighteen, so your grandmother took ownership as your legal guardian. The title reverted to you on your eighteenth birthday, even though your grams continued living there and you did not. Ordinarily, under Virginia law, inherited property isn't considered marital property, but Tony made substantial renovations."

"But—but he insisted!" I protest. "A freak sinkhole threatened the foundation. Our neighbor's house was condemned because of it. I didn't even ask Tony for help —I wasn't even living with Grams at the time to understand the extent of it. He just had it fixed. The workers had to bring in heavy machinery to make it safe again."

"Well, that heavy machinery was expensive, and because Tony substantially contributed to the property's value, he can now claim it as marital property. The bastard wants it, El. And one of his lawyers told me he's willing to go the distance. This is heading to court unless you can buy out his share of the property."

"Which is?"

"Five hundred thousand."

A strangled squeak escapes my throat. It's like I've reached the end of a rollercoaster, rattled and nauseated, only to find the lap bar is stuck, and the attendant says I'll have to ride again. I grip the armrests of my chair until my knuckles turn white and send a pleading glance across the desk to Maeve. "How is that possible?"

"Property values have increased considerably since your great-grandparents settled in Echo Mills, especially on the river."

I clear my throat. "I don't have that kind of money."

From behind the thick rim of her glasses, Maeve's dark gaze flicks to the corner of her office. Her voice is soft as she says, "I know."

She understands better than anyone. I'm broke. Tony is loaded, and we'd shared an account when we were married, but I no longer have access to a dime of that money thanks to an ironclad prenuptial agreement he insisted I sign. I can't even afford Maeve. She's representing me pro bono. I'm also unemployed, thanks to Tony. He made me quit my job as an art teacher six months into our marriage to "focus on managing the household." What a joke. We have no children. We don't even have a dog. But I quit in an attempt to be someone he could love. Turns out nothing could fix what was broken between us.

It's been a week since I left and moved in with Grams. Harcourt Manor is the only reason I'm not sleeping on the street. Now he wants to take that too.

My heart thumps faster. This is happening. Tony— cheated-with-his-secretary Tony, struck-me-*twice* Tony, dominated-the-last-two-years-of-my-life Tony— is rearing his reptile fangs and attempting to snatch my ancestral home right out from under me.

I scoot to the edge of my chair and rest my wrists on

her desk. My hands are trembling so violently, I have to couple them like I'm about to pray. Honestly, that's exactly what I should be doing. "I *can't* move my grandmother. It's not an option."

Maeve sets down her pen and leans across the desk to cradle my fingers in hers. "I know this is awful, El. Your grams has lived in that house her entire life. I remember her stories about giving birth to your father in one of the guest rooms."

"I was the first child born in a hospital."

She licks her bottom lip. "This isn't fair. But if Tony wins the property, he has to pay *you* for your portion. You and Grams could get a nice place for 500K."

"It's not just that." Denial is a comfort I can no longer afford, and I spill the news I haven't been able to bring myself to tell her until now. "The cancer is back, and it's in her bones. Grams is dying. She started in-home hospice this week."

Maeve's already pale complexion turns ashen. "Oh, Eloise..."

Tears well and spill over my lower lashes, even though I hold my breath in an attempt to control them. Frantically, Maeve tugs tissues from the box on her desk and hands me the wad. I bury my face in them. When I speak again, I have to force the words past the massive lump in my throat. "If it were just me, I'd leave. I love the place, and it would kill me to lose that connection to my parents, but I'd survive. Grams... she wants to die there. She wants to be buried next to my parents in the family cemetery. I won't let him take that from her. Please tell me there's a way to stop him."

Maeve's expression shifts into the determined, more

than a little intimidating one I've come to love over the years we've been friends. She's scary as hell when she wants to be and not just because she looks like the spawn of Wednesday Addams and Machine Gun Kelly. Her normally chocolate-colored eyes turn as dark as her nails with her anger. I hug myself against a sudden chill and cast a glance toward the window. A storm has moved in.

It's always this way with Maeve.

"Answer me honestly." She glares at me. "Does Tony know your grams is sick?"

I chew my lip. "He does. The cancer came back a few months ago, although Grams didn't tell me until recently how serious it was. I paid a few of her medical bills from our joint account before I moved out, stuff that wasn't covered by Medicare." I give a sarcastic snort. "God, please don't tell me that gives him a right to half of her too."

Maeve bristles at my dark humor. "Fuck, I hate that guy. I really do."

I blot my face with the mass of tissues. "I know."

She wrinkles her nose. "Do you? Because I tried to hide it before. Even when you started wearing..." She gestures toward my dress.

I sniff. "What's wrong with what I'm wearing?"

She touches the tip of her tongue to the corner of her blood-red lips. "It's just a lot of beige, hon." Beige with tiny flowers that match the darker beige of my pumps. Her attention darts to my bleached hair and then down to my ballet pink nail polish. "The hair, the nails." The way her head tilts and her eyes narrow makes me feel like an abandoned, flea-ridden kitten. "The pearls."

Indignant, I raise my chin a full inch. "I'll have you

know this shade of nail polish was a favorite of the Queen of England. It's very sophisticated. And pearls never go out of style."

"The queen died years ago… at the age of ninety-six. You're twenty-five." Maeve folds her arms. "You wouldn't have been caught dead in that before you met him."

She has a point. Over the years I was with Tony, I changed almost every aspect of myself to meet his standards, including my wardrobe. It was never enough. "I appreciate your help. I really do. But the last thing I'm worried about at the moment is my outfit."

"Right." She drums her fingers on her biceps. "He's just taken so much from you. I can't remember the last time I saw you smile. And your art. How long has it been since you painted anything? The gall of that man. When I think about the woman you were when you met him—"

She's right about the smile and the art, but that's not the whole story. "I was a kid with a death wish. Tony took me under his wing and forced me to get serious about my life. If it wasn't for him, I probably wouldn't have my teaching degree."

"You would have done fine without him. You were an accomplished artist by then—one big break from being as big as your mom."

"It's true I had a bright future as an artist before my parents died. But Tony made me see how impractical a career in the arts is. Besides, I could barely pick up a paintbrush from grief after I lost them. A teaching degree just made more sense."

"And if it wasn't for him, you'd still be using it," she snaps. I shrink at the harsh truth and her face softens. "I'm just appalled on your behalf."

"I know." I blink back another onslaught of tears. "Just tell me what can be done about the house."

She reclines in her leather chair, elbows on the armrests and fingers steepled over her lap. A dark queen on her throne. "There are a few legal avenues I can try, but honestly, your best bet would be to convince him to back off. Can you confront him? Maybe guilt him into letting the house go?"

"I don't think it would end well." I hug myself against an inner quake that leaves me clammy.

"You think he'll hit you again."

"Tony doesn't like to be confronted. He almost broke my jaw while we were married. I hate to think what he'd do now that we're getting divorced. I won't rule out trying, but I'd be lying if I said he doesn't scare me."

"Fucking asshole." Maeve heaves a deep sigh. "Any way to manipulate him? Got any dirt on the bastard?"

"Nothing I can prove." She shoots me a knowing glance. Maeve has long suspected Tony is involved with organized crime, but if he is, he never admitted as much to me, even when things were good.

She sighs. "Then I think there's only one way to guarantee Tony doesn't win Harcourt Manor."

"How?"

"Magic." I swear I see her eyes twinkle behind her glasses.

What? "Magic?" The word comes out strangled. Is she joking?

She leans toward me. "Come on, Eloise. You must have suspected over the years. That time we went camping and it rained on everyone else's tent but ours. Our grades on that calculus exam neither of us studied for. The tea I gave you that helped you lose five pounds the night before your wedding."

I inhale sharply. All those things were weird but... "Are you implying that *you* made those things happen?"

She gathers her raven black hair into a twist, holds it in place with one hand as her other forms an L with her thumb and forefinger and circles the knot three times. When she removes her hands and turns so I can see, it's secured in a perfect updo without the benefit of a single hairpin.

My heart jackhammers in my chest as I try to deny what is right in front of me, while knowing in my heart that it *is* the truth. Knowing in the back of my mind that I suspected... maybe not magic, but *something*. Knowing, like everything else today, that this is really happening. "Why didn't you tell me?"

"Why didn't you ask?" Maeve smooths her hand along the edge of the desk. "Goddess knows, it wouldn't have been the craziest question you've ever asked me."

"So, you're a..." I can't say it.

"A witch."

"Like a Wiccan or something?" I try to get my head around it and can't. I think of witches the same way I do Tibetan monks. I know they exist, but I've never actually met one. At least I thought I hadn't before today. And aside from a few suspect videos I've watched online, I have no reason to believe the ones that do exist can make their hair levitate.

"No. A witch as in the magical sense." She shakes her head. "Magic is real, El, and I can wield it."

Slowly, I lick my lips. My muscles are sore and tense

from processing everything, and I rub the place where my shoulder meets my neck. "What exactly can you do?"

"Enough." She cuts the word short like it's all the explanation I'm going to get, but there's one thing I have to know.

"Can you heal my grams?"

"No," she says immediately. "I'm sorry. I wish I could. But healing something like cancer, especially when the disease has progressed, is not within the Gowdie wheelhouse."

"It's a family thing? You're all, um—" I still can't say it.

"Witches. We're all witches."

"Even your dad?" I raise an eyebrow. Her father is a khaki-wearing accountant who looks about as magical as a Swingline stapler.

She lowers her voice. "He can brew a potion that would make Tony sleep through his fiftieth birthday."

I lean in. "Seriously? Is that what you're proposing?"

She waves a hand dismissively. "No. I mean, it would work, but it's too close to home. Too risky. We need plausible deniability here. A third party to handle the situation at a time when both of us are accounted for."

"Do you have someone in mind?"

She folds her hands beneath her chin. "That depends. What are you willing to do to save your house?"

I scoff. "What am I *not* willing to do? I'll do anything. *Anything.*"

Maeve's mouth bends into a wicked grin, and her dark hair falls from its twist, landing in perfect waves around her shoulders. "Good. Then I know someone who can help you... for a price."

I toy with the pearl around my neck again. "I can't afford much."

"He won't want money."

"Then what kind of price?"

Her dark brows rise above the rim of her glasses. "Exactly what you have to offer, Eloise. And you're going to give it to him."

2

THE SPELL

ELOISE

I'm one thousand percent sure I'm not comfortable with this. Once again, I peruse the items in the box Maeve gave me that morning, then pop the cork on some rosé and drink straight from the bottle. When she'd asked me what I was willing to do to save Harcourt Manor, I assumed certain logical boundaries. No one was going to ask me to charge through a fur-packed wardrobe into the magical land of Narnia because that wasn't real. It didn't *exist*, right?

Never assume.

The spell Maeve told me to perform will conjure a supernatural advocate, a creature she claims will handle Tony and save my house. Only, the details about said advocate are rather nebulous, and the directions, clutched in my sweaty palm, are far crazier than I could have ever predicted.

Each tick of the grandfather clock reverberates in my

head as the gold hands inch toward twelve. It has to be done at midnight, she explained, when the veil between the living and the dead is thinnest, and the ghosts of my ancestors can help amplify the spell. I take another nip from the bottle before setting it down on the triangular art deco end table beside me, careful to center it on a coaster. I remember a time when I wouldn't have given the wood finish a second thought, but those carefree days are long behind me.

I'm in the front parlor of Harcourt Manor, perched on the edge of an ancient green velvet sofa. This room was decorated by my great-grandfather Henry Harcourt in the 1920s. He was a photographer who traveled the world before settling in Virginia, and this room is filled with the spoils of his adventures.

Tick. Tick. Tick. The antique clock in the corner won't let me forget exactly what time it is. The ticking is annoying as hell, an audible accounting of the seconds of my life passing by. Ten minutes until showtime. *Fuck.*

I pace the room at the edge of the circular symbol I've drawn to Maeve's specifications in chalk on the wood floor. Its diameter is as wide as I am tall, and it's divided by a pentagram, the lines of which bear the shaky evidence of my trepidation concerning this plan. I hope to God its construction is good enough for the spell to work.

Opening the box again, I bring it nearer to the fire for a better look. Shadows dance across the contents. Inside, a dingy, yellowing candle stub stinks of beeswax, incense, and dust—the scent of an ancient church or maybe a tomb. Beside the candle is a knife, its bone handle giving way to a curved blade. Clutching the collar of my pink bathrobe tighter under my chin, I reread the instructions.

Light the candle.

Stand naked before the symbol.

Offer your blood.

"Why does there have to be cutting involved?" I place the box on the mantel and cross the room to take another swig of the wine. It doesn't help. I'm afraid there's not enough liquid courage in the world to make this easy.

Gong. The clock chimes. Midnight. I'm out of time.

I abandon the wine, rush back to the box, and position the candle at the head of the symbol. Grabbing matches off the mantel, I fumble for one and strike it against the gritty strip along the side of the box.

Gong.

When it doesn't light, I steady my hands and strike again, relieved when I hear a chiff and the match head sparks to life. Bending carefully, I touch it to the wick, my heart thundering. The flame burns black.

"What the actual fuck?" I toss the match into the fireplace.

Gong.

Stand naked before the symbol. With a deep breath, I shrug out of my robe, letting the fluffy cotton pool around my ankles. I glance at the wall of windows behind me and the red oak whose gnarled branches wave in the breeze beyond. Harcourt Manor stands at the end of twenty acres of remote land and borders a cliff over-looking the Rappahannock River. No one will see me, but I can't help feeling exposed.

Gong.

A chill snakes through the room, tightening my nipples to hard peaks. I thank my lucky stars Grams is a heavy sleeper. I'd die if she walked in right now. I snatch the blade from the box and extend my hand over the candle.

Gong.

What am I doing? Cutting myself? Fuck, this is messed up.

Gong.

I close my eyes. This is for Grams. For my parents' memory. For the ancestors who are buried near the forest behind this house. I take a deep breath.

Gong.

I slice across the fleshy heel of my palm. Blood pools in the hollow. I turn my wrist and let it dribble onto the edge of the symbol.

Gong.

Everything tilts and the world takes on a dreamy quality, but I know I'm awake because my hand throbs. My eyes bulge as the chalk rises off the wood, the symbol twinkling like it's constructed of tiny stars. The lamp on the end table flickers and goes dark.

Gong.

A bolt of lightning illuminates the yard outside the window. Is it even raining? I swear I see a figure standing next to the red oak tree—a decisively male silhouette, massive in stature. Someone is watching me.

Lightning strikes again and the figure is gone.

Gong.

With only the fire to light the room, I can't trust my eyes as shadows gather in the corners—thick, smoky masses that tangle, then close in, bleeding into the symbol. The scent of dark spice overwhelms me. Goose-flesh marches up my arms. If the clock chimes again, I can't hear it over the pounding of my heart.

All that darkness coalesces into a great, black, beastly form with demonic horns, wings, and a barbed tail. But as the thick smoke becomes corporeal, something else takes shape. A pair of leather shoes. Black slacks straining over thick thighs. Tapered hips. A narrow waist that widens into a broad chest. Heavily muscled shoulders. Corded arms. He is dressed in a loose white shirt, ordinary enough, but there is nothing ordinary about the face that forms from the ether. He is stunning. A dark-haired angel. A marble sculpture brought to life.

This is the advocate? God, the man is huge, six-four, if I had to guess, and built like he chops wood for a living. Menace bleeds off him, even before I see his scowl. And when he turns brilliant silver eyes on me that seem to glow in the dim light, I almost wet myself.

My throat gives a loud reflexive gulp.

I offer my cut hand, trembling hard enough to cause the blood to spill, and force out a raspy plea. "I need your help."

He takes a step toward me, his mouth bending into a look of disgust as he scans me as if I've just climbed out of the sewer. "You are no Gowdie witch."

His voice reminds me of the sound of the struck match.

My chest rises and falls too quickly, and I attempt to slow my breathing so I can speak. Maeve prepared me for this. In a strong voice, I declare, "I perform this spell by the power of Maeve Gowdie."

He sneers, studying me. My pulse races under his scrutiny, my breath coming fast again. This man of shadows, this advocate, whatever he is, an aura of intensity surrounds him. Undeniably beautiful, there's a shrewdness in his eyes, and a hollowness to his cheeks that's... hungry... wanting. The way he studies me makes me want to run.

"Your heart is fluttering like a sparrow's," he says, staring at my neck. I feel his gaze like cool fingers pressed to my pulse. "Maeve should know better than to allow little birds to call on me."

"I'm not—"

"What is it you need, little bird?" His face is suddenly close, and I make out the glistening tips of two pearly white fangs peeking from below a full upper lip. My breath catches. *Oh my God.* I glance down at the blood dripping from my hand, still hovering over the black flame of the candle. Has Maeve given me a spell to call a...

"Are you a vampire?" I blurt the question even as a new, prickling chill coasts over my skin.

He draws back, lids narrowing. "Are you a human? Is this why you called me? To talk about what we are and what we aren't? Do you want pictures of my coffin?" He rolls his eyes. "I hate to disappoint you. I don't sleep in one. Now take that candle and return it to Miss Gowdie and remind her that I am only bound to serve her direct bloodline."

The edges of his elbows start to blur. Shit! He's leaving! I fist my hands and find my voice, even as my heart threatens to break through my ribcage. "Please! I'm sorry if I offended you. I don't care what you are or who you are bound to serve. I need your help, and if we could come to an arrangement... " I thrust my bloody hand toward him again.

His smoky outline solidifies. Nostrils flaring, his gaze darts to my hand. "Hmmm, the sparrow is willing to make a deal with the serpent in her tree?" His laugh is grit and cinder. "You're either brave or a fool."

"Neither," I blurt, flustered. "I'm desperate. Maeve lent me the candle because my ex-husband... well, my husband still, I suppose... we're going through a divorce. He's abusive. Physically and emotionally abusive." My God, it's like talking to a statue. He stares down a blade straight nose at me, an impenetrable scowl on his face. At least he isn't leaving. I take that as a sign to keep going. "After he hit me the second time—"

"What is your name?"

"Eloise. Eloise Harcourt."

"Are you asking me to exact vengeance against this man for abusing you while you sleep in his house and eat his food?" He glances around the room, seemingly puzzled by a set of Egyptian boxes stacked in the corner.

"No. This is *my* house. I left him and moved here, where I care for my grandmother, who is ill... dying."

He takes a step closer, those shrewd eyes on me again. "You are free of this abuser, safe and warm in your own home?"

"He's using a technicality of human law to try to steal this house from me. He's trying to cast me and my dying grandmother out. This is where I grew up. It's where my family is buried. And if I don't do something, he's going to take it from me. I don't care about vengeance. I need your help saving my house." A tear falls and I wipe it away.

The creature creeps closer until his toes are at the border of the symbol. "What do you offer me in exchange for solving this problem for you?"

I dart a glance toward my cut hand. "Uh... don't you want my blood?"

Fast as a serpent strike, cool fingers wrap around my blood-tinged ones, and his tongue lashes out to lick across my wound. I gasp at the feel of it, warm and wet. Intimate. How could it not be? Naked in the dark with a man's tongue on my flesh. I swallow again, not entirely out of fear this time.

"Does that mean you'll help me?"

Those brilliant silver eyes lock on mine. Now that he is closer, I can see they are actually winter blue. The blue of ice. The blue of December twilight.

"Oh, my little bird. That was only me tasting what you have to offer."

3

A MONSTER CALLS

DAMIEN

The damned witch did this on purpose!

I scan the trembling human, livid at the effect she has on me. I haven't been able to tear my eyes away from her since I tasted her blood. At first, I assumed she was an entitled brat, looking for an easy way out of a problem she'd made for herself. But Gowdie baited the hook with a juicy morsel by having her friend perform the spell naked. Eloise Harcourt is undeniably beautiful. Her long, straight hair is bleached a platinum color that doesn't particularly suit her, but the rest of her is stunning —a heart-shaped face with a smattering of freckles, defined shoulders, full breasts, a stomach with just the right amount of curve, and a smooth mound at the juncture of two muscular thighs. I fantasize about spreading those thighs and exploring what I find between them. I grind my teeth to keep myself from acting on the impulse.

My throat burns with desire to taste her sweet blood

again. Sweet, electric blood that I can almost hear singing in my veins. Gods, the smell and taste of her have given me a diamond-hard erection that presses painfully against my zipper. I'm tempted to free myself and show her the throbbing need she's ignited. But fuck if I'd give her any more power than she already holds in that cursed candle.

She's delicious. Mouthwatering. Naked.

If that's not enough of a temptation, the faint bloom of her arousal breaks through the stench of her fear. Interesting. Not unaffected then. As I war with myself over forming a pact with this human, I catch the reflection of her back in the window. She has a tattoo. I'd call it a sigil but I've tasted her blood and she is no witch. Still, she wears the mark of a witch family, although I haven't seen this particular one in my almost four hundred years in this realm.

I move in for a closer look, until I'm almost nose to nose with her, and draw her scent into my lungs. *Fuck.* My fangs throb as bloodlust and physical need barrel into me. I was a fool not to leave when I had the chance. Now I must have her.

"I will help you, in exchange for blood taken from your throat," I grit out.

"My throat?"

Her pulse flutters but again I catch the slightest hint of arousal beneath the fog of acrid terror. I press a nail into the fragile hollow of her throat, trace my fingers along her collarbone. So delicate. So vulnerable. Saliva pools in my mouth and I swallow it down. "Would you prefer the inner thigh?"

"No," she answers quickly, but it pleases me that her neck flushes with excitement. My little bird isn't entirely opposed to the idea. Interesting. "Blood from my throat, and you will save my house."

I nod once, then hook a hand around her waist and pull her flush against me. Only the edge of the symbol between our ankles divides us. Once I do this, take her blood, I'll be bound to her will. Again, I see the folly in it. My curse does not extend to friends of the witch family I serve. Why hand this human woman another leash to yank on my soul?

But her skin is soft, her smell like pomegranate and narcissus, and her blood— Gods, the taste of her still lingers on my tongue.

My hand splays across the middle of her back. I want her. It's been a long time since I've wanted anything. An even longer time since I experienced this... this—it takes me a second to name the lightness that bubbles in my oddly stirring blood—hope. I don't understand why the woman in my arms makes me feel hopeful. There's nothing about her that should. But maybe it is only the idea of something new, someone who is not a witch and might be controlled as much as she controls. Yes, I suppose that must be it.

"You feel warm," she says with a note of amazement. "And I can feel your heart beating."

I scoff. "Are we back to asking what I am, little bird?" I am not the creature her human mind thinks I am.

She shakes her head. I flatten my palm over her heart, then trail my fingers along the side of her neck to the base of her skull, delighting in the way the tips of her breasts turn hard at my touch, even as her pupils dilate and her breath comes in pants. She's terrified. Terrified and aroused.

"What is your husband's name, and where can I find him?" I lower my head to bring my nose closer to her skin.

"Tony Denardi. His office is on Parkview Avenue in Richmond, on the twentieth floor. Denardi Enterprises."

"Then we have a deal." I start at her shoulder, lips brushing her skin as I trace the line of her neck. She arches into me, those lovely breasts pressing into my chest even as she tips her head to give me easier access. "So accommodating," I say against her throat, and then I strike.

She jolts in my arms a second before her blood hits my tongue. It's heaven, the nectar of the gods, and when I swallow, a hot tingle surges through my veins. She's sunlight. She's a ripe peach on a summer's day. I grind my cock against her and drink and drink and drink.

Her body sags in my arms. Fucking hell, I've taken too much. With one last lick, I close my bite wound and then lower her unconscious body to the floor. "Sleep, little bird. By this time tomorrow, you will be free of Tony Denardi."

Crouched by her side, I tell myself I must stay until I know I haven't inflicted permanent damage. What the hell was that? I might have killed her for want of her blood. Relief fills me when I hear a strong heartbeat. She's fine. She'll sleep it off and be as good as new tomorrow.

Yet, I can't bring myself to leave.

Instead, I stand and pace to the other end of the strangely decorated parlor, licking my lips. No human should taste as good as she does or make my blood sing in my veins as if someone has plugged me in. And that tattoo. It's in the wrong place to be a sigil, but its shape promises magical abilities. Still, I've tasted witch blood before; it always holds the tang of the element the witch wields. Hers holds no such flavor. And I've met representatives from all the magical families. The pattern on her back is not one I recognize.

Human, she has to be. But then, why does she enchant me? What is her story?

Hellfire, if that Gowdie witch is up to something... Although what her motives could be, I haven't a clue. I'm already her slave. Why enslave me again to this human?

Wine rests on the end table near her head. I sweep it up, and bring it to my lips, drinking it down. I wish it was something stronger. Bottle still in hand, I give myself leave to explore the room.

Dark, handcrafted furniture. A heavy rocker, arms carved with lion heads, is positioned near the fire. A grandfather clock with astronomical gears of a type I haven't seen in a century stands sentinel in the corner. Even the fireplace itself is something from a different time, oversized with a gilded mantel.

Out of curiosity, I move closer to the gallery wall on the far side of the room, where black and white pictures of men and women are clustered in a decorative pattern. A few of them portray people participating in séances around a table carved with symbols. Mysterious white smudges float between their coupled hands. I chuckle. That's the motif. I see it now. Vintage 1920s. The room is a time capsule to the decade. I should know. I lived through it.

My gaze locks on a man dressed in safari gear with one of the first cameras of the era. I cut a look over to the woman on the floor. A relative, undoubtedly, based on the resemblance. The man is in a few of the séance photos as well. Pictures of big game are peppered into the others, but no hunting trophies are in the room. No animal hides or tusks either. Whoever decorated appreciated photography and was perhaps an amateur archaeologist, but not a killer. A spiritualist, I'd guess, given the time period.

I drink again from the bottle until it comes up empty. Shit. Setting it back on the end table where I found it, I turn to go, then catch my reflection in the gilded mirror on the wall. My cheeks are pink, and my eyes are a dark sky blue, almost as if I were home again, back in my world and at full power. I glance at the woman in alarm. What has Maeve Gowdie sent into my path? I need answers.

A fluffy pink bathrobe lies in a heap beside the woman. On a whim, I fold it and gently put it under her head. The candle has snuffed itself out now that the deal has been struck. I toss it into the box along with the knife and place it all on the mantel. I'm procrastinating. I can hardly bring myself to leave her, which is exactly why I must.

With a growl, I sift into shadows and travel the web of darkness.

I manifest in Maeve Gowdie's living room only seconds later. She's waiting for me, a floral teacup in hand.

"Advocate," she says by way of greeting.

"You had no right giving her the candle," I snarl. "My obligation is to you, not your human friend." I make no effort to disguise my anger even though Maeve has the power to hurt me if she chooses. Gowdie magic is formidable.

That wicked smile of hers stretches wider. "Then, I take it, you agreed to help her."

I snort. "You made certain of that. Why was she naked, Maeve? In all the centuries your ancestors have called upon me, never were any of them naked."

She leans back and crosses her legs. "I thought it would increase her chances of enlisting your support."

"You baited me with her beauty and her—" I swallow, remembering "—blood."

"Yes, I did." She brushes lint from the arm of her black T-shirt.

"Why?" I snap. "You already keep me like some sort of genie in a bottle. Why bind me to her? What is she?"

"You noticed her tattoo?"

"Of course I noticed it."

"Then you've never seen it before, either?"

"No! Why are you asking me? You're a witch. If anyone would know it would be you. Look in the book."

"I have, Advocate." She levels a hard, unsettling stare at me. "There is no record of a family with that sigil. As far as I know, she's human. Although, I admit, I've wondered about the tattoo."

I ball my hands into fists. "You allowed a woman who you suspected might have latent magical abilities to call on me?"

She brushes her dark bangs out of her eyes and blinks behind her glasses. "I gave her the candle because her husband is a truly awful human being who needs to die, and she is my best friend. I would do anything for her. But as for allowing her to call on you directly, I admit, I did hope you'd be able to solve the mystery of that tattoo."

I sniff the air, scenting genuine feelings of friendship

toward the human. Interesting. And rare. Witches don't normally associate with other species, especially not the Gowdie witches.

"Her blood was… unusual," I offer.

"Unusual how?"

"Exceptional."

"Exceptional, but human?"

"As far as I could tell, it did not hold the flavor of elemental power."

"As I expected. She's human," she says more confidently, then sips her tea.

I take some comfort in Maeve's confirmation that her friend is non-magical. Exchanging blood with other magical creatures is a danger to my kind. It's how I was captured by the Gowdies to begin with.

"Now that that's settled, you have a plan to solve her problem, I presume."

I flash my most insouciant grin. "Never fear, Gowdie, her husband will be dead by this time tomorrow, and your human friend will be free to go on with her life."

"Good."

I step in closer, baring my fangs. "But hear me, *witch*, the candle may preclude me from harming you, but not your human friends. If I'm called by anyone else, don't be surprised when I drain them dry. I am not some *thing* to be lent like a cup of sugar."

She holds up both hands. "Understood, Advocate. This is the last time I request your services... for a friend."

Disgusted and hardly satisfied, I break into shadow and return to the darkness, desperate to distract myself from the taste of the woman that still lingers on my lips.

4

HINDSIGHT AND HANGOVERS

ELOISE

In the dream, I sit on the edge of our property, wind battering the sandstone cliffs and churning the river below. Mom yells something, but I can't make her out over the deafening rush of wind and water. My father hurries toward us, our old dog Max at his side. Max reaches me first and pokes me with his nose—harder and harder—until I can't ignore him any longer.

I wake to a slippered toe delivering a hard nudge to my ribs. "Owwww!"

Grams leans over me, blinking rheumy eyes that nearly match the turquoise turban she's wearing. "Are you an alcoholic, Eloise?"

I rub my side. "No. Why would you ask that?"

"Because you're sleeping naked in the middle of the parlor next to an empty bottle of rosé."

My eyes widen. Last night comes back to me in a maddening rush of images and sensations. Mortified, I slide out from under her and snatch my bathrobe from... where it's folded under my head? Weird. I wrap it around myself, doing a double take when I see the wine bottle is empty. I definitely left at least half the bottle. It seems my vampire advocate has helped himself to the rest.

Not a vampire. Why didn't he want to be labeled with that term when he so obviously fits the description?

My hand shoots up to rub the spot where he bit me, but the skin is smooth. I check the slope of my neck in the decorative oval mirror on the wall. Perfectly intact.

I whirl. The symbol is gone. The floor is clean, although the rug is still rolled. The candle and the knife are not where I left them. The box is squared on the mantel. Did he put them away? I rub a hand down my face.

"You're awfully jumpy this morning. What's going on? And why is the carpet all rolled up like that?" Grams folds her skinny arms over her French terry sweater and pops out her hip.

"You look good today," I say, hoping to redirect the conversation.

"Well, once they take you off the chemo, all you have to deal with is the cancer, not the damn side effects." She sighs. "Today is a good day."

"Let's have breakfast." I place a hand on her shoulder and turn her toward the kitchen.

"Don't try to distract me, Eloise. What the hell went on here last night?" She points a knobby finger at the carpet.

I don't like lying to my grams, but if I told her the truth, she'd probably have me committed. "Just something I'm trying. Um, exercises to help me manage stress. You know, getting in touch with nature and my inner warrior." When Grams stares at me blankly, I add, "It was Maeve's idea."

That seems to appease her. "Well, that explains it. Crazy follows that woman wherever she goes."

"She's a highly accomplished lawyer. She's representing me, you know."

Grams shuffles toward the kitchen. "Don't get me wrong, dear. I was crazy, too, when I was your age. All my favorite people are."

A ball of lead forms behind my sternum. Do I have a responsibility to tell Grams that Tony is suing me for the house? After all, if things fail to work out with this... *advocate*—my God, I don't even know his name—she should be prepared for what will inevitably happen next. She deserves to know the truth.

I hide my mouth behind my hand as a yawn splits it wide open and make a beeline for the coffee machine. I'll break it to her after breakfast. No sense ruining what is left of her meager appetite. "I'll put the parlor back together later. Good as new, I promise."

"No rush." Grams gives a deep, choppy chuckle as if she's heard a dark joke. "It's not as if I'm expecting guests. Not while I'm alive to greet them anyway." I cringe but she keeps going. "I do love that room. It reminds me of my father-in-law. He used to photograph séances there, you know. Everyone in town wanted an invitation to one of his spirit soirees."

I avoid addressing her earlier comment and latch on to the soirees. "Do you think he really believed in all that stuff?"

"Oh, he believed. It was all the rage in the '20s. Photography wasn't overly sophisticated then, and there were often artifacts in the old photographs that people assumed were ghosts. And when would there be more ghosts in the room than during a séance?"

"Creepy." I poke the coffee machine button as if it will make it brew faster. Poke, poke, poke. I mumble a warning to it about buying a Keurig.

"What's that, dear?"

"I didn't know great-grandpa was an honest-to-goodness spiritualist."

"Oh yes. Actually, it was why he settled in Virginia. According to his journals, he saw fairies on these lands and that's what convinced him to stay."

Brows coming together, I turn and lean my bottom against the counter. My head throbs like it has its own heartbeat. "Great-grandpa thought there were *fairies* here?"

"He was sure of it. Sometimes, if I watch carefully at night, I see lights bobbing beyond the family cemetery. He never found any proof, but I think they're still here. Maybe that's why this family has always been so lucky."

A huff bursts out of me before I can stifle it. When she eyes me strangely, I shake my head. "Mom and Dad were murdered, I'm going through a horrible divorce, and you—" I cut myself off.

"I'm dying," she fills in for me, matter-of-factly.

"Excuse me if I fail to see the luck in our current situation."

She waves dismissively. "That's only because you're young and you don't have perspective. I'm far closer to heaven than you. I can see things you can't from this height."

The coffee machine beeps and I whisper, "Thank God." I spin around to pour us two cups. Nabbing the creamer from the fridge, I bring them to the table, hoping the caffeine will stop my brain matter from melting like a clock in a Salvador Dali painting. I take a sip then refocus on the conversation. "Perspective, huh? Like what, Grams?"

"Well, we've always had each other, haven't we? And we've always had this place. Howard was born here, you know. In the guest room." She points one arthritic finger toward the ceiling. I've heard the story a thousand times but tilt my head and nod. "And your father, I gave birth to him in the same room. Lord, he was a holy terror of a child. I loved every minute of it. Broke my heart when James went to school overseas, but when he brought your mother home with a ring on her finger, it made it all worth it. Diana loved it here too, you know. Used to run along the edge of those cliffs like she could fly. A few times, I thought we were going to lose her."

My dream comes back to me in full color. "I had a dream last night that Mom was standing on the edge. Dad was there too. And Max. Do you remember Max?"

"Oh yes. I loved that dog."

I take a fortifying gulp of coffee. "What can I get you for breakfast? How about some oatmeal?"

"That would be perfect, dear. With chocolate chips and brown sugar."

I snort. "Are you supposed to have sugar and chocolate?"

She shrugs her bony shoulders. "At this point, what's it going to hurt?"

I sigh. "Chocolate chips it is." I take my coffee to the

counter with me and dump water and oats into a saucepan.

"Anyway, it's not surprising you would dream of your mother there. She loved the river. Many of her paintings were influenced by the cliffs and the wind. You know, if you need money, you could take up painting again."

At one time, my goal had been to become an artist like my mother. She'd had a following before she was murdered, and her art has gone up in value since her death. Income from her paintings used to be what supported us. My father owned a greenhouse and landscaping company in Echo Mills, but his income was negligible compared to my mother's. But when they died, grief smothered my creative flame. The only time I've held a paintbrush since is to teach painting, and even that was derailed by my failed marriage. "I'm nowhere near ready to paint for profit, unfortunately. I'm not sure I ever will be again."

"Pssht." She smacks her lips in disapproval. "Fine, then sell one of your mother's pieces. A few are left in her studio. Everything on loan has been returned from the galleries."

Most of Mom's work was done on commission. A few she'd painted for us, pieces that hang on the walls of Harcourt Manor and line her studio. Her paintings sold well and quickly. I'm surprised the galleries had any pieces to return. Now that she's gone, parting with any of them would be akin to selling my soul.

"I couldn't possibly."

Grams frowns. "You're welcome to anything I have, of course, but I don't have much, I'm afraid. Once I'm gone, you'll have a nice nest egg—"

"I thought I'd call Principal Singer and see if he has any openings," I say loud enough to drown out yet another reminder of her mortality. The oatmeal is done. I divide it into two bowls, add brown sugar and chocolate chips to Grams's and a handful of raisins to mine, and bring both to the table.

Grams stirs her oatmeal, contemplative. Relief eases through me when she takes a bite. Being with her this morning, having breakfast, I can almost forget her time with me is limited. Well, I could if she stopped insisting on reminding me at every turn.

"I remember when you came along," she says wistfully. "All that wild energy James had was in you too. The house came alive. James and Diana raised you without inhibitions. It was refreshing. Everything was exciting again."

"I'm sure Mom thought I was exhausting. Until I met Tony, I had no goals in life, no fear of anything, especially not failure." I sip my coffee, trying to put it all into words. "As much as I hate Tony right now, I have to admit that he was kind initially. Remember how he was right after Mom and Dad were killed? Always stopping by to check on the two of us?"

"But then he hit you."

"Yes, but before that. He did fix the house. And he was the one who encouraged me to go to college and become a serious adult. Who knows where I'd have ended up without his influence?"

She grunts. "Tony certainly changed you." Her gaze slides down her nose with all the no-nonsense attitude of Judge Judy. "And then he hurt you. He's still hurting you."

I spoon in another bite of oatmeal to distract myself from a storm of conflicting emotions. Tony. My mind wanders to last night, flashes of my interaction with the advocate coming back to me. He said he'd *free me* from Tony. What exactly does that mean? His serious-as-hell tone sounded almost... nefarious. But Maeve is a lawyer; she wouldn't send an advocate who would do anything illegal, right?

I chew my lip. Can I be blamed for being too overwhelmed at summoning a freaking shadow monster to ask for specifics?

Grams's spoon clangs against her bowl. Pain has crept into her bony body like a demon whose exorcism didn't take. I pop out of my chair and snatch her meds off the counter. Only one pain pill left. She's been taking more lately.

"What time does the nurse come today?" I bring the pill to the table and help her take it.

"Any minute now. She'll refill those. Can't give me too many at once. Wouldn't want me to become addicted." She rolls her eyes.

"When she gets here, do you think you'll be okay if I go into Richmond to discuss something with Maeve?"

"As long as it doesn't involve you drinking another bottle of wine and sleeping naked in the parlor."

I slant a wry grin. "You said you enjoyed the days when I had no inhibitions."

A laugh rocks her body and she braces herself against the pain. "Oh, Eloise, I love having you home. Yes, I'll be fine."

I stay with her until the nurse arrives.

5

THE FINE PRINT

ELOISE

F riendship is a funny thing. Two people choose to care about each other for no other reason than a spontaneous, unexplainable bond. I met Maeve on the first day of high school during my freshman year. Some girls decided they didn't like her goth style. After calling her a witch didn't get under her skin, they cornered her in the locker room, and things turned dark. When I saw what was about to happen, I walked right up to the head-bitch responsible and punched her face. As expected, little miss mean girl could dish it out but couldn't take it.

Maeve and I have been friends ever since.

Over the years, I've learned to love her unique quali-ties. Maeve's always been strange: the way she dresses like every day is a funeral, the tattoos, how she likes to stroll through old cemeteries and trace the engravings on worn tombstones. Once, after she experienced a particularly tough breakup, our college dorm was thrashed by thunderstorms for almost forty-eight hours straight. It seemed like a truly awful coincidence at the time. Now, as I sit in her waiting room with an enchanted candle in a box on my lap, I wonder if I know my best friend at all.

An elderly woman with bright red glasses stops in front of me and, in a smoke-stained voice, whispers, "Ms. Gowdie will see you now."

I get the distinct impression she's trying to keep the other people in the waiting room from hearing. Some of them fidget as if they've been there a long time. I don't even have an appointment. I immediately feel guilty for barging in and vow to keep this short. With a quick nod, I gather the box containing the candle and its accoutrements into my arms and hurry into Maeve's office.

"You didn't have to bring that back right away," Maeve says, the second she notices the box in my hands. Her gaze lifts to my face, and she frowns. "What's wrong?"

I don't bother to sit down. "I'll make this quick." I give her the cliff notes version of what I remember about the night before. "So... the advocate is a... what exactly? He didn't like it when I suggested he was a vampire, but the descriptor seems apt."

"Uh... sort of." Maeve squints at me through her glasses, resting her elbows on her desk. "You might say he's a special kind of vampire."

"There are different kinds?" I mumble incredulously, then hold up a hand. "You know what? Never mind. Based on the look of your waiting room, I sense you only have a few minutes, and I don't want to waste them talking about vampire varietals. But, um, I remember him biting me, only, there's nothing on my neck." I run my fingers along the smooth skin covering my jugular.

Maeve turns one palm skyward. "Oh, the advocate's saliva can close and heal wounds. He likely licked it away while you were asleep. Anyway, the spell worked. You have a deal. Your problem will be solved tonight. Make sure you're out in public when it happens, preferably somewhere with a record of your attendance."

I shift uneasily, gripping the box to my midsection. Tucking a strand of hair behind my ear, I lower my voice to a whisper. "When what, exactly, happens?"

Maeve digs in her drawer for a red lipstick and starts to touch up her makeup using a small gold compact before answering me. "When the advocate kills Tony, of course."

All the air leaves my lungs, and I have to suck in another breath to grit out, "You're kidding, right?"

She smooths a hand through the air as if to comfort me. "Don't worry. He'll make it look like an accident. He's very good."

My jaw drops, and my entire body goes cold. "You told me he was an advocate who was going to help save my house! I didn't think I was taking out a supernatural hit on my husband."

"Stop calling him your husband. Tony is an abusive creep who has ties to some very dark people." She narrows her eyes at me. "How did you think the advocate would solve the problem, if not by killing Tony?"

I gape, my head starting to pound. "Oh, I don't know, intimidate him? Maybe go rough him up?" Box on hip, I punch the space between us with two quick jabs. "Show his fangs and scare him into signing his rights away? Pull an Ebenezer Scrooge visit and convince him of the error of his ways so that he voluntarily does the right thing?"

Maeve breaks out into raucous laughter. "Seriously? Once again you underestimate the depths of Tony's depravity. None of those things will work. Trust me on this."

Knees weak, I drop into one of the chairs, hunching over the box. "Maeve, I can't be responsible for Tony's death. I'm not a murderer."

"You won't be. The advocate will do it for you. Distract yourself with something fun tonight, and by morning it will all be better."

"But I hired him! He might as well be a gun whose trigger I pulled."

"You'll get over it once this nightmare goes away and you have your home. If he dies, the divorce does not move forward, and as the surviving spouse, you have a right to receive assets from Tony's estate, even if his will makes no provision for you. It's in your best interest to allow the advocate to do what he does best."

I squeeze my eyes shut for a beat, disbelieving what I'm hearing. "How can you be so flippant about this? We're talking about a man's life!"

With a reflective sigh, Maeve leans back in her leather chair and threads her black-painted fingertips across her belly. "I'm not flippant, okay?" She gestures toward the box. "I lent that to you at great personal risk. He's been in my family for centuries, and you are the first human to employ his services. But what Tony did to you, what he's doing to you, is wrong, Eloise. I believe you're justified."

"Is that why you didn't tell me precisely what the spell did in advance?" I can't keep the edge from my voice.

Her posture stiffens, and the look she gives me is as cold and dark as the eyes of the menagerie of skeletal animals tattooed on her arms. "You told me you were willing to do anything to save your house."

I clutch at the heavy weight of guilt that forms in my chest again. "I was. I am. Almost anything! But I never thought... Listen, I know you only want to help me, but this is more than I feel is warranted. How do I undo it?"

For a long moment, Maeve twirls her hair around her finger, lips pursed in disapproval. Her mouth tugs to the side and she says, "You can call him back the same way you called him the first time and strike a new bargain."

"But I can't perform the spell until midnight, right? He could strike as soon as the sun goes down. In fact, I'm sure he will because I gave him Tony's office address, not his home."

"Right. You could try to call him earlier, but the magic will be weaker. He might ignore you." She drums her fingers on the desk. "If you're absolutely sure this is what you want, and I really wish you'd reconsider, El, the only way to stop him is to intercept him at Tony's office. You can command him not to kill Tony, and he must obey you. Once you have an agreement, as long as the candle is in your possession, if you tell him to stop, he'll stop."

I stand, gripping the box until my knuckles turn white. "That's what I'll do then. Thanks, Maeve."

"He won't be happy about it." Her gaze dips toward the box. "Don't be surprised if the advocate doesn't appreciate your interference. No beast likes to have his chain yanked."

The intense memory of his giant body dwarfing mine as his teeth sank into my throat comes back to me. If that was him on a good day, what would the advocate be like angry? A shiver courses through me. "I understand."

I head for the door, but Maeve stops me before I reach it. She pulls me into her arms until all the tension leaks from my body. "I'm sorry I didn't prepare you. I should have known you weren't ready for this. You've never used magic before."

I wonder why her apology is about magic and not murder, but I figure she means as much, even if she doesn't say it. "No, I uh, thank you, Maeve. I know you only want to help."

She kisses my cheek, and I leave without another word. Maeve and I are good. It would take a hell of a lot more than this to come between us.

6

BREAKING POINT

ELOISE

A few hours later, I arrive on the twentieth floor of Tony's building and walk through the doors to Denardi Enterprises. According to my app, I've made it just in time. Five minutes to sunset. I scan the reception area, wondering where I should wait for the advocate, then remember he can form from shadows. I'll have to be in Tony's office if I'm going to stop him.

"Can I help you?" the woman behind the desk asks.

"I need to see Tony Denardi, please. It's an emergency."

"Name?"

"Eloise Harcourt." I've never been so happy to have kept my maiden name.

Her eyes lift and then widen with recognition, her cheeks staining pink. "Oh, uh, I'm afraid he's booked for the afternoon."

I study her for a moment, the way she shifts in her chair, her gaze darting everywhere but to me, and realization dawns. Oh God, this is awkward. I know Tony's been having an affair with one of his assistants, but I never knew which one... until now. "You're her," I mutter. "You're the one Tony's been... seeing."

She doesn't respond, but her already pink cheeks turn an alarming shade of red.

"I'm not angry with you," I say softly, checking her badge. "Tamara. Why would I be? I left him."

Her face burns brighter, and she winces, as if warring between humor and pity.

"Oh." My stomach drops as the humiliating realization dawns on me. I've been a fool. "It's been going on longer than I thought, hasn't it? Of course it has."

"Can I leave him a message for you?" The forced professionalism in her voice makes me cringe.

"I'm sorry for you, honestly," I say, although I should keep my mouth shut. "You have no idea what's in store for you once the shine wears off."

She scoffs, the former embarrassment I registered turning on a dime toward anger. My coat hangs open and her gaze drifts judgmentally over the beige cardigan set and pearl necklace I'm wearing. "I think I might have a few more years of shine left than you."

The comment knocks the wind out of me. I'm only twenty-five and only wore this outfit because it's Tony's favorite, the same reason I've pulled my bleached hair back at the base of my skull. He always insisted I dress like this, and I thought it would improve my odds of getting what I want from him if my appearance pleased him. But as I look at Tamara, a deep pit opens in my chest like an ice cream scooper has scraped out my heart. She is what Tony wanted all along—the blond hair, the big boobs. Her cerulean-colored wrap dress accentuates every curve. He'd never have allowed me to wear what she's wearing. It's confusing, and another punch to the gut, even if Tony isn't doing the punching this time.

I clench my eyes shut and just breathe. No way am I going to cry in front of this woman, not over a man like Tony. When I open them again, I look down at my hands rather than at her, see my watch, and remember why I'm here.

"Sunset." I curse under my breath.

"Excuse me?"

"I'll show myself back." I ignore her protests and race-walk down the hall directly to Tony's office. His door is open, and his jacket is on the back of his chair, but he's gone. The darkness outside his window offers a stunning view of the Richmond skyline. Oh hell, am I too late?

"It's better if you're not here when it happens," a deep voice rumbles from the shadows, and all the tiny hairs on my body stand at attention. It's like I've touched a live wire. My pulse quickens with my breath and I'm as aware of the advocate's presence as I would a lion walking into the room. I pivot to find him standing in the shadow of the door, his silver eyes the only thing visible until he steps into the light. Damn, he's wearing a suit tonight in a shade of navy that brings out the blue tinge in his pale eyes. It's stunning. Thickness forms in my throat and I can't find my voice.

But then I don't have to. Tamara bursts in, her finger pointing in my direction. "Leave now, or I'm calling secur—Oh, hello." Her voice softens the moment she sees the advocate, and she flashes a warm smile, her lashes fluttering. "I don't recall checking you in."

He steps closer to her, locking eyes. "You will go back to your desk now and forget either of us is here."

Tamara's face slackens, her expression distant as if her mind has wandered off. "Right. I need to go." She chuckles, glancing around the room as if she can't remember why she's come in. With a flip of her blond hair, she strolls from the room and heads in the direction of the front desk.

"That's a neat trick," I mumble.

He whirls on me, gripping my shoulders hard enough that I can't forget what he is. This is the monster I called, the one who drinks blood and is sewn together from shadows. He brings his face close to mine, his nostrils flaring.

"Leave now, little bird, or it will be difficult to separate you from what I have to do. The longer you're here, the harder it will be for me to conceal that fact."

Conceal as in wipe minds like he did to Tamara? Tamper with the security cameras? What exactly is the advocate capable of?

This close to him, my body tenses in alarm and something else I don't want to admit. I clamp my thighs together and swallow repeatedly to get my voice to work. When I do, it comes out wispy and trembling. I pull away, putting room between us. "There's been a mistake. I don't want you to kill Tony."

He glares, his lips peeling back from his teeth. "You don't—"

"What the fuck?" Tony strides into his office, adjusting the rolled sleeves of his dress shirt before sinking into the chair behind the desk. His bushy brown brows pinch above an aquiline nose and thin, sneering lips. He pointedly looks at his gold watch. "You need to leave, Eloise. I have work."

"We need to talk about the house." I shove my hands into the pockets of my coat and toy with the candle. "You know what's going on with Grams. I can't let you have Harcourt. It's wrong, and you know it."

Tony's eyes lock on to the man beside me. "Who the hell is this?"

If he only knew. I glance at the advocate, who appears even more menacing than before, and realize I still don't know his name. "He's my... counsel."

Tony scoffs. "Is everyone at that firm of Maeve's a damned freak?"

A low growl, almost imperceptible, rumbles from the advocate's chest.

"Why are you doing this to me?" I ask. "You have everything. Leave me my family home."

Tony leans back in his leather chair, hands threading over his abdomen, and lifts his chin to peer down his nose at me. "Half the value of that property is rightfully mine. Pay me my portion, and I'll move on. It's as simple as that." His lips twist into a demeaning smile. "Oh, that's right, you can't. You have no assets but the property itself, and even if you could secure a mortgage on the house, it wouldn't cover my half."

"How do you know that?" *I'm* not even fully aware of the estate's value.

He tugs at one cuff. "I know everything, Eloise. Now take your... counsel and get out of my office."

I stand my ground. "No."

His eyes flash with ire, and his fists clench on his desk. He stands up slowly, never taking his gaze off me. "If you want to talk to me seriously about this, tell your counsel to fuck off. This is between the two of us."

I turn to face the monster. Shit, no wonder Tony wants him to leave. The angles of the creature's face are harsh in the recessed lighting, frightening. Part of me wants him behind me during this conversation. Another part knows that my best chance of getting Tony to change his mind about Harcourt is to do what he asks. I reach into my pocket and fist the candle. "Please go. Meet me later, same time and place as last night."

The advocate seethes in my direction, his lips curling off his teeth in barely contained rage. But he leaves without another word. I turn back to Tony as soon as he's gone. "When you made those improvements, they were a gift, not an investment. Drop your claim to the property, Tony. Please."

He rounds the desk and closes the door to his office, turning back to me with undisguised malice. I try to back away as he swaggers closer, but he hooks his fingers in the pearls around my neck, holding me in place. "You wore my favorite necklace."

"We loved each other once," I force out. "Please, if for no other reason than out of respect for what we once had, let me keep the house."

He twists his fingers in the pearls until they tighten uncomfortably around my throat. "Let's face facts, Eloise." His voice is low and calm, even as the noose he's created forces me to rise onto my toes. "Your grandmother is dying, and you don't have a penny to your name. If I let you keep the place, you'd run it into the ground. The bank would foreclose in six months."

I shake my head. "I won't let that happen. I've already

reached out to my old principal. Once I'm working again—"

"You'll never make enough. No one will hire *you* for anywhere near what you need to maintain that place." He twists again, the pearls threatening to cut off my air. I dig my fingers in behind the strand. "Face it, you're going to lose that house one way or another. Sign the property over to me, and I'll allow you to visit your parents' graves on the anniversary of their deaths."

"Stop," I rasp. "You're choking me."

"Do as I say," he hisses through his teeth. "Sign the house over to me. You can't afford it." Tony's features turn cruel, and the old pattern comes back to me. He's insulted me, degraded me, and now he's physically overpowering me. Tony isn't happy unless I'm groveling at his feet.

Breath barely trickles down my windpipe in a high-pitched whine. Not enough to answer him. Black spots circle at the edges of my vision. I claw at the strand. I'm suffocating, but all I can think of are his words. He'd *allow* me to visit my parent's graves. *Allow* me. Red-hot anger pulses through me. This morning, I remembered his kindness, but now I need to remember his spite. Tony is an abuser, and he always will be. I dig both my hands into my flesh, wedge my fingers under the pearls, and tug.

The strand breaks. Pearls drop and bounce across the wood floor, rolling like marbles. I back across the room, putting space between us and wheezing air through the roughness left in my throat.

Over the sound of my rasping breaths, I hear him laugh. "Think about it, Eloise. As always, I'm the best offer you have. Even Maeve Gowdie knows it, whether or not she's admitted it to you yet."

Coughing, I lunge for the door, but I've got to walk past him to get there. He reaches out and grabs my wrist, squeezing until I'm sure he's left a bruise. "Oww. Tony, you're hurting me."

He pulls me to him and brings his face close to mine. "You know what's sad about all of this? You could still be married to me if you'd just learned your place. We could've had a nice arrangement. You by my side as my wife, your grandmother safely cared for."

"And Tamara in your bed."

He nods. "It's not an uncommon arrangement. I'd have kept you comfortable."

"That's not good enough for me," I rasp, yanking my wrist from his grip and charging out the door.

The last thing I hear as I slip into the hall is, "My offer just expired. Forget about visiting your parents' graves once that property is mine."

Massaging my bruised neck, I walk faster toward the exit, hating Tony with everything in me. I'm not a murderer, but as God is my witness, I wonder if I've done the right thing in stopping the advocate from killing him.

7

BOUND IN SHADOW

DAMIEN

From the darkness, I seethe at Tony Denardi and curse the candle whose power keeps me from intervening. Eloise commanded me to leave. I'm already pushing the boundaries of my curse by watching from a distance, the candle's power grinding painfully against my bones every time I try to hold my physical form or inch nearer.

Gods, I can smell the man's murderous intent. Eloise's ex carries the acrid stench of the truly evil. It kills me to watch him twist her pearls like a noose along that long, delicate neck, to see the pain and panic in her eyes. Not that I have any feelings for the human woman but because I've been cheated out of killing the bastard. I'd have gloried in draining a snake like Tony dry. Over the centuries I've been alive, I've known many men like this one, arrogant narcissists who believe to their marrow that the rest of the world exists for their pleasure.

If Denardi spills Eloise's precious, delectable blood, so help me I'll find a way to circumvent the candle's hold and skin the bastard alive.

I ready myself in the shadows, but then my little bird surprises me. Those fragile fingers succeed in breaking the necklace's hold. Pearls rain down onto the floor and roll across the room. One of them finds its way into the corner, into my waiting hand. I crush it into powder.

It seems my little bird is not as fragile as I assumed. With an air of confidence, she exits the room. I follow, slipping through the darkness until I see her climb behind the wheel of an ancient-looking Jeep, lock the doors, and bury her face in her palms.

A possessive growl rumbles from my chest. I stop the sound as soon as I recognize it for what it is. This human does not belong to me. She's a walking meal. A complication. A joke played on me by the Gowdie bitch.

I need to feed before I see Eloise again. Only my hunger for her blood can explain my lapse in judgment when I chose to watch over her. Last night, I was tempted to drain her dry. Best that when I return to her at midnight, I'm fully fed.

I surf the shadows to Night Haven, the subterranean city ruled by vampires where I've lived since the Gowdies brought me to the new world. I am not, strictly speaking, one of them. My kind are called shades, and we hail from a world named *Tenebris*. Shades are rare in this realm. As far as I know, there are only two others like me here, forced through the same interdimensional rift I was drawn through. When the Gowdies conjured us from our home world, they made it impossible for us to return. Fortunately, our physical needs are similar enough to a vampire's that living among them in this world is comfortable. Like them, we require blood as well as other sustenance to survive, and sunlight is toxic to our composition. We also share a mutual disgust for witches. As such, the underground city of Night Haven has become a home away from home.

I manifest in the marketplace, navigating the vibrant network of shops and services that line the underground streets. The smell of grilling meat meets my nose, and a woman sways a section of silky fabric at me from her booth under the strands of white lights. But I'm in no mood for an early snack or a quick shopping binge. I want blood, human blood, enough to ease the temptation that is Eloise Harcourt.

In Night Haven, there's only one place I trust to have what I need, the red-light district. I slide open the shoji-style doors and step into the foyer of Marabella's where a blond man dressed in a black silk robe reminds me to remove my shoes. I do, sliding on a pair of the house sandals meant for guests. A stone waterfall bubbles along the wall next to a cherry tree that's enchanted to always be in bloom. I've never asked how Marabella managed the spell.

"Back again, Damien?" the voluptuous madame says when she sees me. She's human and has been serving Night Haven for over thirty years. "Haven't you figured out yet you can get it for free?"

"I'd rather have a willing donor than a free one." After being forced into this life when I was trapped into serving the Gowdies, I can't stomach tricking or forcing human donors. Unless, of course, it's in punishment for their crimes. I would've gladly drained Tony Denardi, for example. His blood would've tasted like shit, but the sweet knowledge that there was one less asshole on this planet would've chased away the bitterness. Considering that is no longer an option, I'm left with either animals or a blood brothel. I prefer the brothel. The humans here know what they've signed up for, and I pay them handsomely for the use of their veins. It's better this way.

Marabella laughs. "Have you looked in a mirror lately? I think you'd find many topsiders willing, especially the women. And you being a shade, I've heard your name on the lips of vampire women as well."

It is true I can subsist on the blood of vampires as well as humans, something I learned from my friend Cassius, one of the two other shades in this realm. I've never tried vampire blood, though. Once Cassius shared that his partner considered his blood a delicacy, I ruled the option out. Feeding from another vampire would presumably lead to them asking to feed on me. That isn't happening. No fucking way.

"Not my taste," I say.

She smiles wider. "Good for me, then. I should stop giving you ideas. Don't want to chase away my best customer. Who are you interested in having today?"

"Hazel," I say without hesitation. The elderly woman has been donating for decades. She was raised on a farm in the Appalachians, far away from modern chemicals. Her blood is as pure as you can get on this planet. More importantly, she's an expert at keeping things clinical, just the way I like it.

"Sorry, Love. She's off today. Now that she's over seventy, she only works every two weeks."

Disappointing. I rub my temples against a brewing headache. "Then give me someone like Hazel."

Marabella's brows lift, a furtive smile tugging at the corner of her mouth. "I have just the thing. Room 110." She hands me a key.

Snatching the gold-tasseled end, I glance at my watch before striding down the hall to the room. I have just over an hour to scratch the itch before I see *her* again. Just the thought of Eloise makes electricity surge in my veins. The memory of her scent sends a swirl of heat through me, and for a second I'm transported to the moment I first touched her, the soft curves of her body, the tattoo along her spine. *Fuck*, the girl is dangerous.

I unlock 110 and stop in the doorway. A beautiful young woman with long, shiny black hair waits inside, a black silk robe decorated with cherry blossoms wrapped around her supple body. She stands from her chair and pads toward me on bare feet, her pupils dilating as she takes me in. When she reaches me, she places her hands lightly on my chest. "I'm Liang. Can I help make you more comfortable?" She grips my lapels and tries to push the jacket off my shoulders.

I grab her wrists, spin her around, and brush her hair off her neck in quick, efficient movements. "That won't be necessary."

She clears her throat. "You know I'm available for more than blood, right?"

"Not for me." I strike. I'm not interested in sex with my donors. Not interested in any attachments that might make it harder for me to leave this godforsaken realm if I ever find a way to break the Gowdie curse. All I want is a full stomach so I can go about my work.

There's nothing special about Laing's blood. I drink until I'm satiated but it's not a particularly pleasurable experience. Then again, I wonder if it would have tasted better before. Before *her*. Before I understood how delicious blood could be.

Once I've had my fill, I pay and rush out the door, prepared to face my little bird and the mess she's made of things.

8

A NEW DEAL

ELOISE

By the time I climb the winding drive to Harcourt Manor, I've run out of tears. I've also burned through all the adrenaline my body produced during my escape from Tony's office. I barely have the energy to keep my eyes open.

I stop in the driveway and stare up at the two-story colonial home with its sweeping wraparound porch. The pedimented dormers always give me the impression of eyebrows, like the house itself is watching over me.

This place is a treasure trove of memories. Built in the early 1910s by my great-grandfather, every generation has added something, but it remains distinctively Harcourt. My heart clenches at the mere thought of letting it go.

Of one thing I am positively certain, Tony retains no affection for me whatsoever.

I suspected he didn't love me anymore. Maybe, if I'm

being honest, true love wasn't what brought us together in the first place. Deep down, though, I believed he possessed some affinity for me. But tonight, I searched for an emotional lever to pull, some memory I could tug to get him to work with me on this house thing, and came up empty-handed. My pleas were met with nothing but cruelty and contempt.

I wish I could say the experience made me angry. Anger is a useful emotion that can motivate, spur action, and bring clarity to a situation. I'm too tired to feel angry. What I feel is small. Tiny. Inconsequential. A fly trying to take on Goliath without the benefit of a slingshot. I have little money. No prospects. And my only remaining family member is at death's door.

A ping comes from my dashboard. The red oil light blinking on. *Fuck.* My ancient Jeep is bleeding black gold. The gas is low too. "Pick some up tomorrow, old girl." I rest my forehead on the steering wheel. She was my dad's once. I pray there are still some miles left in her.

Things are going from bad to worse. I did manage to squirrel away some cash before I left Tony. I'm not a complete idiot. After the first time he hit me, I started secretly stockpiling every bill I could get my hands on. I have a little over two thousand dollars to see me through, but it isn't going to last long unless I start working again.

Mentally, I move *find a job* up on my to-do list.

Once I park the car, I shuffle inside and cruise down the hall to check on Grams. The moment I see she's okay, fresh tears start to fall. I wipe them away, returning to the parlor where she won't hear me cry. I click on the table lamp and check my reflection in the gallery mirror. A chain of red bruises ring my neck and wrist. They'll turn purple in time. I'll have to find ways to cover them until they're healed.

"Fuck. Fuck. Fuck." I promised myself this would never happen again. It's why I left Tony in the first place. He's now physically abused me three times.

More tears come. Do I have *victim* tattooed on my forehead? Why did I allow myself to be alone with him? Did I really think I could convince him to give me five hundred thousand dollars worth of property? For God's sake, Tony used to fume when I tucked five dollars into a homeless person's cup. He isn't known for his generous heart.

My spiral of self-loathing is interrupted when the lamp flickers, and the room plunges into darkness.

"Have you had your fun?" a gruff voice says from behind me. I turn to find the advocate leaning against the unlit fireplace in a column of moonlight. He snaps his fingers, and the light comes back on. Better to see how positively pissed off he looks.

"I thought you were coming at midnight." I wipe under my eyes again, although there is no hiding my blotchy, mascara-streaked face.

"It is midnight, little bird."

I glance at my watch. I guess it is. Time flies when you stop three times on the drive home because you can't see through your tears.

"It doesn't have to be midnight, you understand." He pushes off the mantel and glides toward me. Darkness incarnate. The night itself in a dress shirt and trousers. At the rate he's moving, I should easily be able to follow where he is in the room, but somehow I lose track and then he's standing behind me. Hot breath caresses the back of my neck. My nose fills with the scent of dark spice. "You've already cast the spell."

I draw a shaky breath.

"We have an agreement," he continues in a lethally quiet voice that makes the hair on my arms stand on end. He circles me, close but not touching. "You have the power to command me to visit you as necessary. I would have expected Maeve Gowdie to explain as much, but then maybe she did, and you simply didn't understand. This evening's *spectacle* suggests you don't understand a number of things about how a magical agreement works." He's in front of me, his nose almost brushing mine. Behind me again. My heart thunders. My palms break a sweat. Shadows play around us and I swear I can feel one brush my ankle. "Are you a child, playing with magic like you might play with matches?"

His words strike a blow, but I'm already numb. I've withstood too much tonight. My eyes lose focus. I'm here but not really. Suddenly cold, although I'm still wearing my coat.

His gaze settles on my neck, the bruising there, and he goes perfectly still. I think I see fury contort his features, then it's gone. When he speaks again, his voice is softer, almost kind. "Our agreement still stands. The man is not beyond my reach. Say the word, and I will kill him."

I blink slowly, swallowing through a throat still gritty from being choked. "What's your name?"

"You don't need it to employ my services," he counters. "The Gowdies call me *the advocate*."

I slip my hand into my coat pocket and squeeze the candle. "Please, your real name. I want to know."

A puzzled look tightens his features. "Damien."

"Damien." When I say it, he closes his eyes for a beat, and I'm glad I asked. He is a person, maybe not human, but an individual. He deserves to be addressed by an actual name. "You're right that I didn't fully understand the spell. Maeve told me you were an advocate who would help me save my house, not that you would murder Tony."

He tips his head, scrutinizing every part of me with that seemingly perpetual scowl on his lips. "You knew I was a monster when you called me. I deal in death. How else did you expect I'd solve your problem?"

I want to give him some insightful retort, but in my exhausted state, my mind has gone completely blank. "I don't know. I guess I made a mistake."

His brilliant silver gaze settles on my neck again. "Then why, when the man has made such a mess of you, won't you free me to kill him now?"

I release a deep breath. "Because I'm not a murderer."

The corner of his mouth lifts into a sneer. "No, you are a trembling sparrow who's been knocked out of the sky and insists on flying back into the window again and again. How many times will you smash your head into your reflection before you understand that it's killing you?" The steely edge of his tone cuts through me.

"Now you're being cruel."

"Am I?" He circles me again, that scornful expression frozen in place. "I've lived a long time. Many of your lifetimes. I can tell you without a doubt that Denardi is evil. He wears his viciousness like armor. He stinks of festering, insufferable arrogance. If there is any man alive who deserves his comeuppance, it's him."

"How could you possibly know that?"

"The same way I can look at you and see a bird who's had her wings crushed."

I shrug out of my coat and toss it on the couch. "Maybe. Considering I'm standing here with you, a self-confessed monster and murderer, and feeling perfectly safe, I think it's clear I'm missing a crucial instinct for self-preservation."

"Then allow me to kill him!" Damien paces like a caged lion.

"I can't. Tony being evil is about Tony. Me exchanging my blood for his death is about me. I'm not evil. I can't do it."

Damien studies me, suddenly astutely curious. "Tell me this, if you are nothing like him, how did you end up married to him?"

I lower myself onto the green velvet sofa with a groan. "It's a long story."

"I have nowhere to be." He crosses his arms and settles into his stance as if he has no intention of leaving until I tell him my sorry tale. I suppose I owe him an explanation, considering I reneged on our agreement.

"My parents were murdered right after I turned seventeen. They'd gone into Richmond to do some shopping and stopped at a gas station on the way home. A twenty-eight-year-old man chose that moment to rob that gas station. The police think my parents got involved somehow. My dad was a hero. Doesn't surprise me at all he might have tried to help the attendant. Both my parents were shot and killed, along with the employee. They caught the man who did it. He's doing life in Virginia State."

"I'm sorry for your loss," Damien says in a way that's disturbingly human.

"Thanks. Anyway, afterward, I couldn't eat or sleep. Maeve and I were already a little wild, but I went crazy. Crazy enough for even her to worry about me."

"What counts as insanity to a human like you?" Damien inches closer, as if he's genuinely interested.

"I drove my mother's Camry into a light pole on purpose because I wanted to feel the airbags hit my face. I wanted to feel something. I wanted to be reminded I was alive."

Damien hisses.

"At the time, Tony's family was renting the farmhouse next door. After the Denardis found out about the death of my parents, they came to check on us and brought food. Every other day, Tony was on our doorstep with something for Grams and me. I'd see him on the grounds sometimes too, just looking out for us. I was seventeen. He was five years older than me. I wasn't attracted to him. I was too busy juggling knives to be interested in anyone. But then, one day, I was standing on the edge of the cliff at the back of our property, watching the river. I had the strongest urge to jump. I didn't want to die so much as I wanted to know what it felt like to fall. I don't know if I would have done it or not, but suddenly his arms were around me, and then he was kissing me."

"And you liked that. Him kissing you?"

I meet the monster's diamond-colored gaze, and it's like he can see into my soul. So, I go ahead and bare it. "I liked the distraction of it. I liked that he was older. I liked how rough he was, I mean before the abuse, when he kissed, he kissed hard. When he held me, it was tight, almost painful. It shocked me out of my reality." I can't believe I just admitted that. I've never told anyone, not even Maeve, but the truths just keep gurgling to the surface like raw sewage. "We started dating, and he snapped me out of the self-destructive spiral I was in. Talked me into going to college when I graduated high school that May. Looked out for my grandmother while I was away. And then he asked me to marry him four years later when I finished my degree."

"Sounds like a real hero," he drawls.

Damien doesn't shift on his feet or seem like he needs to sit, even though my story has grown long. He stands like a statue, still as marble, his full attention on me. I might've found that kind of attentiveness flattering once. Might still if I thought it had anything to do with attraction and not hunger for what is pulsing through my veins. Absently, I rub my bruised wrist. "I married Tony because I thought he was what I needed. But as soon as we were married, he changed."

"What a surprise."

I frown at the judgmental snark. "Actually, first he fixed this house, and then he changed."

"He fixed the house?"

"Sinkhole under the property. Grams found a huge crack in the foundation, and Tony paid for and managed the extensive repairs. That's why he has a claim to it now. But afterward, it was like he thought he owned me. He treated me like a pet, including hitting me when I did something that made him angry. A black eye and a broken rib later, I left him."

"Is that when you filed for divorce?"

Averting my gaze, I take interest in my tangled fingers.

"Actually, *he* filed for divorce once I moved out. No effort at reconciliation. He was happy to see me go. Tonight, I learned he was sleeping with his secretary the entire time we were married." I rub my temples. "Honestly, that shouldn't have been a surprise. He rarely touched me, even in the beginning. He is the only man I've ever been with. God, tonight he suggested he wanted us both. Her for her body and me to control as his little robot wife. Sick, right?"

Damien rubs his chin, expression dark like he's late for an appointment to kick kittens. The grandfather clock's incessant ticking fills the wordless space between us. "Am I to gather from this pitiful story of yours that you refuse to allow me to kill Tony because he provided you with a few casseroles and told you what to do with your life?"

I snort. "Fettucine and the patriarchy. I was helpless to resist."

Damien ignores my failed attempt at humor. "Very well, little bird, if you wish to call off our arrangement, so be it. But undoing one bargain requires another to take its place. I will agree not to kill Tony... in exchange for more of your blood."

Finally. "Deal."

His icy gaze rakes down my body. "Then, stand up and take off your clothes."

9

STIPULATIONS

ELOISE

"My clothes? I thought the deal was for my blood?" I stare up at him from the couch, sliding forward so that I'm perched on the edge. My heart bangs against my ribcage like an angry prisoner.

"You know how this works."

"But I don't need to light the candle or draw the symbol?" It doesn't make any sense. "Why just the nudity?"

"The candle and the symbol are to summon me. I'm already here, and these are my terms."

"The blood and my nudity are your payment?"

"You catch on quickly."

"Why not just my blood?"

Damien begins to pace again, his eyes never leaving mine. "Because I wish it."

That isn't good enough for me. I already feel vulnerable as hell after my run-in with Tony and desperately unattractive after meeting his mistress. The idea of exposing every roll and mole makes my stomach turn, not to mention that my face is puffy and streaked from crying. I must look like a clown. "So, you want to humiliate me? Do you get off on that sort of thing?"

He stops in his tracks and rushes me until I have to lean back on the sofa to avoid his fangs. His nose almost touches mine and his brilliant eyes flash with inner fire.

"I'll tell you why, little bird." His low, rough timbre sounds like he's dragged his throat through hot cinders. "First, I want you to remove that god-awful sweater because I don't want anything that reminds you of him between us when I take your blood. Second, I want the rest of it gone because your body pleases me, and I want your fragile skin against me when I'm at your neck. Third, I want to taste you and not this caricature he's made of you. And finally, you will do it because if you don't, I will hold you to our original agreement and show Tony what it feels like to be strangled by a string of pearls." His teeth clack together when he finishes.

"You saw what happened. You were watching."

"From a distance," he growls. "You commanded me to leave. You didn't say how far I had to go."

I gulp so hard it seems to echo in the room. Once again, my body and brain are at odds. My mind tells me I should be afraid, but I'm not. My muscles grow warm and loose. My lids lower as my face tips up to look at him. My lips part. The intensity of his stare sends my pulse skittering. Heat blooms low within me. It's been a long time since I've wanted sex, but all at once I ache for him.

His nostrils flare, and I wonder if he can smell my arousal. I don't care if he does. Damien's words make me feel seen. They make me feel wanted. And I don't care if it is only for my blood. After a night where Tony made me feel worthless all over again, it feels good.

Without further hesitation, I stand and remove the cardigan and the matching sleeveless sweater. He takes a step back, watching me with hungry eyes as I toe off my shoes and shimmy out of my slacks. When I'm done, I stand before him in nothing but a black lace bra and thong.

I reach behind me to undo the clasp, but he raises his hand. "Those are yours."

"Yes. I chose this set."

"Better."

"How did you know? That the outfit wasn't something I chose, I mean."

The hard edges of his face soften. "Even little birds are wild things. A wild thing with a tattoo like yours wouldn't choose that outfit." He frowns. "It was also how he grabbed your pearls. Denardi is a wicked man and I sensed that's why he wanted you to wear them. He twisted them like a man who has dreamed about choking a woman."

That's a pleasant thought. I shiver.

"I've upset you, but you know I'm right."

"I don't want to think about him tonight." I wipe my mind of everything but this room, this moment. "Do you want me to stop undressing?"

He shakes his head slowly.

Reaching behind my head, I pull the elastic from my hair and let the platinum-blond sweep across my shoulders. I try not to think of how much I hate the color or how many hours I've spent straightening it because that's what Tony wanted. I unhook my bra and let the straps fall down my arms, then bend over to slide off my panties. Naked, all my insecurities rush back tenfold. I focus on the carved foot of the sofa.

Strong fingers clasp my chin and lift. His diamond eyes cut through me with their intensity. "Beautiful," he grits out.

I shake my head.

"I have lived several of your lifetimes and have no reason to lie. Do not take my words lightly, little bird."

"So... " I tip my head and wait for him to strike.

"I don't take what is not freely given. Ever." His eyes drift to the window behind me and the reflection of my tattoo. His fingers trace along my spine. "This is yours as well. Your choice."

"Yes."

"What made you choose this design?"

I look over my shoulder at the reflection. A collection of archaic symbols make up the abstract figure of a key. At the top, a diamond shape marks the base of my neck, flanked by two triangular figures that form a winged handle. A parade of interconnected symbols progress down my spine, forming the shank of the key and ending in a point, with two bits extending toward my right hip. The tattoo is purple and black, composed entirely of angles and spirals. Tony hated it. More than once, he'd asked me to have it removed. It was the one thing about myself that I refused to change.

"My mother was a professional artist, and this figure is featured in many of her most personal works. When I look at it, I see a key but others see an insect or—"

"A dragon," he says softly.

"Right. It was probably inspired by many things, but this particular piece of art was important. Both my mother and father had it tattooed on their chests, right over their hearts. After they were killed, I wanted it to remember them. I wanted them in my skin. I was only seventeen, but Maeve knew a guy."

He strokes his long fingers along the tattoo again, sending shivers through me. I arch, inhaling as my breasts press into his shirt. "How does a woman with a tattoo like this become such a helpless, trembling little bird?"

"I'm not helpless," I say weakly. The feel of Tony's fingers twisting in my necklace comes back to me in a rush and I don't know if my words are truth or lie.

"But you are trembling." Damien's eyes meet mine.

"It's drafty in this room." *And I'm naked and pressed against a monster's gloriously handsome body.*

He toys with a strand of my hair, rubbing it between his fingers. "You have the power still. I haven't yet taken your blood. You hold the candle. You should know, Isobel Gowdie was much like you. She was the first of the family to call on me. She was accused of witchcraft by a spurned admirer. At first, she didn't want to hurt the man who she'd once thought of as a friend, but when they beat her and told her she would burn at the stake in the morning, she understood she had no choice. She lit my candle and commanded my help. I killed her accuser, the magistrate, and the would-be executioner and used some compulsion on the guards to have her freed by sunrise."

I grasp onto that last part, remembering how he'd compelled Tamara. "Why can't you use compulsion on Tony to save my house? Make him drop his claim to it?"

He shakes his head. "It only works if a person's will is

weak around a situation. Tamara left Tony's office because she didn't deeply care about being there. She found the situation awkward and embarrassing. I sensed in her the desire to leave and simply bolstered that thought. The same with the guards. They liked Isobel, and some part of them knew it was wrong to hold her. But the men I killed—men like Tony—their will was strong. Tony covets this house. I don't know why, but he's firm on this. I felt it."

"He wants to hurt me," I hypothesize. "Because he can't control me any other way."

Damien slants a curt nod and pulls me tighter against him. "You want to take the moral high ground. You don't want blood on your hands. But it wasn't wrong for Isobel to use me to save herself, and it isn't wrong for you either. This is a game of kill or be killed, and if you don't find the strength to fight him"—he runs a hand over my tattoo—"I'm afraid you may not survive this, little bird." His voice becomes as low and smooth as a caress, his breath brushing my bruised throat. With his hand petting my back in long, fluid strokes, the temptation to obey him is strong. "Free me to do this thing for you. Be free of him."

I sag in his arms, wanting to say yes, wanting to agree to anything this seductive creature proposes. Tony *does* deserve it, I tell myself. But when I think about giving the command, I can't. "A burning stake is different from a house, Damien. I wouldn't be saving myself from an excruciating death. I'd be saving my home, my memories, and a place for Grams. Those are big, important things, but they aren't the price of a person's life. Even Tony's. It's not the same."

Damien cups my face in one massive hand and it's like

he's looking straight into me again, as if his ability to travel through shadows extends to the darkness in my soul. "So be it." His words come down like a hatchet. He strikes quickly, sinking his fangs into the side of my throat. Once again, there is a mild sting and then pleasure —deep, calming pleasure. I fist his lapels.

His hand drifts down my spine to cup my ass and squeeze. A moan escapes my lips, and my lashes flutter as my eyes roll back. I clench his jacket tighter to keep myself from embracing him. He's a monster. He's a monster.

Too soon, he retracts his fangs, licking the wound again and again. Last time, he spent much longer at my vein until I passed out. This time, I'm not even woozy. He's taken less blood, but it's his touch that lingers, his hand smoothing over my butt cheek, back up my spine, to massage the base of my skull. He licks his way to the other side of my throat, and I tip my head, wondering if he'll strike again. He doesn't, but he lifts my hand and kisses trails along my bruised wrist, scraping the flesh with his fangs. I watch the deep red splotches fade to almost nothing and remember what Maeve said about his saliva having healing qualities.

"Thank you," I say softly.

He meets my gaze and for a split second there's this look on his face, like a kid who's seeing his first dinosaur. There's wonder and pleasure and warmth, and then the scowl returns and the softness I thought I saw is gone. He backs away toward the shadows.

"You can stay," I blurt. It's a terrible idea I'll most certainly regret tomorrow, but I want him. If he asks me, I'll let him take me right here on the floor. I don't care about the repercussions or that I'd possibly be inviting my own death. For the first time in forever, I feel beautiful and wanted, and I welcome the pleasure I know he can give.

But he refuses with a shake of his head and a look loaded with challenge. "No, I can't. But call me again if you change your mind about Tony."

Damien blends into shadow and is gone with a flick of that smoky barbed tail, leaving only the crushing realization that he was my only plan to save Harcourt Manor.

IO

THE LIBRARY

DAMIEN

I'm royally fucked. I manifest underground outside the west wing of the Palace of Night Haven, feeling like I have a full-body case of blue balls. I need answers. Eloise Harcourt has sunk her claws into me and is performing some kind of voodoo on my inner workings. Maeve Gowdie may not know what she is, but she's something. A godsdamned enchantress I haven't encountered in five hundred years on two different worlds.

Even now, every molecule that makes up my shadowy body is aching to return to her, and not just for blood. My mating drive urges me to claim her. I'm strung out and wanting. Should I have stayed? The taste of her blood was pure ambrosia, and just like the ancient drink of the gods, it's both delicious and deadly. I can feel it coursing through my veins like bottled lightning, throbbing in my still hard cock.

When she invited me to take her, I almost gave in. The

idea of fucking her until she screams my name is more than tempting. Coming inside her while drinking that sweet nectar from her vein would be paradise. The only thing that stopped me was seeing that sigil on her back. She admitted that her parents had worn the mysterious pattern over their hearts. Strange place for a tattoo with no magical power.

No, there's more to this little bird than meets the eye. I can't risk her binding me further to this place. The last thing I need is a complication like Eloise Harcourt, no matter how soft and delicious she may be.

Since the night the Gowdie's tricked me into their service, my only goal has been to find a way to break their hold on me and return home, and I'm finally onto something. I've made a friend , a scribe who spends his days in the palace archives among books ancient enough to hold secrets even the Gowdies aren't privy to.

Which is why I'm here.

I jog up the steps of the palatial building. Sunrise is coming topside, and the vampires of Night Haven, tired from a long night of activity, have headed home to sleep the day away, leaving the streets conspicuously empty aside from the occasional courier. This section of the royal palace houses an ancient collection of texts and scrolls that inform vampire kind. And vampires are nothing if not well-educated about their world. Being immortal gives one plenty of time for intellectual pursuits.

I hurry inside, hoping to catch my new friend before he leaves for the day. But I needn't have worried. I find Lazarus hunched over a massive dusty tome. The ancient vampire truly loves his work and would likely sleep in the stacks if it were allowed.

"Oh, Damien! It's so good to see you again, my friend." Lazarus shuffles over to embrace me, thumping my back vigorously. Truth be told, I get the sense that Lazarus exists in relative isolation. He's old, even for a vampire. While this species is immortal, they do age, albeit far slower than a human. His skin has a thin, parchment-like quality, and his nails are thick and yellowing. Everything here eventually decays, and Lazarus, as far as I can tell, is thousands of years old. I asked him once if he was the Lazarus of biblical fame and he told me he was not, but he remembered the man from when he was a boy. That's when I realized just how long he'd been toiling on this planet.

I try to remember to make my visit about more than just me. Lazarus doesn't entertain many guests here in the stacks.

"It's good to see you too, Lazarus. Have you been well?"

"As well as can be expected given the changing of the guard." He lowers his voice. "I'm afraid the new queen has earned her reputation for being short-tempered."

"A well-studied vampire like yourself should have no problem avoiding her attention." I gesture toward the shelves. "I can't think of a better place to hide from her than under a stack of books."

He gives a low laugh. "True. From what I've heard, she's not much of a reader."

"Just who we need running the largest vampire nest on the East Coast." I'm not the type to take much interest in politics—ironic considering I was heir to a kingdom in my own world once. That was centuries ago, though. I'm more slave than prince in this world, and what happens here is none of my business. This isn't home for me. The second I find a way to break the magical chains that bind me, I'm gone.

But living in Night Haven, it's impossible not to hear the rumors. The last vampire queen and her consort died under suspicious circumstances. Rumors that they were murdered by the current queen, chosen from the same powerful bloodline, seem probable. "Maybe things will get better once her position becomes more... stable."

Lazarus grins, his abnormally large eyes glowing in the dim light. "Once she takes a consort? Yes. It has been so in the past. I've lived through three matriarchies, and always it is so."

The issue for these vampire royals is always safety and protection. Without a consort, the vampire queen is at constant risk of usurpation, usually by the very people she trusts most, those who share the royal bloodline—her family. Almost every queen chooses a consort from the military ranks, a male who can serve as a guard dog, lover, and politician. Even then, it isn't always enough as the last consort's untimely death proves. Poor schmuck.

As if he's only just remembered something, Lazarus jolts, his expression becoming excited. "About your problem... I've found something."

My muscles draw tight as a bow string. He gestures for me to follow him and I do, trying to tamp down the hope that rises in my chest. This wouldn't be the first false lead I've had on an antidote to my situation.

"I have to say, the hold the Gowdie's have on you has proven to be a most complex challenge for this old scribe.

Their magic is rare and we are particularly vulnerable to it. The spell that holds you is in the marrow of your bones." He points at the page of a book with a diagram of a vampire and an illustration of the inside of a bone.

"I don't know this language."

"Few do, my friend. It's an offshoot of Gaelic that was used by a band of faeries in northern Scotland during the eighteenth century." He picks up a set of reading glasses and perches them on his nose. "The clan was wiped out about a hundred years ago. Poached by shifters they say. Werewolves found them utterly delicious. Lucky for you, I spent some time among them and remember quite a bit."

"I count myself extremely lucky to have met you," I say, and the yellow-toothed smile the vampire gives me tells me he appreciates the sentiment.

"We've always known the Gowdies are animators, their magic can be used to bring almost anything to life. In one famous case that occurred in the fourteenth century, an ancestor animated an entire army of wooden toys to storm a castle and kill the lord of the manor over an argument concerning land rights. But what sets them apart from other witches with this power is their ability to use it to exert control over sentient beings, like you. And they do this by animating their bones."

"Bones?"

"The closer to dead the bones are the better, but animating a vampire is quite easy for them. The spell that binds you, Damien, is rooted in your bones."

I wait for more, but he just stares at me as if the answer is obvious. "I'm rather attached to my bones, Lazarus. Please tell me that you have a theory of how to undo it that doesn't involve liquefying my skeleton."

He chuckles. "Considering you're able to become shadow, if liquification could fix what ails you, I suspect you'd be free already."

I rub my jaw. "It doesn't work like that. When I'm shadow, everything that is me simply separates, but every part of me still exists."

"Exactly." He holds up a finger. "This curse isn't like a tumor. It can't be cut out. It's systemic, like a virus."

"Neither your kind nor mine can catch viruses."

"Not human ones. But this, this is close."

"Then how do I cure this virus?" I find myself holding my breath that he has an answer.

Lazarus rubs the back of his head. "I'm afraid it won't be easy. In humans, their medicines block the receptors in their cells where viruses attach. Hypothetically, in you, a counter curse could do the same, one that goes all the way to your bones and crowds out the Gowdie magic."

"A counter curse... So, another witch."

"Or fae. Any other magic-performing creature might be able to do the same if they were strong enough. The problem, of course, aside from finding such a creature, is knowing who to trust. Anyone strong enough to free you, would of course be—"

"Strong enough to bind me again."

"Hypothetically."

"Great." I groan.

"I'm sorry I don't have better news for you."

We stand in companionable silence, breathing in the stale and dusty air. It's well past dawn now. Fatigue weighs me down. I need to get to bed, but there's one more thing I feel compelled to ask. "Lazarus, I wonder if you might help me with something else. It's a particularly difficult bit of research."

The vampire beams as if I've offered him a gift. "I'll give it my best."

I lift my hands and command the shadows to form Eloise's tattoo in the air before him. "I am attempting to find the origins of this sigil. It's not in any of the modern witch records, but I thought perhaps in one of the older tomes."

"Where did you see this?" Lazarus asks in wonder. "Interesting. Very interesting." He ruffles through a desk drawer and produces a pen and notepad, creating a quick sketch of the design.

"It was on the back of an ordinary human woman. It struck me as strange."

"Strange indeed. Some of these symbols are Norse in origin, others Egyptian, Celtic, pagan. The more I look at it, perhaps none of those four. It might predate them all. Are you sure this is an accurate depiction?"

"Positive. I commanded the shadows to record it exactly as it appears."

Lazarus finishes his sketch and holds it up to check its accuracy. He makes a few adjustments. Once he's satisfied, I pass a hand through the shadows and erase the design from the air.

"It will take some careful digging. The tomes I think will help are in the archives."

"Take your time. I'm only curious." I'm not sure why I lie except that I'm still lying to myself. I am far more than curious. If Lazarus confirms she is human and no threat to me, I will take her. I will seduce her and taste her again.

"Understood. Whatever I find, I'll use it as an excuse to enjoy your company again soon."

"Thank you, Lazarus. And no excuse is needed."

"Have a pleasant sleep, Damien."

I leave the library and travel the few blocks through the empty streets to the simple dwelling where I live. I'm so tired, I don't even bother unlocking the door but shift into shadow, re-forming on my bed. My last thoughts are of Eloise before I slip into an easy and dreamless sleep.

II

THE BAD DAY

ELOISE

After my monster—*Damien*—left last night, I spent hours racking my brain for some way out of this mess that didn't include killing Tony. Nothing came to me, other than the obvious—there's no way I can raise or earn $500k in time to save this house. Still, I know one thing for sure, I need a job. No matter what happens, being gainfully employed will keep my car running, pay for health insurance, and stock groceries in the fridge, not to mention what it will do for my mental well-being. If I've learned one thing, it's that I never want to be dependent on someone like Tony again.

I plan to start my hunt for employment at Echo Mills High School. With any luck, Principal Singer will give me my old teaching position back. It's mid-school year, though, so I'm not holding my breath. Still, I've got to try.

But the moment I see Grams, I know my plans will have to wait. Today is a bad day. She can't get out of bed and is running a fever. I wrap her in a comforter and hold her when the chills come. Even through the puffy down, I can feel her bones. It's easy to forget how frail she's become when she's wearing bulky sweaters. She's lost so much weight. She's literally wasting away, and I silently curse the cancer that eats her from the inside.

When she vomits her pain pill, I clean up the sick and call the hospice line. Thankfully, the nurse has foreseen this turn of events and directs me to where she left the medicated patches. She reminds me that this is a normal part of the process, as is her loss of appetite, as if my grandmother's death is like a pregnancy, a natural event that's progressing to an inevitable end. I push her words out of my brain the moment I hear them. I'm not ready. I don't want to think about it.

I administer a pain patch to the back of her shoulder and am relieved when the muscles of her face finally relax. With my back propped against her headboard, I hold her in my arms, her mostly bald head tucked under my chin, and rock her until she falls asleep. It's past two in the afternoon when I sense I can safely leave the room and let her rest. I haven't had anything to eat or drink since the night before, and I tiptoe to the kitchen to see what I can throw together.

Halfway through a ham sandwich, I phone Maeve.

"I have a client in my waiting room. Try to make it quick," she says.

"Okay, um, sorry. I found out yesterday that Tony's affair with Tamara started before I left him. Doesn't his infidelity count for anything?"

"You called off the advocate." A disappointed sigh fills the line.

"Yes. Damien agreed not to kill him. But now I'm back where I started."

"Damien?"

"That's his name. The advocate. His name is Damien."

"You're on a first-name basis with the monster now?" Maeve laughs incredulously.

"Wait. Aren't you? He's worked for your family for centuries, and you don't know his name?"

"Just call him the advocate, Eloise. He's not a friend. He's not even a person. Think of him as a tool. You're compelling a creature of the night to do your bidding, not getting to know him over tea."

"I'm not comfortable with that."

Maeve groans and abruptly changes the subject. "Unfortunately, neither Tony's infidelity nor his domestic abuse of you dissolves the prenuptial agreement because the contract has a no-fault clause. Basically, that means that it doesn't matter if one of you caused the divorce through your actions or inactions. It doesn't nullify the agreement."

With my fist pressed against my forehead, I lean an elbow on the table and close my eyes. "I confronted Tony about the house last night after I stopped Damien from killing him. It didn't go well." My voice cracks and my eyes sting with the memory.

"What did he do?" Maeve demands.

"Tried to choke me with my necklace." My cheeks heat.

"Fucking asshole."

"I'm embarrassed to admit I let it happen again."

She blows out a breath. "You didn't let anything

happen. He assaulted you. Is there evidence we can take to the police? Bruises or—"

"No," I say, remembering how Damien healed me. I consider sharing that tidbit with Maeve, then hold it back. If she doesn't like me calling him by his first name, she definitely won't like hearing about our make-out session. "No bruises."

"Shit. Don't try it again. It's clear he won't budge and next time it could be worse. He's an evil bastard. You should have let the advocate do what he does best."

"Yeah, yeah, murder him. I've heard you, and I'm taking it under advisement. You mentioned before that you're still pursuing a legal way to stop Tony."

"It's a long shot."

"Tell me more."

I hear a door open, mumbling, and then papers shuffling. Maeve whispers to her secretary to give her five minutes. The door closes again. "There are three ways to nullify a prenup in Virginia," Maeve says, coming back on the line. "The first is to prove that you signed it under duress."

"I didn't," I admit. "I thought it was a formality and that we'd be together forever."

"I knew you'd say that. Gods, girl, has anyone ever told you that you're honest to a fault?"

"You."

"Right, that's why I immediately threw that possibility out. The second way is if we can make a case that it's unconscionable. That means that it's so grossly unfair to one party that it wouldn't be ethical for the court to allow it to stand. I've asserted this all along and already filed this with the courts. What he's done to you, restricting your ability to work but then not allowing you access to any of his assets, is cruel in every sense. However, you were married only two years and have no children. His lawyers will likely say you entered the marriage with nothing, and you were the one who left Tony, so therefore, you are no worse off than before you met him. And honestly, that one could go either way with the judge."

"What's the last way?"

"If you can prove that he had or has assets that he did not fully disclose before you signed, it nullifies the prenup. That wouldn't immediately save Harcourt Manor, but with half of his assets on the line, it gives you a hell of a lot more to negotiate with."

I rub my jaw, memories storming back to the time he whacked me across the face. "I think he does have undisclosed assets," I say quickly, and I can't believe I didn't think of this before. "The first time he hit me, it was because I found him paying an invoice charged to a company with a logo I didn't recognize. Gold Weaver. He told me to mind my own business. He was so defensive. His reaction was just crazy. There's something there. I know it."

"Can you get your hands on that invoice?"

I think for a second. "Probably not, but I bet Damien could if I called him again. Is it okay if I keep the candle a little longer?"

"As long as you need it." Maeve clears her throat. "Eloise, just be careful, okay? The advocate—"

"Damien."

"I've watched him kill men without a second thought.

The candle gives you the power to control him, but that doesn't mean you should necessarily trust him."

The line goes silent for a beat while I consider how to respond to that. "Understood. Thanks, Maeve, for everything."

"You're welcome. One day this will all be behind us. I'm not sure we'll ever laugh about it, but someday we will sit on your porch, drinking mimosas, so far beyond this that we couldn't care less about Tony Denardi."

"We won't even remember his name."

"That's the spirit."

"I should go. Grams is having a rough day, and I need to prepare the symbol if I'm going to call Damien back tonight."

"One more thing before you go... " Maeve's voice sounds serious. "We have a court date."

"Oh? When is it?" Maeve previously told me to expect six months to a year to get a date.

"October 19th"

"That can't be right. That's a month from today."

"Yes. It's the fastest date anyone in my firm has ever heard of. Even in cases without a prenup where adultery and domestic violence can be proven, it usually takes longer. The only explanation I can think of is that Tony paid someone off to accelerate the proceedings."

I close my eyes and curse. In the back of my mind, I always thought Grams might pass before my court date, which would give me time to follow her final wishes and have her buried on the property before Tony took possession of the place. I hate thinking that way. I want to believe that Grams can hold on for another six months, maybe even a year. But in the back of my mind, I've counted on the probability of a scenario where the timing works out.

That fucking weasel. This is too fast. It's cruel and spiteful.

"That's terrible timing, Maeve. Grams is getting worse. In a month, moving her will be painful for her."

"I know. And I can try to use that to have the date moved. Only, if Tony can manage to get a court date in thirty days in this state, he likely has the judge in his back pocket. My recommendation is that whatever skeletons you think you can pull out of his closet, you do it quickly. If we go to court without some hard evidence, we will lose."

I push away the rest of my sandwich. "I understand."

I don't understand. Not anything. Not how my ex can get away with what he's doing or why God, if he exists, would take Grams from me right when everything is going to hell. I try not to think about what could go wrong and instead focus on what's in front of me—spending quality time with Grams while I have the chance.

Evening falls on Harcourt Manor. Grams wakes, but barely eats, although I manage to get some herbal tea in her. I tell myself that we have time, and I try to make the most of what moments remain. I cuddle next to her in bed and read to her from one of her favorite novels. She pays for internet service and has Wi-Fi, but it rarely works out here, which means we have a choice between five television channels. I pop in one of her favorite movies, *Somewhere In Time*, and we pretend to watch it while we talk about her childhood. She tells me all her favorite stories again, and I whisper that I love her as she drifts off to sleep.

Only when I'm sure she's out for the night do I creep from her room and prepare again to call Damien.

12

THE PRICE

ELOISE

I need to convince the advocate to strike a new bargain with me, and I can only hope he's still willing. Last night ended awkwardly. He said I could call on him again if I changed my mind about having him kill Tony. I'm not sure how he'll react when I ask him instead to search for an invoice I haven't seen in months.

I do my best to sweeten the deal. He's mentioned liking things I've chosen for myself, so after I shower, I leave the pink bathrobe hanging on my bathroom door and don a thigh-length, kimono-style robe from the back of my closet, one of the few things I still own from before Tony. It's silky, black and strikes me as something a creature made of shadows would love.

After that, I go through the motions of preparing myself and the parlor almost robotically. My grandmother's failing health, my impending court date, my gloomy financial situation, and Tony's cruelty take up too much room in my head. I try not to think about anything but exactly what's in front of me. I roll the carpet back. I draw the symbol. I ready the candle.

When the grandfather clock strikes twelve, I light the match, lowering it to the wick. The black flame flickers to life. With no hesitation, I draw the blade across my palm, sucking air through my teeth at the sting. The pain is mildly comforting, a reminder that I can still feel.

As before, shadows gather in the corners of the dim room, and in the blink of an eye, Damien is there. My heart beats a mad tattoo in my chest, but paradoxically my body loosens, air entering my lungs in a long, deep inhale. Suddenly, mercifully, all I can think of is him. It's hard to think of anything else in Damien's presence. He commands attention, from his sheer size to his dark, preternatural grace, to that inviting spice that clings to his skin.

His gaze rakes over me, nostrils flaring with surprise and intensity. He's the first man to ever look at me like that, like he's hungry for me. I thought Tony had, in the beginning, but that was nothing like this. Damien prowls toward me like a predator. As frightening as that should be, I am eased by the simplicity of it. He wants me. His desire might be only for my blood, a desire to consume me, but I don't care. I love the feel of it, of being wanted. And my physical reaction to his presence requires no thought, no concentration, no decision.

It just is.

"Little bird, have you changed your mind so soon?" His voice is smoke made flesh. His lids sink low over those silvery eyes until he's looking at me through his lashes. His full lips spread into a wicked grin. "Come to your senses?"

"Not entirely," I say. "I still don't want you to kill Tony."

He balks. "Then why am I here? You do realize, despite what you told him, I am no lawyer."

"But you are a monster, which gives you certain powers. Powers that could be useful in finding out information that would otherwise be inaccessible to someone like me."

He leans back on his heels and folds his arms. "A monster. Is that what you've decided I am? Given up on vampire?"

"It seems like an encompassing enough label."

"Fine. The monster is listening."

"The first time Tony hit me—"

"It happened more than once?" Damien hisses through his teeth. "Let me kill him."

"No." I take a deep breath and center myself. "I found an invoice on his desk charged to a company called Gold Weaver, Inc. I wouldn't have thought twice about it if it were a typical invoice. Denardi Enterprises does business with thousands of other companies. But this was an invoice he was paying. He was acting as Gold Weaver and the name he was signing was not his own. It was weird."

"What does that have to do with me?"

"I believe Tony is running a secret business on the side. The way he lashed out at me at the time was unusual, even for him. He hadn't wanted me to see that invoice. Maeve says that if we can prove he has undeclared assets, we might be able to dismantle our prenup and negotiate for the house. I want you to find that Gold Weaver invoice and bring a copy to me."

A low rumble emanates from his chest. "Killing him would be faster."

I tilt my head and pop out a hip. "Are you telling me you can't do this? You can turn yourself into smoke and compel information out of people, but a little private investigation is beyond your capabilities?"

With a look of condescension, he drawls, "Not beyond my abilities, but it is a new agreement, one that will cost *more* to secure."

"More than our first?"

"If I kill him, I have the added reward of his blood. The task you ask of me now is far less... appealing."

"Fine, what's your price, then?" I release a deep breath. "Just so you know, I have very little money and only so much blood."

"I have no use for your money." He moves toward me, his gaze raking down my body in a way that makes my skin flush hot, and I realize I'm still wearing the black kimono. "I do want what blood you have to give, but this time, I want to touch you too."

"Touch me?" I know what he means but I want to hear him say it. "Why?"

His gaze traces along my exposed neck, the vee of flesh at my chest, then skates to the belt knotted at my navel, lingering at the place the silk ends halfway down my thighs.

"Yours?" His brow quirks higher, along with the corner of his mouth.

I nod.

He takes a deep breath, and I wonder what he's learning from the scents in the air because he steps to the very edge of the symbol and stares down at me with a new intensity. "Because I wish it."

God, I want his touch. My nipples harden under the silk, and inside, my body is begging me to say yes. I hate that a part of me, however small, hears Tony's voice in that moment. *Who would want you?*

But even if I were attractive, I'd expect Damien to be interested in my blood and nothing more. Granted, the first time I performed the spell, I presumed there might be sex involved, considering it required me to be naked, but when he hadn't tried anything then, I gathered it wasn't his primary interest. And while he'd grabbed my ass last time, he hadn't taken it any further, although I flat out asked him to stay.

"You could have *touched* me more last night, but you didn't."

"I may be a monster to you and your kind, but as I told you, I do not take what isn't offered me." He curls his lip as if the thought is distasteful to him. "Make no mistake, Eloise, what I'm asking is to touch you between your thighs where even now I can smell you're wet for me. I want to touch those breasts I so enjoyed you holding against me. If we make this agreement, I will touch you... everywhere."

I must be crazy to entertain this idea. I chew my lip, tempted, aching to say yes.

When he speaks again, his voice is scorched velvet. "What will it be, little bird?"

I could say no. I could renegotiate the agreement.

I don't want to.

"Okay. You'll investigate Gold Weaver, and, in exchange, you can touch me wherever you like, in addition to taking my blood." I raise my chin a notch and meet his gaze. "We have a deal."

The symbol rises off the floor, twinkling like a million sparkling stars, and then crashes, disappearing like dust on the wind. Damien steps over the now non-existent line, but he doesn't come straight for me. He circles me, slow and deliberate. He's making me wait, probably listening to my pulse ratchet faster as he closes in. One strong hand wraps gently around my throat, fingers cradling the back of my neck while his thumb strokes toward my chin. My lips part on a jagged breath. His eyes never leave mine, but I gulp at the brush of his fingers untying my kimono. The sides swing open, and cool air skims across my belly and between my breasts. He sweeps the silk off my shoulders and it ripples to the floor.

Only then does his gaze trail down my body. My breath hitches at the heat in his eyes, some primal essence triggering an instinct to run. I jerk back, but his hand cradles the base of my skull. "Shhh, easy."

His other hand settles in the small of my back and he pulls me closer. Two deep breaths and the urge to bolt morphs into something else, a hot, tingling sensation that swirls low in my abdomen. I submit with a sigh, calming in his hold.

"Good girl," he coos. The praise sends an unexpected thrill through me. And when his lips brush mine, my heart lurches into a gallop. When he said he wanted to touch me, I hadn't thought he meant to kiss me, but his full lips meet mine, in a breath-stealing battle of mouths and tongues. His fang nips my lip, and he swallows my cry with another kiss. He licks the spot, closing the wound, then plunges back into my mouth, the taste of him mingling with the taste of my blood. I moan at the way he strokes against my tongue, exploring the hidden depths.

This kiss is a firebrand, a catalyst. I can feel it changing me, drawing out a long-dormant need like an animal coming out of hibernation after a long winter. I turn molten and slide my hands inside his jacket, feeling the hard planes of his chest. My fingers find their way to his buttons. I've managed two when he pulls back, grabbing my wrists and twisting them behind my back where he pins them inside one massive hand.

It doesn't stop me from spotting the tattoo on his chest through the open neck, a skull and crossbones pattern right over his heart. I wonder if he has more. Inspecting every inch of his body for tattoos seems like a good idea at the moment, but when I tug against his grip, he holds firm.

"Easy," he whispers again, as if I'm a skittish animal to be calmed. He strokes down the front of my throat, his fingers splaying between my breasts, my nipples tight and hard with wanting to be touched. His hold behind my back tightens, and I arch. The new position lifts my breasts and he bends his knees to lower himself, catching one peak in his mouth, sucking greedily until I moan. His fangs scrape either side of the hard bud, but the pain is a wicked counterpoint to the pleasure of his tongue. Just when it begins to be too much, he moves to the other side, tongue flicking, teasing, nipping.

"Damien," I whisper. "I need... I need." I can't complete the thought. I want to touch him. I want to taste his skin. But I need to ease the ache between my legs. I straddle his knee, shamelessly rubbing myself against his tree-trunk-sized thigh. He releases my breast with a feral growl.

"I'll show you what you need." His fingers find my center and slide easily through my wet folds. I pant as he dips inside me. "Oh, you do want this." Never breaking eye contact, he withdraws his fingers and thrusts them into his mouth, sucking them clean.

I moan at the sight, fighting against his hold on my wrists, wanting desperately to touch him, to get closer.

Mercifully, his fingers find my center again and this time they stay there, massaging with delectable pressure. I shamelessly ride his hand, my eyes widening at the jolts of energy his touch sends through me. He sinks his fingers deeper, all the time working my clit with his thumb. "Let me feel you come, little bird."

A command issued in moonlit silk.

Already I can feel the pressure build, coiling at the base of my spine. I circle my hips, climbing higher. Almost there. I tip my head back just as the pleasure crests.

That's when he strikes. His fangs sink into my throat at the exact moment a tsunami of ecstasy washes through me. My eyes roll back in my head and my toes curl. If he weren't holding me up, I'm sure I'd slump to the floor. I come and keep coming. Every draw at my neck amplifies the supernova exploding inside me. It blinds me in white light.

Minutes or maybe hours pass. He stops drinking. Licks the wound closed. Gently, carefully, he balances me on my feet, releases me, and backs away.

He's not unaffected by what transpired between us. He's hard and his long dark lashes are low.

I reach for him, prepared to return the favor, but he dodges my touch.

"The agreement is made." His voice is curt and gruff as a bear's growl. At once, he breaks into shadow and is gone, leaving me standing naked in my parlor, my body still ringing from the most intense pleasure I've ever experienced.

13

TELL ME HOW IT IS

ELOISE

The moment sunlight streams through my window, I spring from my bed. My alarm hasn't even gone off. Considering how late I stayed up putting the parlor back together and reevaluating my life choices, I should be exhausted. This entire week has been a whirlwind of stressful situations. Nothing is right. My grandmother is still terminally ill. I'm still in danger of losing my house. And my bank account is still running on empty, as is my gas tank. But somehow, the sun shines brighter. My heart swells with a strange and unexpected buoyancy.

It's hope, I realize. I feel hopeful.

Is it because of Damien? Has the orgasm rewired something in my brain? I loathe to admit it. One climax from a bad boy should not improve my mood. If anything, the replay of the encounter in my head is worthy of the hashtags #unsafe, #foolhardy, and #badidea.

Still, the truth is I haven't ever experienced that kind

of pleasure. Learning my body is capable of it is like learning I have a hidden talent for acrobatics or can speak another language. Last night was eye-opening and empowering. Damien wanted me. I saw it in his eyes. And today, standing in the sun, I am a woman worth wanting. An individual, separate and distinct from Tony, capable of powerful choices, and of performing magic. Even if I never have another encounter like that with Damien, it happened, which means it could happen again with someone else.

I guess my good mood is about Damien. Even if it isn't.

After checking on Grams, I seize the moment to call my old principal, Ed Singer, and ask for my job back. Ed is an octogenarian who's been running Echo Mills High School since before I was a student there. All the jobs and applications are online these days, but Ed predates all of that and always appreciated the personal touch.

"I didn't think I'd ever hear from you again," Ed says. "Weren't you supposed to be living the good life with that new husband of yours?"

A prickle of embarrassment seizes me, but I cast it aside. "Actually, we're getting divorced. I desperately need to work, Mr. Singer. I submitted my application on the website, but you told me to call if things ever changed."

"I'm glad you did. We miss you here at EMHS. Both the kids and the staff loved you, Eloise. Unfortunately, after you left, we brought back Ms. Adams, so your position has been filled for the year, although I'm happy to take you on as a substitute if you're willing."

"Yes. I'll take anything you've got. Thank you."

"I don't think it'll be long before something opens up. I wouldn't be surprised if Ms. Adams retires at the end of this year. Anyway, I'll send a note to Dolores to get your paperwork processed and put you on the list."

"Thank you. Oh, thank you so much."

"See you soon, Ms. Harcourt."

I end the call, beaming at the kitchen window. This is a good day. A very good day.

"Did I hear you talking to Ed Singer?" Grams hobbles into the kitchen, dressed in an aqua-colored terry cloth lounge suit with her usual matching turban. For a woman who spent the entirety of yesterday in bed, she looks remarkably put together.

I pull out her chair and help her sink into it. "Morning, Grams. How about some cream of wheat?" It isn't her favorite, but it would be the easiest to swallow.

"I'll try a few bites."

I grab the enameled cast iron saucepan from the cupboard. The red color is chipping around the edges. It has to be a fifty years old. Still works though. I add water and start a burner on the old gas stove.

"Are you going to tell me about your call?" Grams asks.

"Mr. Singer is hiring me on as a substitute. I think it's actually better than full-time. This way, if you need me, I can be here." Grams becomes conspicuously quiet, and I glance over my shoulder at her.

"Teaching." She shifts. "You haven't given a second thought to opening up your mom's studio and painting again."

My brows shoot toward my hairline. "I have to actually make money. I appreciate you letting me stay here for free, but that's not a long-term solution. I have expenses. This house is paid off, thanks to Mom and Dad, but there are the taxes and the upkeep."

She spreads her gnarled fingers on the table. "I have a life insurance policy. All the paperwork is in my office and my agent, Marilyn Maples, has it on file. You remember Marilyn. After I'm gone, see her and use the proceeds to pay the taxes and to live off of while you're creating."

I walk to the table and take her hand. "That will still be a while. I need the income now."

Grams raises her chin defiantly. "For what?"

"Utilities. A better data plan considering the Wi-Fi here is awful." I hold up my phone. "My car needs some serious TLC, and then there's food, health insurance premiums."

She frowns. "Oh, Eloise, you know there are a million casseroles in the deep freeze from the neighbors. Everyone brought one when I was going through chemo. I had to tell them to stop when I ran out of room."

"I shouldn't eat all your casseroles," I say, then instantly regret my words.

She shakes her head, a cackle bubbling up from deep within her. "Who else do you think is going to eat them, darling? I can't stomach more than a few bites. There's plenty there to see you through. And once I'm gone, you'll have enough for the rest of it."

"I'm an adult. I should be able to take care of myself." I squat beside her chair and take her hand. "That's why I need this job. I need to stand on my own two feet."

Grams closes her eyes for a second, then opens them on a sigh. "I don't know why everyone is so obsessed with independence these days. Even the strongest among us needs a little help now and then. You're talented, Eloise, just like your mother. You could be more if you gave yourself time and a chance. Your work sold before James and Diana were killed. You could have made a go of it, if you'd kept going. If you hadn't met Tony and let him fill your head with practicalities, you'd have a career to rival your mother's by now. All your mom's gallery contacts are in her studio. I'm sure if you—"

"I haven't painted in years." The full feeling I woke up with deflates, and my shoulders hunch. "It wasn't just because of Tony. I was in pain after they died. Holding a paintbrush reminded me too much of Mom. I couldn't focus or concentrate. I only made it through school because teaching gave me a separate framework to distance myself from the creation process. Painting in her studio? I still don't think I could do it."

Grams leans forward and clasps my hands between her own. I can hear the water boiling behind me and need to finish her breakfast, but I can tell whatever she wants to say is important. I stay where I am and let her speak her peace.

"Now you listen to me and listen good. You have something special inside of you, something other people don't have. A true talent. And God won't forgive you for wasting something like that. When you're gifted like you are, you've got to share it. And I know sharing it with those kids is important, but you, you have something that should be shared with the world. And right now, you're wasting it, honey. I think you're afraid to face that studio because some part of you thinks a part of her still lives there. Some part of you thinks that if that space becomes yours, it won't be hers anymore, and you'll kill her last memory. But I'm telling you, a person's soul does not live in a room or a house. Diana and James live in you, as I will after I'm gone. If you paint again, you won't forget us. You'll be keeping us alive."

Our eyes lock for a moment, and I try to digest everything she's said, but it's too much for me. Too much to take in all at once. I stand and turn back to the stove, dumping the cream of wheat into the boiling water and stirring. Removing it from the heat, I pour it into a bowl, adding butter and brown sugar the way she likes it. I can feel her eyes on me, watching me. This is important to her. She wants me to understand.

I slide the bowl in front of her and drop in a spoon. "I'll try," I say, sitting down beside her and raising a hand before she can respond. "Maybe not right away. I'm not ready yet. But I will try. For you."

Grams leans forward and embraces me. She feels tiny in my arms, even more feeble than before. My burning eyes release a few tears and they drop onto the shoulder of my pink T-shirt. I kiss her on the cheek before easing her back into her chair when I notice her grip on me weaken.

"How about if I help you with this?" I lift the bowl and scoop some cereal. She nods, and I bring it to her lips.

She swallows the tiniest bite. "Can I ask you something?"

"You've never held back before." I snort.

She rolls her lips together in a tight grin. "Did you have a man over last night?"

I choke on my spit and have to set the bowl down and cough furiously into my hand.

"I'll take that as a yes." Her cheeks turn pink, and she giggles.

"How did you know?"

She shrugs. "I thought I heard a man's voice, but I wasn't sure if you had someone over or if it was Howard talking to me."

I pick up the bowl again and spoon a little more into her mouth. "Does Grandpa talk to you often?" I can't keep the skepticism from my voice.

She nods. "More and more, the closer I get to joining him. I see him, too, sometimes out my window, standing in the cemetery, waiting for me among the fairies. He's so proud of you, Eloise, for leaving Tony. Did I ever tell you that?"

A lump forms in my throat. My grandfather died when I was fourteen, but we were close when I was young. I know Grams isn't really talking to Gramps, but I appreciate the thought anyway. "No. You never told me, but it sounds like something Gramps would say."

"Well, I thought it was him at first, but the voice sounded too low. And then I realized maybe you'd brought someone home and were truly moving on from Tony."

I lick my bottom lip and feed her another half bite. "He's a friend. Nothing serious. But I'd like to think I'm moving on from Tony on my own."

"Hmm." She studies me with her soul-searching grandma eyes. "I'm glad you have a friend then."

I feed her another bite, but she barely nibbles the edge. My gut tells me she's done but is going through the motions to keep me talking. "Anyway, if my friend visits again, I may move on some more." My cheeks blaze, and I know I'm as red as a summer tomato.

She gasps and claps her hands. "Move on all you like, darling."

I stare down into the bowl. "You're done with this, aren't you?"

"Two bites ago."

"You're not eating much."

Her expression softens. "This is how it happens. It's natural. Don't worry about me."

Impossible. "I love you, Grams."

"Love you, too." She kisses my forehead. "Now help me back to bed."

14

THE INVITATION

DAMIEN

I wake before twilight, the rich, dark-wine scent of Eloise lingering in my nose. Fucking siren of a woman. Why did I allow myself to take her blood again? Already she occupies more than her share of space in my mind. I'm becoming obsessed. And now I can add the softness of her skin to things I can't stop thinking about. Worse, the way she looked at me when she shattered in my arms, rattled me to the essence of my being. That bastard husband of hers tore off all her leaves and branches, left her a stump of her former self to die in the dirt, but she looks at me like I'm the sun and all she needs is more of me to grow again.

I am no fucking hero.

It's been centuries since I've been truly needed. Used, yes. I've been used by the Gowdies regularly. But being used for the benefit of others is different from being needed. Eloise reaches for me as if who I am matters to who she is becoming, like I can honestly free the part of her she's locked away these past years. And I fucking love it. My name on her lips steals my breath.

If she won't let me kill Tony, I'll find this Gold Weaver invoice for her and save her from the bastard the only way I can. And then... And then... *Fuck*. I'll probably never see her again. I'll be a dog on someone else's leash. That thought makes me morph into a dense cloud of darkness and reform in the middle of my apartment. Perhaps a long, cold shower is in order.

An unexpected knock comes on my front door. Who could that be at this hour?

The knock comes again, more insistent. I cross the small apartment and open the door, ready to tear into whoever is on the other side, but when I see the crimson, onyx, and gold braided cords that signify a member of the queen's personal security detail, I clench my teeth and offer a formal bow.

The lanky woman bows back, the heels of her heavy boots snapping together. "Please excuse the hour of my visit. I have a missive from the queen." She thrusts a parchment envelope in my direction, the royal seal pressed into the red wax securing its flap.

"What's this about?" I ask. I don't like this. Not one bit.

The guard smiles and gestures toward the letter. "All of the details are there."

"Care to give me the gist of it?"

She tips her head as if she finds my request baffling. "The queen is actively seeking a consort, and your company has been requested for an interview."

"I think you have the wrong address. I'm not a member of the military."

"You are Damian Hymir of 32 B Evermore Lane?"

"I am."

"Congratulations. The invitation is for you." She bows again and retreats down the long empty hall outside my apartment.

I close the door and tear into the envelope. *Her royal highness Queen Valeska requests the pleasure of your company...* Fuck!

I know why the queen wants to meet me. As one of only three shades in this realm, I have abilities that no ordinary vampire enjoys. Only, I have no interest in the job. In fact, I can't think of any position I'd enjoy less. At least my Gowdie curse will come in useful this one time. She *can't* choose me. Bound to the Gowdie witches as I am and have been for centuries, I'd be a security risk. My loyalty may lie with the crown, but I'd be helpless to deny a direct command from a Gowdie candle bearer. If one of the family ordered me to kill the queen, I'd be magically compelled to obey.

I dig in a drawer for a piece of paper and a pen and, in the formal language of my kind, respond politely to the invitation, revealing the Gowdie curse and detailing why I can't serve in the role of consort. I'll find a courier to deliver my regrets to the palace. I slide the letter into an envelope and seal it with black wax and the generic circular press that all commoners use.

The circle brings back dusty memories of my true family signet. Once, my seal held the power of a kingdom and consisted of a griffon, wings spread, behind crossed swords. If I was still that prince, I could claim Eloise Harcourt and make her mine forever. I drop the letter on the table and shake my head. What a stupid, reckless thought. If I was still that prince, I would have never met Eloise Harcourt, and I'd likely be married to a neighboring kingdom's princess. Damn it, even if I freed myself from this curse and returned home, she shouldn't come with me. She's human. She belongs here.

Running a hand over my face, I cast aside the rogue thoughts and head for the shower. I have work to do.

AN HOUR LATER, I MANIFEST IN THE SHADOWS OF DENARDI Enterprises's waiting room, dressed in a suit that matches the moonlit sky outside the windows. Tamara, the receptionist I compelled before, is behind the front desk, filing papers while she hums to herself. The area is blessedly empty.

I approach the desk silently and wait for her to notice.

"Oh, hello!" Her lashes flutter. "Can I help you?"

"Is Tony Denardi here?" I have no intention of actually meeting with the man; I only need to know if he'll be a factor tonight.

"Sorry, no. Um, actually, we're closed." She glances at the glass doors and frowns. "I thought I locked up."

I lean forward, casting a shadow in her direction. As she breathes it in, I gaze deeply into her eyes until I see the ring around her iris pulse with our mind link. "You did exactly what you were supposed to do," I say, feeling the thought slide into her brain as if I'm feeding a shoelace through an eyelet. "Now, you will allow me behind the desk to search your computer."

She smiles warmly, dipping a flirtatious shoulder in

my direction. "Come on back. What are we looking for today?"

I pass through the door that leads behind the front desk and lean over her shoulder. "Any reference to Gold Weaver, Inc in your files."

She snorts, her lashes fluttering again. "Oh, you won't find any."

"Why won't I find any?" Inwardly, I cringe. I have a bad feeling I know the answer.

"Tony shredded everything with that name on it a little over a month ago and brought in some computer guy to wipe every trace of it from the system."

I squeeze my eyes shut. I was afraid of that. Denardi never trusted Eloise to keep quiet about what she saw on that invoice. After he beat Eloise, he destroyed the evidence. I'm beginning to think this fucker is a master criminal. I refocus on Tamara, curious how much the woman knows. Her mind is as weak and pliant as a child's. Might as well empty the contents. "Why would Tony destroy everything about Gold Weaver?"

She shrugs. "He told me it wasn't a real company, just made up to use for training. You know, like teaching staff to do things before they do them in the real system. We wouldn't want some newbie sending a test invoice to one of our customers by mistake."

My stomach clenches. Damn it. That is a reasonable explanation. Is Eloise's last hope simply a mistake? "What do you use for training now?"

Her face goes blank. "You know, I'm not sure."

Hope surges inside me again. *Training system, my ass.* "You're doing well, Tamara. Such a great help. I wonder if you could tell me one more thing. What was the address on those Gold Weaver invoices?"

Her pupils dilate, and she stares at the wall. "I don't..." I push deeper into her psyche. Her conscious mind may not remember, but I might be able to nab it from her subconscious if she saw the address. "883 Junction Lane."

For the first time, I give her a genuine grin. "Excellent. Now all I need is Tony's login information, and you can head home."

She giggles. "But I'm supposed to finish this filing before I go." She glances at the stack of folders to her right. "Tony gets mad if I leave them out."

I lower my voice to a whisper. "You can come in an hour early tomorrow and finish then. He'll never know."

"He'll never know," she repeats.

"Write down his login credentials." I hand her a Post-it note, and she scribbles the ID and password combo. "Now go. You deserve a break."

She pops out of her chair. "I deserve a break." Grabbing her coat and purse from the closet, she strides out the double glass doors toward the elevator. I lock them behind her, then head to Tony's office to do some searching of my own.

15

A SHADE ABOVE

ELOISE

After applying for positions at a few more schools in the area, I do laundry and clean while Grams sleeps the day away. At least she's resting comfortably today. Whenever she wakes, I try to get her to eat and drink something, but she refuses. When I help her to the bathroom, she can't wait to return to bed and resume staring out the window toward the family graveyard. It's as if she's waiting for an appearance from her beloved Howard. I'm not sure how I feel about that. I've accepted that she's dying, but part of me wants to hold her to me for as long as possible. Another part, a part I'm not ready to acknowledge fully, is starting to understand that she's ready to go.

Grams has the look in her eye of someone who has better places to be.

She's fast asleep by the time I roll the two big black garbage bins down the lengthy driveway to the curb for tomorrow's pickup. I always enjoy this walk. The grounds of Harcourt Manor are extensive. It's a little over a quarter mile to the road. As the sun sets behind the pine, hackberry, and sycamore trees that populate our property, I admired the stars and the half-moon in the clear night sky. A person could see eternity from my front yard.

I take my time walking back, allowing the night to seep into me through my coat and the skin of my cheeks. Its touch is reassuring. The universe above me is constant and eternal, unlike my small, inconsequential life, caught in a maelstrom of change. Maybe long after we're all gone, we'll become part of that great, star-filled expanse. Maybe there will be a day when Tony, this house, the money... none of it will matter. It should be a depressing thought, but somehow it's comforting.

"Is staring at the moon a regular habit for you?" Damien appears beside me in the blink of an eye a la David Copperfield, and I lurch back, barely managing to muffle my scream and not wet my pants.

"What the actual fuck?" I hiss through my teeth, then charge forward, slapping his head and shoulders and giving him a solid shove in the chest. My tantrum has zero effect on him. I might as well have shoved a brick wall. "Damn it! I have a human heart, Damien. Do you even know CPR if I went into cardiac arrest? Worse, if I screamed, you might have killed my grandmother with worry about me."

The corner of his mouth twitches. "My apologies."

I smack his shoulder again fruitlessly. "Don't sneak up on me like that."

He sticks his hands in his pockets, his stuttering smirk telling me he's trying not to laugh. "I'd hate to send your little bird heart into cardiac arrest, but if it eases your mind, I do know CPR."

I squint at him. "You do? *Why?*"

He arches a brow. "I've lived here hundreds of years. It's a useful skill."

"Really?" It makes no sense to me. Why would a shadow monster need to know CPR?

"One reads," he says, shrugging a shoulder.

I notice he's wearing jeans and a sweatshirt. I've never seen him in casual attire before. "Why are you dressed like that? Actually, I don't care. What are you even doing here so early? It's barely ten."

That twitch in the corner of his mouth takes on a smug quality. "Our weak-minded Tamara was able to retrieve the address of Gold Weaver, Inc from her memory. It's a warehouse, but I'm not sure it's what you are hoping for. I'm dressed like this because anything else would stand out where we need to go tonight. I came to ask if you'd like to accompany me there to see it for yourself."

"Tamara gave up the goods?"

He flashes me a conspiratorial grin. "She is truly as simple as they come. Barely a glance in her direction and she emptied the contents of her mind like a spilled candy dish."

I'd like to say I'm a big enough person not to revel in that, but I'm not. I thoroughly enjoy the idea of Tamara contributing to Tony's downfall, and I cackle at the thought of Damien coaxing all the info out of her. "So, where is it? When do you want to go?" I fold my arms against a night breeze that chills me to the bone.

"Now would be best. There are only so many hours before dawn."

"Okay." I hold out my hand.

His brows sink and he stares down at my offered palm. "What exactly do you think is going to happen here?"

"You're going to take my hand and whisk me away in a column of smoke to show me the warehouse."

He snorts, then gives a low, gritty laugh. "No."

"No?"

"I'm afraid it doesn't work that way. Only shades can travel through shadow. If I tried to take you with me, the transmutation would split you into a million molecules, never to be put back together. The process would make quite a mess and result in your death."

Inhaling sharply, I point at his chest. "You just called yourself a *shade*."

He rolls his eyes. "Yes, I am a shade. Not a vampire. Not the boogeyman. A shade."

"Oh." I scratch my neck. "What exactly is a shade?"

"The clock is ticking, little bird. Would you like a lesson on supernatural creatures of the universe or to find a way to stop your husband from taking your home?"

"Hmm, you're a grump tonight." I plant my fists on my hips. "How are we supposed to get there?"

He peers at me as if I'm dim. "I assume you have a vehicle?"

I sigh. "Yeah, I do, but we're going to have to stop for gas."

"Lead the way."

After a quick detour to grab my purse and keys, I load Damien into my Jeep, a feat that requires adjusting the passenger's seat all the way back to accommodate his grizzly bear sized height and girth. He tells me the warehouse is in Richmond, so I take off in that direction, glancing wearily at the oil light. I've added the last quart from the garage. With any luck, we'll make it to Richmond and back without it needing more.

After a few miles of riding in silence, I glance over to his side of the Jeep. "It must be hard for you to travel like this when you can basically go anywhere you want in the blink of an eye."

He doesn't say anything for a moment, but a muscle in his jaw tics. "It is no inconvenience spending time with you."

I do a double take, then stare at the road. Another glance over, and he's impassive, but my mind toys with his comment. It was... nice? "It's no inconvenience spending time with you either," I say.

"Why would it be for you? I'm serving your needs."

"I don't have the candle with me. You don't have to be here."

"You don't have to be touching the candle for it to work," he grumbles. "We have a spellbound agreement. That's enough."

"So, whatever I tell you to do, you'll do?"

"If it pertains to our agreement." His eyes shift over to me. "Why? Would you like me to repeat what I did for you last night?"

He did not just go there! A distracting throb starts between my legs, and I shift in my seat. No way am I going to let him have the satisfaction of thinking he's undone me. Not when the undoing has been so fretfully one-sided. The glow of a Mobil station is my salvation.

"No. I want you to pump my gas for me." I pull up to a

pump and get out. "Fill 'er up, Damien. I'm going inside for a cup of coffee. Do you want anything?"

He gives me a withering stare and unfolds himself from his seat.

"Or don't you eat... snacks." I have no idea if shades live on blood alone or also eat like humans do.

He rounds the car to the pump and flips open the tank. "For your information, I do occasionally eat *snacks*, as well as other things, but nothing you might obtain in there appeals to my palate." He tips his head toward the building.

I shrug. "Suit yourself." As I head inside, I think about how comfortable I've become with Damien. Our exchange tonight seems almost normal. I was frightened of him before but now he's pumping my gas. Do I think of him as a friend? No. A lover? Maybe. I'm not sure how to classify our relationship after last night, honestly, but I do know his fangs don't seem quite as long or sharp at the moment. Could it be that Damien, the shade, is more man than monster?

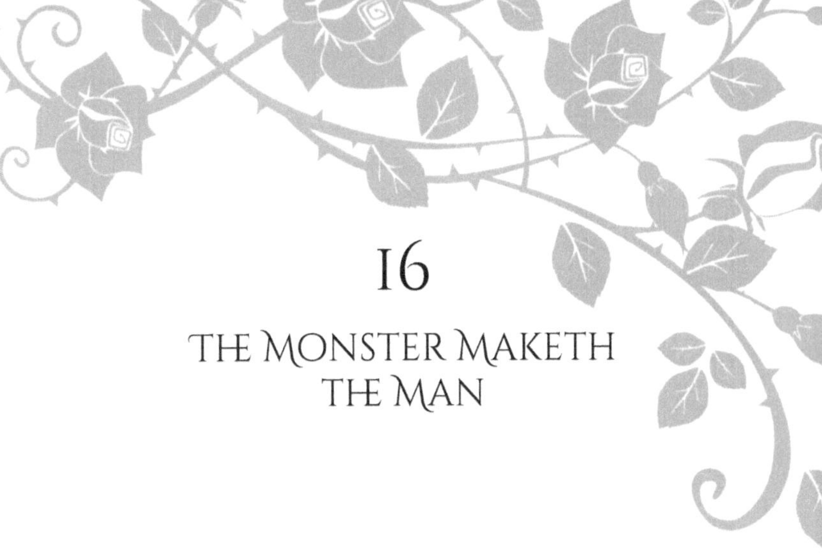

16

THE MONSTER MAKETH
THE MAN

ELOISE

Inside the gas station, I pour a cup of coffee, add some hazelnut creamer, and grab a roll of chocolate donuts from the rack, then carry it all up to the counter. "This and pump four."

The man behind the cash register is painfully thin, with the rough, yellowing skin of a person who has spent his youth chain-smoking in full sun without a hat or sunscreen. The oval name tag on his chest reads Hank. I notice there's a tip jar and plan to put something in it once he gives me my change. Hank hasn't had an easy life.

"That'll be $59.84," he says.

I curse at the high gas prices and hand him a hundred from my wallet. I've had to become comfortable paying for everything in cash since I left Tony. He closed all our credit cards immediately, and the only bank account I have left is the same one I had before we were married. But I don't dare deposit the cash I've siphoned off him.

Those transactions would have been a red flag during discovery, and if his lawyers found out, he'd have his thumb on my money before I could say bankruptcy. Which means I'm stuck carrying cash everywhere.

Hank takes the hundred and holds it up to the light, his eyes shifting from me to the bill. Then he clicks a few keys on the cash register, and the door pops open. He puts the hundred in the empty slot next to the twenties, then counts out sixteen cents into my hand. I wait patiently for the other forty dollars. He stares at me, then pushes the drawer closed and hands me a receipt.

"Thank you. Come again." His voice holds an edge of finality, his eyes issuing a challenge.

"You owe me forty dollars. I gave you a hundred."

"No, ma'am, you did not. You gave me three twenties. Check your receipt."

I look down at the paper in my hand. The faint, almost unreadable ink says I gave him $60. Not today, Satan. "I watched you place the hundred I gave you in the last bin of that drawer," I say disbelievingly. I lean over the counter and point at the register. "Open it, and you'll see it's in there."

"Can't open it unless you buy something." He chuckles dismissively.

"I just bought something!" My mouth drops open, and I look around the store for any witnesses to this crime against me, but we're alone. Flabbergasted, I slide my phone from my pocket. "I'm calling the police."

He leans his elbows on the counter and rests his chin on his fist. "Sure you are, sweetheart. I've got to be here all night anyway. You, on the other hand, are going to have a long wait ahead of you for a chance to explain to a police officer that I gave you the wrong change. Last time someone called the cops in this town, it took them three hours to arrive."

I huff and search the corners of the ceiling, pointing at the black bubble that must be a security camera. "I hope you don't like this job, buddy, because one look at the security video, and you are going to be fired."

He flashes a patronizing grin. "It hasn't worked in years. It's your word against mine, and let's face facts, I don't see anyone having a whole lot of sympathy for a blondie like you in a cashmere sweater who pays for her gas with hundred-dollar bills." He squints at me. "I may not know your story, but I know you don't want the cops nosing around in it."

I glare at him, my thumb poised over the call button. *Fuck!* I don't have time for this. And if what he says is true and there are no cameras, there's no evidence I've given him a hundred. Worse, I really need the other forty. I may be wearing cashmere, but the amount of money I have stored in the drawer in my bedroom is in no way as flashy.

Tears well in my eyes. "Please, Hank, I need that money. You don't understand—"

"Sure you do, honey." He turns back to his magazine, ignoring me.

Rage heats my blood. Even as thin as he is, he's bigger than me. It's not like I can physically make him give me the cash. But he's also not watching me anymore. In fact, he's doing his best to ignore me. *Hmm.* I calculate how long it would take him to get to me through the little locked gate that leads behind the counter, then I take justice into my own hands.

Striding to the back of the store, I grab a bottle of rosé from the cooler, tucking it into my purse. Then I head for the door, gathering every snack within reach and shoving them first into my bag and then under my cashmere sweater like a squirrel stuffing his cheeks with nuts for the winter. By the time I reach the door, M&M's are spilling out the neck of my shell.

Hank finally notices my vengeful act and moves for the locked gate. "What the fuck do you think you're doing?"

"Go ahead and call the cops, asshole!"

Cradling my goods like a pregnant belly, I shoulder through the door, then notice a jug of motor oil. I hook my only free hand through the handle of the 10W-30 and high-tail it out of there. Hank is right on my heels. I'm mere feet from the tailgate of my Jeep when my head snaps back, and I drop, hard. All my muscles brace and I manage to keep my head from slapping the pavement, but bolts of pain shoot through my backside and scalp where Hank still has me by the hair.

"Fucking cunt!"

I scream as he lifts my head as if he plans to crack my skull on the asphalt.

But before he has a chance, a massive hand wraps around Hank's throat. "Release her."

Hank abruptly lets me go, but the back of my head taps the pavement anyway.

"Oww." I rub the spot.

Damien flashes me a withering gaze. Then he turns his attention back to Hank.

Like a dark wind, Damien's shadow form sweeps the cashier off his feet and toward the mobile station, slamming his back into the side of the building hard enough to knock chunks of concrete off the wall. For a second, Hank's widened eyes register pure terror, and then Damien lifts him straight up. All I see is a blur of black and then Damien is standing on the roof, dangling Hank over the edge by his throat. The advocate's eyes glow silver in the darkness, and his rage is a palpable thing that seems to silence the other noises of the night. The man doesn't cry out, and I'm not sure if it's because Damien's grip on his throat is too tight to allow a scream or if his neck is already broken. Before I can make a sound of protest, Damien releases him. Hank drops like a brick, landing face-first in the parking lot, his limbs splayed at odd angles. Blood pools near his head.

Oh my God.

Sound turns back on. The whir of fluorescent lights. The songs of insects and mating frogs chirp from the woods around us.

Damien funnels his smoky form to my side, reaches down, and helps me up. "You're not bleeding." A statement. Not a question.

"You killed that man," I say breathlessly. My thoughts race too fast to say anything more. Damien is not harmless. When Maeve called him a monster, this is what she meant. He's a cold-blooded killer who dropped a man off a roof without hesitation.

"No. Not dead. Very badly injured, though. This would be a good time for us to depart." Damien loads the oil and my purse into the back of the Jeep, then helps me into the front.

Hank groans from the asphalt.

"Wait." I realize he's put me in the passenger side as he

closes the door and rounds the Jeep to climb behind the wheel. "What are you doing? Do you even have a license?"

Hank's groans are loud enough I can hear them through the ragtop. Damien takes off at a speed that makes the Jeep's engine growl. I reach for my seatbelt and clip myself in. "Fuck! Easy!"

"Is there a reason you have Funyuns spilling out of your bra?" His gaze darts in my direction.

I glance down and see the small bag sticking out of the scoop neck of my sweater. I toss it into the backseat, along with all the other boxes and bags I've stashed in my shirt. I keep a sleeve of Reese's Peanut Butter cups and tear off the end of the package. "Hank stole my change."

Damien shoots me a sideways glance, then laughs darkly, his entire body rocking from his amusement. It's the first time I've ever seen the monster laugh like this.

"What? It's forty dollars! I need that money."

Still laughing, he eyes the wine and motor oil in the backseat. "Looks like you came out ahead."

I run my hand through my hair, still tangled from Hank's fist, and rub the spot on my scalp where my skull tapped the pavement. "I think we're even, considering the loss of hair and the bruises I'm going to have tomorrow. Fuck, that hurt." I catch myself. "Of course, not as bad as he must be hurting right now. Shit, Damien. You threw the man off the roof."

Damien grins wide enough to show his fangs. "But the inside of your skull isn't oozing onto the pavement."

He has a point. My attention catches on the wine and Twizzlers sticking out of my Coach tote and my mouth fills with bile. What have we done? I fish my phone from my bag and dial 911 as guilt snakes around my chest and squeezes. "Hi, I was just driving by the Mobil station on Highway 17, and I think I saw a man jump off the roof. Can you send an ambulance?" When the dispatcher asks for my name, I hang up, feeling not at all better about myself or the monster at my side.

17
GOLD WEAVER

DAMIEN

I've frightened her. The bitter scent of Eloise's fear fills the cab and makes it impossible for me to ignore. She barely says a word as I drive her to the warehouse in the Richmond industrial district. Her reaction is a good reminder of how human she is and how persistently altruistic. Only she would regret hurting someone who meant to injure or kill her. It's Tony all over again. The woman has a soft heart, even for the wicked.

I grind my teeth. This is why what happened between us can never go any further. I'm a shade, a monster to her, and she's a soft, pink, vulnerable mortal who wouldn't last two weeks among my kind.

This area of town has seen better days, peppered with broken-out windows and barricaded doors slapped with orange foreclosure stickers. I park across from a large brick building under a streetlight flickering its last breath.

"This can't be right," she mutters, climbing from the Jeep. "Tony would never do business here."

The street is empty, but the chemical stench of meth cooking on the breeze has me moving closer to Eloise on high alert. If I crack another skull in front of her today, she's liable to dismiss me again. But she needs me, even if she doesn't believe she does.

"The location isn't half as surprising as what's inside," I mumble. I lead her into the yawning concrete maw of a perfectly empty warehouse. At the rear of the vacant building, a rat skitters across a beam of moonlight cascading through the broken windows.

"What the hell is this? Where is Gold Weaver, Inc?"

"Exactly my question." I walk deeper into the empty room, the sound of my footsteps echoing in the voluminous space. "This is the address Tamara remembered."

Eloise taps on her phone's flashlight, reminding me she can't see in the dark. "Hey, there's something over here." I follow her to the corner where a pile of paper trimmings waits. "Do you think he used this place to shred documents?"

I sift through the scraps, sending a stampede of cockroaches scampering for a hole in the wall. Eloise shivers and takes a step closer to me. I'm tempted to put my arms around her, but stop myself, holding my breath rather than breathing in her scent. "Tamara said he shredded anything related to Gold Weaver over a month ago, but these are blank. It seems unlikely that Tony would rent a warehouse to shred blank sheets of paper."

"What the hell was he doing here?"

We both whirl around when the door we'd entered through gives a head-splitting squeal. Uneven footsteps herald a haggard-looking man in a hoodie who steps into the light. The pungent, chemical scent I smelled on the street wafts off him. Tensing, I growl low and step in front of Eloise.

"Wait, he might know something," she whispers.

I enhance my illusion to appear more human, dimming the glow of my eyes and shifting my weight the way their kind does.

"You hiring again?" the man asks her.

Eloise walks around me and approaches the man with a warm smile. "Hello. Did you say you worked here before?"

The man glares at her through dull eyes, his face marred with scabby sores. I don't like how close she's standing to him and have to dig my talons into my palms to keep from forcing myself between them. "Just looking for work, if it's back."

"If what's back?" she asks.

The man winces. "Never mind." He starts for the door, but I'm already there. I grab him by the throat, prepared to compel the truth out of him. His eyes widen the moment he registers the points of my teeth, the way the shadows cling to me, and the hard light I've allowed back into my gaze. I smell his fear but also his confusion. This man doesn't trust his own mind.

"Don't hurt him," Eloise commands, and there's that note of compassion in her voice again. Her green eyes are misty with it, her expression pleading.

Unbelievable. Must she sabotage her best interests at every turn? I sneer at her. "I was only going to help him remember."

She pulls out her wallet and holds a ten dollar bill in front of the man. "I think he'll tell us without any *help*."

The man's gaze snaps to the money, and he licks his lips. It takes only a moment for his resolve to crack. "Yeah, I used to work here off and on. This place hired a lot of us. Paid us in cash."

I release his shoulders. "Us?"

"Uh, vagrants. Street people." He folds his arms and casts me a sideways glance. Yeah, I'm between him and the door, and I'm not going anywhere. "A lot of us don't like regular jobs. Ask too many questions. This one, you just showed up, and they gave you work."

Eloise nods encouragingly. "What is it you did here?"

"Me? I just moved reams of paper to keep the presses going." The man shrugs.

"Presses? They were printing something?" she prompts.

He nods slowly. "I take it you're not with them, then."

She shakes her head and holds up the money between two fingers. "What did they print here?"

He inhales, then blows the air out slowly. "That magazine, Echo Mills Today."

I've never heard of a magazine by that name, but Night Haven has its own periodicals. I do know that Echo Mills is the tiny rural town where Eloise lives.

Eloise frowns. "When did you say this place stopped printing?"

He scratches the back of his head. "'bout six weeks or so. It was weird as hell. Place was cleaned out overnight."

"Just one more question." Eloise taps her phone and brings up a picture of Tony. "You ever see this guy here?"

The man's eyes widen slightly before shifting to the

side. "Not sure. A lot of guys have his colorin', ya know? Besides, I don't have a good head for faces."

"But if you had to say..."

His eyes focus on the money in her hand. "Yeah... I think he was here before."

She hands him the cash and then gestures for me to step aside. I don't.

"Damien," she says through her teeth.

Reluctantly, I shift out of the man's way. He starts for the door but stops and turns back to her. "You won't tell nobody I told you nothin', right? I really need the work if they come back, and that was the one rule. Don't talk about it."

She shakes her head. "Of course not. I don't even remember who you are. I've never seen you before."

He smiles and gives her a little nod, then with one last apprehensive glance in my direction, leaves.

"Six weeks ago... That's right after I saw the invoice, and he hit me the first time." She narrows her eyes, and I tamp down a resurgence of my desire to rip out Tony's throat.

"Tony went to great pains to cover up what he was doing here."

"Why? Because of the prenup?"

I scowl. "You should have let me interrogate him." Once again she's let the best hope for her salvation walk out the door. "We could have mined him for more information if I'd used my powers."

"Like you did with the gas station attendant?"

I growl, baring my teeth. "We weren't interrogating the gas station attendant. He was slamming your head into the pavement."

She sighs. "True. That wasn't a fair comparison. But I think we have what we need. Tony was here, and he was printing a magazine called Echo Mills Today. I've never heard of it personally, but it counts as a business. That should nullify the prenup."

"If you can prove it exists and that Tony owns it," I drawl, exasperated. "You just let your only witness to its existence walk out the door with the last money in your pocket."

"But... I mean..." She rubs her eyes with her knuckles like a child. "Well, fuck!"

I level a dark look in her direction. "Are you wondering what I think you should do next?"

"No," she says emphatically, but I can see it's a lie. She's young, so painfully young compared to me. And an orphan. She wants my help, she's just too proud to ask for it.

"You should let me kill Tony," I tell her definitively.

"No!" she cries. "We're not killing anybody. How do we find out more about this place and what they were doing here? If he packed everything up six weeks ago, someone must have seen something."

A muscle in my jaw twitches with annoyance.

"I mean someone other than the man who just walked out the door." She waves a hand in the direction of the exit.

Fuck. I can think of someone, but it's risky. I decide not to offer it as a solution. "Come on. I'll drive you home."

She follows after me as I head toward her car, mumbling to herself. I hear her say something about monster instructions under her breath and feel myself smile.

"Vampires are up at night, right?" she says suddenly.

I turn the key. "Obviously."

"Well, do you know any? If they moved this place overnight, maybe one of your vampire buddies saw something and could help us."

I face her, eyes narrowing. "Vampire... buddies?"

"There must be a place they go where you could, you know, ask around?"

I pull the Jeep into the empty street. "Despite what you might think, most vampires don't spend much time topside."

"Damien, please. I need you to do this."

I groan. Why does she have to put it that way? My blood grits like sand inside my veins. I can't deny a direct command. "There is one place. A club for supernaturals who like to live among humans. It's possible one of them saw something."

"Take me there."

I scoff. "Humans aren't welcome. It's too dangerous."

"But I'd be okay with you, right?"

"I'll go alone. I'll report back what I find."

"But I need to be there. It's possible someone will say something that jogs my memory from when I was with Tony and gives us a clue to finding the proof we need."

"It's a bad idea."

"I command you to take me, by the power of the candle." She folds her arms over her chest.

I wince, the bone grinding discomfort building within me again. "You don't have to say it like that," I snap. "A simple order will suffice."

She stares at me expectantly.

"Fine. I'll take you tomorrow. I need to feed tonight, or I won't be strong enough to protect you." Gods, this is a bad idea for so many reasons.

"Tomorrow." She looks relieved it's not tonight. It's close to 2 a.m., and I can tell she's exhausted.

"Wear a dress," I say. "And shoes you can run for your life in."

18

UNWANTED ATTENTION

DAMIEN

After I drive Eloise home, I shadow back to Night Haven before I can do something stupid like taste or touch her again. If our experience tonight has taught me anything, it's that she could never be my mate. She's too fragile. Too docile. But that doesn't mean I can turn off my wanting her.

To keep myself from returning to her, I visit Marabella's for the second time this week and leave slightly sloshy from drinking as much human blood as my body can carry. Normally, I can go weeks on regular food, supplementing my diet with blood when I start to feel anemic. But considering where I have to take Eloise when the sun sets again, I'm highly motivated to stay as nourished as possible.

I shouldn't care. Whatever happens to the human, she's brought it upon herself, commanding me as she did. Unfortunately, I've grown attached. Despite my promises to keep my distance, I've become obsessed with the woman. Even now, with my body so full of sustenance I couldn't drink another sip, I spend the day dreaming of her blood, of her skin, of her smell. The temptation to taste her again is a constant gnawing sensation at the pit of my stomach, a dull ache, a lingering addiction. No blood will ever compare to hers.

I want to deny it, but it's useless to try. Only by admitting it to myself will I break its hold over me.

The antidote is simple. I have to meet the terms of our agreement and get as far away from her as possible. Which means, I must be prepared to defend and protect her. That won't be easy, considering where I have to escort her tonight.

I've just left my apartment for the evening when two of the Queen's Guard hail me from across the street, their crimson, black, and gold corded uniforms unmistakable. With a curse, I realize they've both seen me. No chance of smoking out of there. Nothing good ever comes from the queen, I know that well enough. I grit my teeth as they move in.

Both women bow. "Damien, the queen requests your presence at the palace. We've come to escort you."

I scoff. "A request or a demand? I sent a letter explaining my situation. I am obligated to perform the terms of my curse tonight."

"The queen has read your letter, which is why we're here now. There is still time before full dark. She wishes to see you before you leave Night Haven for the evening."

Biting my lip, I lament the day I attracted the queen's attention but have no choice other than to comply. I follow the two guards to the palace, where I am searched for weapons before being led deeper into the fortress and left in a salon adorned in emerald green and gold. Gods, the pretentiousness of the room makes me itch. Portraits of past queens and consorts stare down at me from gilt frames mounted along the walls, some with the vampires they've turned to extend the bloodline. Gold and diamond chandeliers hang over richly upholstered furniture, shedding soft light that mimics the sun in a way that puts the fluorescent lamps in my apartment to shame. Leaded crystal vases overflow with flowers imported from topside.

I have an irrational impulse to break something. Even when I was a prince, I hated rooms like this. I see it for what it is, an attempt to use wealth to either intimidate or impress. In my case, maybe both.

Jangling metal to my right distracts me from my rogue thoughts, and I turn, bowing low when I recognize the queen. I've never met Valeska in person before, but I watched from the street during her coronation. Even if I hadn't recognized her though, the crown of gold and rubies on her head is as good as a name tag.

"My queen." She's not my queen. She's not even my species.

"Rise, Damien, and for this meeting, you may call me Valeska."

I straighten, noticing the source of the sound I heard earlier. Her dress is made entirely of two-inch gold panels hooked at their apex to a chainmail sheath, forming a body-skimming gown that clinks when she moves. I have to admit, the queen is as stunning as the rumors suggested, with wavy black hair and silky brown skin, red-tipped nails, and full lips. Her oversized eyes are as gold as her dress and put off their own light, a trait common to both shades and vampires.

"I'm honored," I say, although I'm actually repulsed. As beautiful as the queen is, it's impossible to forget that the same rumors that extol her allure claim she's taken her throne by ruthlessly murdering the last queen and her consort. She holds ultimate power. One word from her and the vampires of Night Haven could be using my head as their soccer ball.

"You're probably wondering why I asked you here." She jingles to my side.

"I am." I decide to get straight to the point. "I assume you received my letter. I regret that my curse precludes me from serving the throne directly."

Her smile doesn't falter, but her eyes narrow at the corners. "Right. The Gowdie curse. You've been bound to do the will of their bloodline for..."

"Almost four centuries."

She clasps her hands together in front of her hips and glances up at the nearest portrait. "Shades such as you are exceedingly rare. At the last census, we knew of only three —yourself, Cassius Blackthorn, and Morpheus Maxilla."

Both men are my friends, torn from our world by the same rift the witches used to capture me. Although I haven't seen either of them in some time, we share a lasting bond. "Yes. We are the only ones. The door to my world has been closed."

"Pity. And now you are the only one left in our hive."

My hackles rise at her use of the term hive. Covens have masters. The masters of covens that nest together in a common area often choose a queen with authority over disagreements between covens. Large nests develop shared armies to protect their vampires. Night Haven falls into that category. It is a large, multi-coven underground settlement. But a hive... a hive denotes multiple covens who have been conquered and assimilated, all reporting to the same queen with ultimate control and authority—a queen who replaces or eliminates the individual coven masters. A queen with ultimate control. It is a sign of her ambition to trot that word out, and it makes my skin prickle.

It's my fellow shades I'm the most concerned about though. I would have felt along the shadows if either were hurt or killed, but not necessarily if they were captured or left Night Haven. "What happened to Cassius and Morpheus?"

"You haven't heard."

I shake my head. "As I mentioned, my time is not my own."

"Right, right, you serve the Gowdies. Well, let me bring you up to speed. Cassius left for another coven in the Midwest for reasons unknown, and Morpheus has accepted a place in a triune topside, relinquishing his Night Haven citizenship."

"I wasn't aware." *Fuck.* Becoming a triune requires trusting a witch and a shifter with one's life, especially the witch who must perform the spell to bind the threesome. That type of bond is not something entered into lightly, especially not for a shade like me. It would mean giving up any hope of going home. I suspect Morpheus's decision to accept the bond and Cassius's decision to leave the coven has everything to do with Valeska's rise to power.

The queen's dress clinks as she moves around me. "You are the last of your kind in my kingdom. I must confess, Damien, I've never met a shade in person. Every-thing I know about them comes from books. They say our species are distantly related, vampires having evolved on Earth and shades evolving on—"

"Tenebris."

"Right. I've looked into the three of you. You tend to keep to yourselves."

My jaw tightens. "Nothing wrong with that."

"No."

"The scribes tell me that the witches conjured the three of you from your realm during the European witch trials and that you sacrificed your freedom so that Cassius and Morpheus could escape."

"Something like that." The Gowdies had dragged three of us through the rift. I attacked, breaking the spell long enough for Cassius and Morpheus to flee. It wasn't sacri-fice though, but responsibility. They were warriors for my kingdom, ones I was sworn to protect as their prince. But I never intended to martyr myself. I intended to kill the bitch and go home.

It didn't work out.

"Interesting. It is said that you carry the power of a demon within you, and that is why your heart continues to beat, unlike our kind. Is that true?"

I hide my laugh behind feigned interest in the art above me. "We're not demons. Unlike your kind, we're born alive and stay alive." No one knows for sure what magic makes us immortal. Does any creature ultimately understand the origins of their species? Even humans haven't closed the gaps on that puzzle.

The queen moves closer, fast enough I release a reflexive hiss as her hand lands on my chest. "Your heart does beat." Her eyes widen. "And you are warm to the touch."

"Yeah." I gently grab her wrist and remove her frigid hands from me.

"Is it true you ride shadows?"

"Yes."

"Show me."

I reach out to a shadow behind the sofa and coax it to merge with mine. The moment they touch, I break apart and travel through a web of darkness, reforming on the other end of the room. The queen turns her head to look at me, and with a gentle motion of my fingers, I send another shadow, thin and razor sharp, whipping around her to slice across her throat. It's just enough pressure to sting but not break the skin.

As expected, she jerks away from the curl of darkness.

It's only a taste of what I can do, and I hope it unsettles her. Fear is something all vampires understand, and I prefer she fear me. Nothing good can come from garnering her interest in any other way.

"Fascinating," she says through her teeth. A breath later, she's beside me again, eyes flashing with a sort of greedy hunger. "And what about the reports that your blood can sustain a vampire? That you can subsist on vampire blood?"

I hate that look in her eye. Maybe I've approached this all wrong. I wanted to scare her, but the way she's examining me is like a warlord inspecting a weapon. I play dumb. "I don't know anything about that."

She tilts her head. "Hmmm. You don't know if that conjecture is true or not?"

"I've never fed from a vampire nor been fed upon." I

move away from her. "And I have no reason to test the theory."

"I'm giving you a reason," she snaps, eyes locked on my neck.

"No."

"You would not deny your queen." She snatches my wrist in an iron grip. I could break free, but her wrath is something I don't wish to inspire. Not here.

"No," I repeat.

"No. You *will not* deny a direct command from your queen."

"Are you giving that command?"

She draws my wrist to her mouth. "I am." Before I can say another word, she strikes, and I'm reminded of why I only use willing donors at Marabella's. The feel of her fangs in my skin is a violation. My shadows slip around her neck like a noose and tighten.

"I can't control it, my queen," I warn, although, in truth, it is my temper I can't control. The shadows I can stop at any time. She lifts her mouth from my wrist, and the darkness releases her. I wrench my arm away before she can lick the wound closed and press my opposite palm to it instead. Blood dribbles on the marble floor. "My apologies. That is the first time anyone has attempted to feed on me. It's unpleasant, and it seems I cannot control the reaction of my shadows."

She runs a thumb across her bottom lip. "With practice."

I shake my head.

But she's watching me now as if I'm a prize she's desperate to win. "How many Gowdie witches would have to die to free you from the candle's curse?"

"All of them, and there are hundreds," I say quickly. "Powerful witches with magic capable of controlling vampires like puppets. There's a reason they were able to curse me, Valeska."

"Hmm. I've heard." She places a hand on her stomach, her covetous gaze scraping over me once more, and landing on my healing wrist. "What a shame. You are delicious. A consort like you would be the ultimate weapon."

Dark ice fills my veins, and every molecule in my body urges me to leave that room. Never before have I been thankful for the Gowdie curse, but I am now. "Pity, it can never be," I say dryly. "Now, I do have to go. I feel the candle's draw. The sun has set. I can't delay." I make a show of the shadows circling me.

"*Pity.*" She repeats with a sneer. "You are excused, shade."

I twist into shadow and escape her presence, praying that she'll choose a consort quickly and forget I ever existed.

19
BAD WITCHES' CLUB

ELOISE

What is appropriate eveningwear for a bar that serves supernaturals? As I drive up to a quiet building with white cinderblock walls and blacked-out windows, I think maybe I've overdressed. The place looks more like a prison than a club. Maybe I should have gone more *rave* and less *cocktail party*. "Is what I'm wearing okay?"

Damien glares at me from the passenger seat, radiating exceptionally grumpy vibes. "Your attire is acceptable." He's been acting like that since we left the house. I'm not sure what I've done to piss him off, but he's either angry at me or having a shade mood swing.

I climb from my tan Jeep, tugging my sequined purple minidress down to cover my ass and straightening the waist-length matching jacket. I've never actually worn this dress before, and I'm learning the designer number likes to ride up. The first New Year after I married Tony, we were invited to New York by a few of his clients for a New Year's Eve party. I chose this dress, but when I put it on, Tony yelled at me that it was too short to wear to a professional event. I ended up changing into a plain black wrap dress that could have doubled as funeral attire. But I held onto it, along with the sparkly Golden Goose sneakers I planned to wear. Tonight, I've paired the ensemble with a shaggy black ostrich feather clutch in which I carry my phone and the candle stub, just in case. I think I look cute.

Irritably, Damien walks around the Jeep and marches past me in the direction of the building. I look down at myself again.

Cocktail dress—check.

Shoes I can run in—check.

Hair curled and fluffed to club-ready perfection—check.

What is the problem? "Damien, Stop!"

He does, his feet scuffing the pebbles of the unused drive that leads to the building. He barely glances in my direction. "Little bird?"

"What's wrong? You've barely looked at me since we left the house."

He turns slowly, those brilliant ice-blue eyes raking over me from head to ankles in a way that makes my spine tingle. In the space of a breath, he has me in his arms, my body clutched against a hard, very male body. His frighteningly large erection is sandwiched between us. My breath hitches at the feel of him, the tips of his fangs white in the moonlight.

"Do you want to know why I won't look at you?" His lips brush my temple, the edge of my hair. "All I can think about when I see you in that dress is how easy it would be to bend you over." He coasts his hand over my ass and teases the flesh just under the hem. "Lick your tight pussy until you scream my name, then fuck you while your heart flutters like the tiny sparrow you are. Once I've made you orgasm so many times my cock is covered in you, I'll take your vein, likely the artery in your thigh, and drink your sweet blood until you pass out from pleasure."

"Oh," I squeak.

His jaw clenches, and his voice sounds like he's dragged it across the pebbled drive as he adds, "But I can't do that because we have work to do. I can't look at you because when we walk into that club, I need to protect you from everyone and everything in it, and that's hard to do when I'm thinking about the taste of you and the way the muscles in your neck flex when you come."

I swallow and take a big step back, adjusting my dress as heat swirls in my lower belly. He's right, we're here for a reason, and if I let this go much further, we may never learn what we need to about the warehouse. "Understood. I'll, uh, erm. I'll follow you then."

Damien turns on his heel and strides toward the building, looking sexy as hell and possessing every inch of his massive frame.

I curse under my breath. I'm hot enough to melt a quarter between my thighs. No man of any species has any business being so overtly sexual, so undeniably in touch with his inner animal. He calls to something deep and forbidden within me. The way Damien moves promises wild, uninhibited sex and multiple orgasms. From the tips of my nipples to the center of my core, I want him.

"Control yourself," he whispers at the door. "I can smell your need from two feet away."

"You can smell that?" I mumble under my breath. It's like a bucket of ice water splashes my libido. I crack my neck and shake out my limbs, thinking of anything but men and sex. "I don't know what you're talking about."

"Better," he grumbles. He pulls a gold key from his pocket and opens the door.

Once inside, I'm even more confused. We're in a white room with no doors or windows aside from the one we've just passed through. If there is a club anywhere near here, all its patrons must be dead. It's as quiet as a cemetery. A bare bulb in the ceiling flickers. Damien shuts and locks the door behind us, then takes my hand.

Tugging me to his side, he steps right through the solid white wall like it isn't even there, hauling me with him.

The moment we're on the other side, the thump of house music meets my ears, and my mouth drops open at the sight of a two-story mural depicting an evil queen, her crowned head tipped back in a wicked laugh. The style is familiar, Warhol meets Takeuchi but I can't put my finger on the artist. WELCOME TO BAD WITCHES' CLUB is emblazoned in twinkling gold letters underneath, surrounded by purple fog that wafts from the base, enhancing the overall magical effect.

I glance back at the wall Damien pulled me through. "Holy shit, it's like Platform 9 ¾."

My monster scoffs and shoots me a dark look. "Only if everything on the other side of the barrier between platforms 9 and 10 wanted to eat the young witches and wizards. Stay by my side and try not to look human."

I'm not sure exactly how to accomplish that feat, but I

reach into my clutch and dig out the pair of sunglasses I thought might help, donning them in the already dark room. If anything, it will keep people from noticing that my eyes don't glow like Damien's. I finger-comb my hair forward on my shoulders to cover my arteries so they won't see my pulse either.

He casts a shallow smile in my direction. "Not bad." Taking my hand, he leads me toward the bar.

Bad Witches' Club is a kick-ass nightclub by human standards. A dance floor is positioned at the center of the place, the writhing bodies of nonhumans blurring with supernatural speed to the thump of electronic dance music. Three stories above us, a glass dome offers a stunning view of the stars. Lounge and bar areas surround the dance floor, each level providing a view of the dancers below. It's the perfect place to hunt and be hunted.

"This way." Damien leads me to a section where the tables are surrounded by dark tentacles painted on every wall. It isn't until I see the mural behind the bar that I realize it's an homage to the sea witch from the little mermaid.

"Oh, I get it," I say breaking into a smile. "All the sections are story villains. Bad Witches' Club. That's cute." I instantly want to explore the rest of the club. Is there a Maleficent section?

Damien slants me a withering look, then places a finger over his lips. Fine, I'll be quiet for the grumpy monster.

"Jimmy," he says, approaching someone I assume is a vampire. With wide-set, glowing brown eyes and hair that's too dark to be called blond but isn't quite brunette, he looks barely nineteen, but I'm guessing he's far older.

He sweeps bangs from his eyes. "Damien! I swear to all the gods, I haven't stepped within ten feet of a Gowdie witch."

"Not why I'm here, Jimmy. Do you still hunt in the industrial district in Richmond?"

"Yeah, sometimes. Why?" Jimmy's gaze slides to me. I hold perfectly still and try not to breathe.

"Did you ever see a printing operation there, on the corner of Wakefield and Junction?"

He rubs the back of his head. "Sounds familiar. Why do you want to know?"

"Gowdie business. It's gone now, and I need to know what happened to it."

He shrugs. "One day there, next day gone. They used to hire people off the street. It attracted a good number of prospects. Hunting's been shit as of late."

"Did you see the people who moved it?" Damien shifts so his body is between us, blocking Jimmy's view of me, and I take a slow, even breath.

"No. Sorry. Wasn't there that night." Jimmy shuffles to the right and his eyes catch on me again.

"Do you know anything about the publication?" Damien asks, a note of annoyance in his voice.

"Not much of a reader." Jimmy rubs the back of his neck. "Hey, who's your friend?"

I'm growing impatient and it's clear Jimmy suspects I'm not a vampire because he's tracking me and swallowing reflexively. I step forward and hold out a picture of Tony on my phone. "Did you ever see this man at the warehouse?"

Jimmy freezes, his nostrils flaring. At first, I think it's because he recognizes Tony, but then he lowers his nose to the inside of my wrist and inhales deeply. His mouth spreads into a wide, fang-filled grin. "Damien, you've been a very naughty boy."

Damien slaps a hand over my wrist and shoves it down to my side.

The other vampire scoffs. "Like that'll help. She smells like freshly cut pomegranate and narcissus. I knew she was human the second she was within ten feet of me."

Damien's expression grows dark and he steps closer to Jimmy, looming over him. "Have you seen the man or not?"

"No. I didn't pay attention to the place. It was human stuff."

"Fine," Damien says gruffly. "Is Thaddeus here tonight?"

"I think I saw him in the White Witch section."

Damien gives Jimmy a curt nod, then hooks his hand behind my elbow and escorts me up the stairs. Once we're alone, he jerks me roughly into his side. "Don't ever offer your wrist to a vampire. Do you have any idea what you've done?"

20

BLOOD TIES

ELOISE

"I didn't—" I start to protest, then realize, fuck, I had exposed my wrist to the vampire. When I showed him the picture, my pulse was on full display. "Okay, well maybe I accidentally did, but honestly, he already knew what I was. If he stared at me any harder, he'd leave a bruise."

"It's a dead giveaway that you're human," Damien says. "I knew this was a bad idea. Jimmy has never kept a secret in his life. He's likely spreading the news I'm here with you even now."

"I won't do it again."

He snorts. "We're on borrowed time. Let's move." He makes a growly sound and hauls me up the rest of the stairs. When we reach the top, he opens the door to a gigantic wardrobe at the end of the landing. I enter a dark passageway lined with furs. The back of the wardrobe gives way, and we step into a winter wonderland, complete with falling snow.

I hug myself against a blast of cold air. "Wow." The tables and chairs are made out of clear acrylic to resemble ice, driving home the Narnia theme. "The artificial snow is a nice touch."

"It's all real." His hand smooths to the center of my back. "This section is enchanted to always be winter."

"So these are...?" I touch an unoccupied chair next to me and yank my fingers back from the cold, slightly wet surface. Not acrylic. Real ice. I shiver and clutch my jacket tighter around me. "Shit, it's freezing in here." I look around the lounge. No one is wearing a coat. My shivering is going to give me away as human before I even have a chance to talk to anyone.

Damien seems to realize my predicament the same time I do because he wraps an arm around me the way a lover might and walks me straight through the White Witch's domain and into a corridor covered in spots. The air warms immediately. "It won't help either of us if you're turned into a human popsicle or bitten by some hungry vampire before we get answers."

"Fair assessment," I say, giving one last shiver.

Shadows rise around us, blanketing us, as his hand warms my lower back and he escorts me along a hallway decorated in Dalmatian print to a lounge with Cruella's mural on the wall and couches upholstered in what I pray to God isn't real dog hide. He only drops the cloak he has around us once we're in the darkest corner of the lounge. This section of the club must not be popular because there's no one else in here but a bartender who's more than twenty feet away and busy washing glasses.

"I'll question Thaddeus alone. Wait for me here. Don't move or speak to anyone. I'll make this fast."

Reluctantly, I nod. "Do you need me to forward that picture of Tony?" Does Damien even have a cell phone?

He shakes his head. "Wait here. And put your phone away, the light from the screen will draw attention."

I obey, dropping my phone into my bag, then watch him slip from the empty lounge.

"What. The. Fuck." Maeve appears out of nowhere, glaring at me from the other side of the table.

"Where did you...?" I look both ways but can't fathom where she came from without me noticing.

She slides into the chair opposite me, looking furious. "You shouldn't be here, El. I mean, really. How—"

"I came with Damien. We're investigating a lead on Tony's side business."

Maeve gapes like a fish. "Oh, my goddess, Eloise. I thought I explained this to you. That's not how this works." She leans across the small table and grabs the sides of my face. "You call the advocate. You tell him to do something. He does it. You don't go with him to do the thing. He can't be killed. You can, and believe me, this is where it could happen."

I shrug. "You're here."

Releasing me, Maeve leans back in her chair. "I'm a witch. I have a key. Also, I can hold my own."

Wearing a black dress with spiderweb-patterned tights, she bobs her platform heel out of a level of annoyance I've never ignited in my friend before. Here, in this place, I wonder how I ever believed she wasn't a witch. Her sleek dark hair seems to flirt with the shadows in the room, and her army of skeleton tattoos all stare at me, the ocular cavities becoming blacker, more three-dimensional. I thought I knew everything there was to know about Maeve, but now, I observe her with new eyes. "You're not exactly a love, light, and lavender sachet witch, are you?"

She snorts. "No."

"You need to bring me up to speed on the real you, Maeve. My God, we've been friends for over a decade. Did I ever really know you at all?"

She reaches across the table and squeezes my arm. "Yes, you do know me. All the important parts. Magic, it's a tool, that's all. It would be like me not knowing you could paint. You are still you without painting, right?"

"Right," I drawl. "But art is a pretty big factor in my life, and it seems like magic is a huge one in yours."

"Fair. And we will share everything. I promise we will. But first, I need to get you out of here." She stands and takes me by the hand.

I hold my ground. "No. I have to wait for Damien. Oh, there he is now."

Maeve releases me as Damien strides toward us with his usual swagger. The man moves like a shadow, like ink spilled in water, smooth, intoxicating. I sigh as he nears and don't miss the way that draws Maeve's attention or the way she narrows her eyes at Damien.

"Maeve," he says by way of greeting.

"How could you bring her here? You know the risks," Maeve hisses.

"She commanded me by your magic." His voice is so low I can barely hear it. Resentment causes his teeth to clench and a muscle in his jaw to tic. What must it be like to have all that power and be bound by a centuries-old curse?

Maeve grimaces. "Morpheus is coming. There's been a change. He's—"

"I know." Damien rolls his shoulders back and turns toward an elderly-looking… man? Vampire? Shade? I don't know what he is but his face is scarred, and his skin is sallow. Dark eyes turn my way, and a wave of fear ripples through me at the intensity in that gaze.

An understanding passes between Damien and Morpheus, and they drift off toward an unmarked door in the wall.

"Listen to me carefully," Maeve says in a voice that can only be described as no-nonsense. She's speaking to me like I speak to the children in my class. "I'm not sure what is going on between you and the advocate—"

"Damien."

She scoffs. "Fine. You and *Damien*, but you need to cut it out, El. I mean it. He's a monster, a *killer*. Do not become involved with him. Tell me you haven't… done anything with him."

My cheeks blaze. "Uh, not really."

"Is that why you're blushing like you're fifteen, and your crush just noticed you for the first time? Wicked hell, the way he looked at you! I haven't seen that much lust in a creature's eyes in a long time, Eloise. I have half a mind to take the candle from you right now."

The notion sends a sharp pang through my heart. "Please don't. We're so close to nailing Tony."

She gives me a sideways look. "Seems like Tony's not the only one getting nailed."

"Maeve!" My mouth gapes.

She sighs. "Never mind. Tell me what you found out."

I tell her about Gold Weaver, the warehouse, and what the stranger revealed to us about what went on there. "He has a side hustle, one he hasn't disclosed to me or either legal team."

"I'll get my financial team on it. Maybe there's something in the accounts they've missed," she says. "And I'll trust you to keep the candle because if I take it now, I'm not sure what the advocate will do to you—"

"He wouldn't hurt me—"

"Oh, my goddess. Wake the hell up!" Maeve's pupils constrict, purple sparks igniting in their depths. "He's not a dog or a security guard. Damien is a shade, the most lethal creature ever drawn into this realm. He's a monster. A killer. My ancestor conjured him here from a deadly world of darkness, and he murdered her in cold blood before my coven managed to bind him to the candle. You can't trust him. Not ever."

I stare down at my tangled fingers on the table. "The candle is almost burned through the base. What happens when the wick runs out?"

"That won't happen."

"What do you mean?"

She squeezes my hand. "Later. Damien is currently in a world of shit, and since you still need him, you have to get him out of it."

"Wait, what?" I point a thumb in the direction the two creatures went. "Was that because of me?"

"Non-magical guests are prohibited in Bad Witches' Club. He took a huge risk bringing you here. Risked your life and his." She shakes her head. "He should have tried harder to talk you out of it."

"What's the punishment for bringing a human into a place like this?"

"Morpheus will decide, but it could be anything from a pint of blood to a week chained inside a coffin. Whatever it is, it won't be pleasant and could put a wrinkle in our plans to stop Tony."

"Wrinkle in our plans?" I remove my sunglasses, absolutely gobsmacked. I'm far more concerned about Damien being locked in a coffin and starved than my problems at the moment. "We've got to help him. This wasn't his fault."

"We will, okay? All I need you to do is remove your jacket. That dress is backless underneath, right? I remember you showing it to me a few years ago."

"Yeah, but why would that—"

"Your tattoo. Trust me. When they come back here, show Morpheus your tattoo."

"Why?" I hate this. It feels like I'm playing a game, and I'm the only one who doesn't know the rules. But the door opens, and Damien and Morpheus stride toward our table. Maeve nods at me, and I stand, removing my jacket. With my back facing them, I can't see their reaction, but Maeve shoots me one of her secret smiles. I glance over my shoulder to find the two directly behind me.

"Damien, why didn't you explain that your guest was a Harcourt?"

Damien's expression is unreadable. "My apologies, Morpheus. I wasn't sure the young lady was ready to disclose her identity." His attention skirts to Maeve, who shrugs.

"You look just like your mother." Morpheus places a hand over his heart. "We were all sorry to hear what happened to Diana. I do hope you'll visit us again." He bows, then retreats, leaving me gaping.

"How the hell did he know my last name was Harcourt?" I whisper.

Maeve takes a deep breath. "I don't know. I thought the tattoo would convince him you were magical, but I had no idea... Damien?"

"I don't know either, and I'd prefer not to ask after the conversation I just had. Morpheus and I have a history, but his loyalties now lie with the triune he serves." His warm hand lands on my waist. "Let's get you out of here."

But the Cruella mural behind the bar has my full attention now, the way the oversized eyes give the observer a window into her dark soul, the bony protrusions of her shoulders, the lines in her neck that give her a simultaneous look of hunger and insanity. Bright colors. Light, delicate line work. An ethereal quality that adds a fantasy element. I wasn't able to name the artist when I saw the evil queen or the sea witch, but I stride closer to the bar, intentionally studying the far right corner of the mural. There it is, a scrollwork D H.

"What's wrong, Eloise? Breathe. Goddess, you look like you're going to be sick." Maeve wraps her arm around my shoulders.

I swallow the knot in my throat. "My mother painted this mural. She painted all of them."

21
TEMPTATION

ELOISE

A million questions plague me regarding my mother's involvement with Bad Witches' Club, but neither Maeve nor Damien seem to have any answers. Both are anxious to get me out of there, despite my newfound acceptance by the vampire Morpheus. Maeve claims she didn't know anything about my mother's involvement with the murals, but when I press her on the fact that she must have known something considering it was her idea to show Morpheus my tattoo, she promises we'll talk later and escorts Damien and me to the exit. I don't fight her and willingly climb into the passenger seat of my Jeep. My nerves are shot, and I'm too exhausted from trying to process everything to come up with more insightful questions or to fight Damien for the wheel.

For most of the drive home, I close my eyes and curl onto my side, revisiting everything that happened tonight. Maeve says I can't trust Damien, but can I trust Maeve, considering she only told me she was a witch after eleven years of friendship? My mother worked with the supernatural. Did my father know? Why didn't either of them tell me? Tony ran a secret publishing company called Gold Weaver. At one point, I trusted him too. Does everyone in my life harbor some dark and mysterious secret? Will I wake up to learn my grandmother runs a gambling ring?

I must have fallen asleep thinking about it because the next thing I know, we're pulling up the drive to Harcourt Manor. When Damien notices I'm awake, he says, "I found the other vampire I was looking for, Thaddeus. He knew about the warehouse but had never seen Tony there. He hadn't heard of the magazine. Morpheus interrupted our conversation before I could tell you. Bad Witches' Club was a dead end."

"Did you know my mother?" I ask. He claims to have been on Earth almost four hundred years, which means he could have been around when the murals were painted.

"No. And before you ask, I'm not sure how she became involved with the Caspian Triune."

"Caspian Triune?"

"That's the group of supernaturals who run Bad Witches' Club. They only recently completed the spell to bind to one another."

"It's not just Morpheus in charge?"

"No. A complete triune consists of a vampire, a witch, and a shifter." When he can see that I have no idea what he is talking about, he explains. "Vampires are immortal."

"So I've heard."

"But they're vulnerable during the day. Sunlight is lethal to all vampires."

"At least some of the folklore is true."

He laughs. "Much of it is. Shifters are innately powerful but mortal. And their power is incredibly volatile. They have normal human abilities during the new moon and supernatural strength, speed, senses, and healing capabilities around the full moon, but ironically that's when their inner animal makes them prone to impulsivity. Many shifters lose their lives to hair-trigger tempers when they're at their strongest."

"Shifters are drunk frat-boys. Got it."

The smile he shoots me lights up the cab.

"Witches aren't physically powerful, but as you know, they are a force to be reckoned with due to their ability to wield elemental magic. But witches are mortal and surprisingly fragile. All that power in a pitifully human body."

"I'll try not to take that personally." I lean my pitifully human body against the door.

He reaches over and brushes my cheek with his knuckle. "In a triune, a witch, a shifter, and a vampire are bound, and something remarkable happens. The vampire imparts their immortality on the shifter and the witch, and in return, the vampire receives the ability to walk in the sun. The shifter imparts supernatural strength, speed, senses, and healing on the witch and, in return, gains full control of his animal and an almost endless source of energy. The witch receives immortality, strength, speed, heightened senses, and accelerated healing from the shifter and vampire and, in return, is the source of the vampire's ability to walk in the sun and the shifter's dominion over their animal. Together, they are almost unstoppable. Morpheus is a shade like me but we're close enough in an evolutionary sense to vampires for the magic to work. We were conjured here together but only I was bound to the Gowdies. He's been a co-owner of Bad Witches' Club for decades, but the triune is new. The witch he's bound himself to is of the Caspian line, a water witch family. His shifter is a Davies. They draw power from their tiger forms. Together, I predict they'll rule the supernaturals of Richmond soon. It's the first triune with a shade in history, and Morpheus is a powerful warrior."

Gooseflesh parades up my arms, and I hug my jacket around me. I'm just getting used to the idea that shades, vampires, and witches are real, and here I am, learning there are also shifters. Will the world ever look the same to me again? I suddenly miss the false certainty that humans are all there is. Never again will I experience the peace that comes with that misconception.

The notion should keep me from delving deeper, but my curiosity gets the better of me. "Maeve said her coven conjured you from a dark and dangerous world."

"Her assessment of my world is misguided, as were her ancestor's actions."

"You mentioned that Morpheus was with you. Why were you bound by the candle and he wasn't?"

Damien turns introspective. "It's late, and this is a long story."

"I'm not tired, and after the night I've had, I plan to open up a bottle of wine. Why don't you come in?" He nods once, although I sense reluctance in the way his body tenses, and he stares over the steering wheel. "That wasn't an order or anything. I wasn't candling you," I clarify. "I'd just really like to talk. Would you care to come in and have a glass of wine?"

I might be imagining it, but the muscles in his face and neck seem to ease. "Yes, I would."

He parks in the garage, and I lead him into the parlor, where I leave him to check on Grams before retrieving the bottle of wine I took from the Mobil station from the kitchen. I unscrew the cap and pour us a couple of glasses. It isn't bad for gas station wine.

"I wonder what happened to Hank." I've thought about Hank more than once since the incident. He did a bad thing stealing my money and attacking me, but the memory of his broken body on the pavement still haunts me.

Damien folds himself into the green velvet sofa beside me, making the heavy piece of furniture groan under his weight. "He's still recovering in Richmond Memorial. He claims someone robbed him, but unfortunately, none of the security cameras were working, and no money was missing from the register, so the police are going on the assumption that he did, in fact, jump off the roof."

I sip my wine. "I hope he doesn't mention my Jeep or remember my license plate."

"That would be difficult, considering I wiped his mind before I dropped him." He flashes me a little fang.

My jaw drops. "Brilliant. How did you think of that in the moment?"

"I assumed you'd have to buy gas there again." The corner of his mouth twitches.

"I'm not sure what it says about me that I'm relieved. Shouldn't I feel more guilty for what happened to him?"

"Guilty for what? You didn't do it." His diamond eyes study me.

"I might as well have. You did it because of me."

"And if I hadn't, he'd have put you in a hospital bed, or a grave." Damien believes that, just as he believes that Tony is a bad man, an evil man. Maybe he's right.

"Maeve told me tonight not to trust you. That you murdered her ancestor."

"The one who magically tore me and my two brethren from our world in an attempt to enslave us. Yes, I killed her and I do not regret it." He says this through his teeth and I can tell the memory is still fresh, even after hundreds of years.

"I'm sorry," I say. I love Maeve and it's hard for me to believe that her family would do such a thing, but I can see the pain in Damien's eyes. "Maeve didn't tell me the whole story."

He softens at my show of empathy. "Maeve may not know exactly, being a relatively young descendant of the witches who cursed me. I, on the other hand, will always remember that time. Unlike her, I lived through it, and it changed my existence forever."

"Will you tell me, the way you remember it?" I pull my legs underneath me, squeezing a pillow to my middle, and hold my breath. I want to know the truth about how Damien became the advocate, but I won't force him.

He grows serious and stands to pace the small room, almost like he's not sure where to start. "To understand how I ended up here, you first must understand where I come from. My home is on Tenebris, a watery planet much like Earth. Maeve might think of it as a world of darkness, but for me it was a world of life. My kind, shades, we are like vampires in that sunlight weakens us. Unlike vampires, we can survive it, but it makes us vulnerable. We are immortal in the dark. If a sword pierces our flesh, we simply blend into the darkness and come back together somewhere else. But in sunlight, we are mortal. In sunlight, we can be captured. What you need to understand is that before I was abducted and brought here, I was heir to the southernmost kingdom of Tenebris, the Kingdom of Stygarde."

"Wait, wait, wait. What?"

22

FLESH AND BLOOD

DAMIEN

Eloise straightens. "Are you telling me you were, like, a *prince* in your world?"

I rarely speak of my past life as a royal of Stygarde. Those memories come weighted in considerable sadness, but she needs to understand. "It's been a long time since anyone called me that, but yes. My parents ruled Stygarde, and I was the oldest of three siblings, although still too young to lead by my people's standards. I'd barely completed training as a warrior when a neighboring kingdom attacked. The elf mages of Willowgulch have magic much like your witches. A long bloody war ensued that drained my kingdom. The elves learned to magically produce sunlight and used it to trap and kill our soldiers. We'd slayed a fair number of theirs as well. I couldn't see an end to the violence."

"What were you fighting over?"

My brow lifts at her question, surprised she wants

details. "Land. Specifically, a forested area between our two kingdoms. A wild, neutral territory until a hunting party found a dragon's egg and everything changed."

"Like from an actual dragon? They exist there?"

"They're not native to Tenebris. All my life they were thought to be extinct, but when the egg was found, there was much excitement. A dragon's body holds magic. The scales and blood can be used in powerful spells. But the elves didn't dare move the egg. It rested near a river of fire, and it is known dragon eggs must incubate in a hot environment. So the battle became not about the egg but about the forest. The elves wanted it, and the dragon they assumed had laid the egg, for themselves. My people fought to keep the forest neutral."

"You didn't want it for your own kingdom?"

"There were times I thought that would be best. How do you protect something if you don't own it? But my father used to say that no one owned the wild. It owned itself."

"He seems like a wise man."

"He was," I say softly. "Is, I hope, still." The grandfather clock behind me chimes twice. Pressure builds inside me as I think about my parents, to the point I'm tempted to break into shadow for the relief it would bring. "The truth is that I don't know if they're alive. When I was captured, we were at war, and as the king and queen of Stygarde, my parents would have been the first executed if the elves broke through our defenses."

"You don't know if they survived the war?" she asks breathlessly. "I'm so sorry."

This is more than I planned to share with her, but I can't stop myself from indulging her curiosity. "The war had waged for years. One night I was fighting side by side with Cassius and Morpheus when the sky tore open and we were dragged through a rift between our worlds. I thought the elves were to blame because the way the night split was similar to how they called the light to kill us. I found myself surrounded by sunlight, walled off from the darkness and unable to escape. I landed in the center of a symbol, trapped by a coven who I would later learn were Gowdie witches. Cassius and Morpheus landed by my side. I slayed the one who smelled the most powerful, Jane Gowdie, and then used my shadows to fight the other witches so Cassius and Morpheus could escape. But in doing so, I drank Jane's blood. Blood exchange between supernaturals is dangerous. In this case, Jane's blood gave the Gowdie's power over me. My friends escaped, but working as one, the Gowdies captured and bled me. They used my blood, rich with Jane's magic, to create the candle that binds me to their coven."

Silence unravels between us, punctuated by the ticking of the clock in the corner. "Why did the Gowdies call you in the first place?" she asks softly. "How did they even know how to open a rift to your world?"

"The why was clear immediately. It was the time of the European witch trials and they needed a protector. Their family survived because of me. Anyone who challenged them, they'd order me to kill. How they knew about my world and how they drew me here—that is not as clear. I have searched far and wide over the centuries for a way to reopen that rift, and it remains a mystery to me."

"You want to go home."

I stare into my glass. "Yes." Only after a long, fortifying sip of wine do I look at her again. "Do you know what the

Gowdie specialty is? Every witch family has a type of magic they are known for, and the Gowdies are unsurpassed in one particular skill."

She shakes her head.

"Animators. They draw their power from the earth element. The Gowdies can animate anything, including the dead. That's how they caught me to do the binding spell. They animated my bones, kept me from using my powers while they collected my blood for the candle." I rub a hand over my sternum at the ache the memory conjures.

"So, you've been bound to serve the Gowdies for centuries." She hugs the pillow tighter.

"Three hundred eighty years, nine months, and eight days."

"*Fuck.* No one deserves to be imprisoned for that long, even if initially the Gowdies considered it a punishment for killing Jane."

I give a low chuckle. "I agree, little bird."

"Wait, didn't you say that the Gowdies have commanded you to kill for them over the years?"

Darkness forms within me, a cold bitterness I struggle to keep hold of. "Yes. Thousands."

"Then most of the people you've killed were in service to a witch who was pulling your strings. You didn't ask to be brought here. You're not a monster. You were defending yourself." She says it with such conviction that the knot in my chest loosens just a bit.

"If only the Gowdies saw it that way."

"But the candle is barely a stub. It won't be long now before it burns down and you're free, right?"

I scoff. "The Gowdies will never let it burn out. They'll make sure I'm bound for eternity."

"Why would they do that?"

"As long as it exists, I can't hurt them, I can't return home, and I am not free to truly join a coven of vampires or other supernaturals. I am their ultimate weapon."

I pour myself another glass of wine. I wish alcohol had the same effect on shades as it does on humans. Still, the mild effects are something tonight.

"You and I are so similar."

Intrigued, I narrow my eyes on her. "How so?"

"People like Tony and Jane Gowdie are bullies. They pull us into their orbit, use us, and then hang us out to dry. Maeve, she probably doesn't know the whole story. She inherited the candle. But this... *servitude* has gone on long enough."

"We'll free you from Tony," I promise.

"And I'll let the candle burn," she says with sudden certainty.

I focus on her with an intensity that makes her squirm in her seat. "What are you saying?"

She swallows. "After we save my house, I'll free you. It's time. I'm not sure how I'll explain it to Maeve, but I'm certain I won't be able to forgive myself if I don't break your curse." She holds out her hand. "Do we have a deal?"

Time and time again, I promise myself I'll stop indulging in Eloise. Every time I touch her or taste her blood, I fall for her just a little bit more. She may be human, but she's enchanted me. Already I find it impossible to accept I'll have to leave her when my work here is done. But tonight, here in her parlor, this isn't about the candle at all.

How can I resist her now that she's proven to be an angel in human skin? Eloise has no idea that the Gowdie candle will *never* burn down. It's taken me a century to learn that truth for myself. The wax is enchanted with my blood, immortal blood, mixed with that of a powerful witch. It will last as long as I do. The only way the curse can be broken is by more powerful magic. Curse-breaking magic.

Eloise doesn't know that, however, and her promise to free me is genuine. She truly intends to try.

And that means everything to me.

Damn, magnificent woman.

Isn't it torture enough to be tempted by her delectable blood, the pleasure of her warm skin, the scent of her that lingers in my dreams long after I've left her? Now I'm drawn to her vulnerability, to her selflessness, to her bravery. Maybe it's too late. Maybe I'm hers already. I was so worried she was a witch trying to bind me that I never considered I might love her, and what is love but the wickedest web.

I stare at her offered palm, overwhelmed by the sincerity in her offer. "Oh no, little bird. We cannot make a deal with a simple handshake."

Her lashes flutter, the corners of her rose colored lips twitching. "What do you have in mind?"

I remove the wineglass from her hand and set it gently on the end table. Fisting the pillow in her lap, I toss it across the room. Then, I lean over her, bracing myself on the back of the sofa.

"Spread your legs for me, little bird."

Her answering gasp feeds my fire. Her eyes lock onto

mine for three long breaths. Slowly, with a hard swallow, she parts her thighs. I drop to my knees.

"You've been taunting me with this dress all night." I nudge the hem of the purple sequined number higher on her hips and toy with the strappy black thong underneath.

She clears her throat. "Damien, I wasn't making a bargain. I'll let the candle burn because it's the right thing to do. You don't have to... do anything. I don't want you to think..." She can't even finish the sentence. Gods, does she believe she's coercing me? Even the thought is preposterous. I skim a palm under her dress, up her lower belly. Her breath falters.

"If you think for a second that you're forcing me to do *anything* right now, you've been willfully ignoring your effect on me tonight." My voice is thick with need for her. "I've wanted you from the moment I first saw you tonight. Unless you intend to command me to stop?"

"No," she says quickly, breathlessly. "I don't want you to stop."

I slant her a wicked grin, wide enough, I'm sure my fangs are showing. Hooking my fingers into the sides of her thong, I slide it down her legs and over her feet, tossing it aside. Her pulse ratchets faster, its soft drumbeat and her breath the only sounds aside from the ticking of the grandfather clock. Spreading her knees wider, I lower my gaze to her most intimate area and lick my lips. As if she could be any more of a temptation, her pretty sex glistens, ready for me, and the scent of her desire makes my blood heat.

"You're perfect." My voice is wrecked, low, and gritty. Tugging her hips forward, I drag a knuckle over her drenched slit, and she rewards me with a moan.

I love her this way, totally exposed to me. At my mercy. Her eyes grow hooded. A light blush stains her cheeks.

Gods, I want to taste her, and I will not deny myself. Not this time.

"Little bird, look at me," I whisper, an unexpected note of reverence in my voice. When her green eyes meet mine, I lower my mouth to her center and lick. The noise she makes is all the encouragement I need. With no place else to be until dawn, I settle in, lapping her folds in long, teasing strokes. When she writhes against my mouth, I flick the tip of my tongue across her clit, then suck on that tender nub as she arches and moans. Quicker now, I flick, suck, circle, watching her chase her pleasure until I fall into a rhythm.

She squirms, digging her fingers into my hair. Gods, she tastes like a fine, dark wine. I reach down to one of her feet, massaging the arch before lifting her leg to set it on my shoulder. The position opens her wider, and I thrust a finger into her, stroking inside while I relish her. Her thighs begin to shake. I want to feel her come, want my face slick from her wet heat.

She digs her nails into my scalp. "Oh God, Damien!"

23

FIRST TIME FOR EVERYTHING

ELOISE

This is a first for me. Sure, I've been married. I'm not a virgin. But Tony was my only sexual partner and my experience with him was limited. He never performed oral sex on me. He said he didn't like it, although he was happy to be on the receiving end.

Damien's mouth is heaven.

I tip my head back as he laps up my center, licking me from one end to the other in a way that is almost too erotic for me to process. I'm torn between telling him again he doesn't have to do this and screaming for him to never stop. In the end, I'm too wound up to do anything but make deep guttural noises of pleasure as he circles and tugs at my clit with his tongue and teeth while he penetrates me with his fingers.

The ache at my core morphs into an insistent throb, the telltale quiver of a building orgasm in my thighs. The base of my spine tingles with it. Tension builds, climbing higher, bigger. I can't control myself. I grab his head and grind myself against his mouth.

The vibration of his answering purr sends me over the edge.

No orgasm has ever been like this for me. Blinded by it, I arch my back as my inner walls clench around his fingers. But he doesn't let up. Shadows curl around him, brushing along my thighs like cool fingers, sinking into my navel, and coiling around my breasts. They tease my nipples to taut peaks. More shadows coast along my belly and then into me, filling me. I've never felt anything like it. While his hands massage my inner thighs and his tongue and teeth tease me higher and higher, his shadows thrust into me, cover me, a thousand snowflake kisses drawing my blood to my skin. My thighs shudder, the pressure building again, more intense than before. One more lick and another orgasm rips through me, this one sending me into the stratosphere.

"Damien," I say breathlessly. He doesn't stop. One orgasm feeds the next until I have to bite my arm to keep from screaming. I lose count of how many roll through me. He only pulls back when my muscles give out from pure exhaustion, and I collapse, loose and panting on the green velvet.

His lips brush my inner thigh, right over my femoral artery. Oh, the blood. I expect he's going to strike. He must be hungry after everything that's happened tonight. I position myself for him, but the bite never comes. He sits back on his heels, watching me with a strange expression somewhere between vulnerability and reverence. Where did that come from? Nothing I could do could hurt Damien. He is more powerful than me in every way.

Not knowing what to say, I shoot him a genuine, somewhat bashful smile. Leaning forward, I gently run my fingers along his hairline and then behind his ear before cupping his chin. Then I kiss him, my heart swelling with gratitude and something more. Once again, Damien has made me feel wanted. Worthy. Valuable. I drink it in like water on parched earth. I open my mouth to tell him what it means to me, but abruptly, he draws back and presses my knees together. He tugs my dress back into place.

All at once, he looks like he's in pain. "I must go," he says around elongated fangs.

"Wait, but don't you want—" I don't get a chance to finish my sentence. Before I can offer him my blood, the lights flicker as he breaks into an inky cloud, those smoky horns and barbed tail making an appearance. He blends into the shadows and disappears.

I sit for a moment in the empty room, wondering if I've done something wrong to make him leave. Snatching my thong off the floor, I pull it on again, my muscles loose and exhausted from the best oral sex of my life.

With a sigh, I turn off the lights, grab my purse and jacket off the chair, and head to my room. Somewhere between undressing, showering, and crawling under the covers, I make my peace with what happened. It might've meant nothing to Damien. It might never happen again. But I'm glad it did. My last thought before I sleep is that I feel lucky. Not lucky that it's probably over—or will be once I free Damien from the candle's bond—but lucky that it happened. I experienced multiple orgasms at the hands of a monster lover, and I don't feel an ounce of shame over it. I slip into contented dreams with a smile on my face.

"You were out late again last night." Grams staggers into the kitchen, leaning heavily on her cane. I pop up from the place I've been nursing my coffee and help her into her chair.

"You should call for me next time. I don't want you to fall." She looks exceptionally feeble today, like an unexpected breeze could take her out. She hasn't even bothered with her turban. The wispy strands of what is left of her white hair are on full display.

Drawing a deep breath, she shakes her head and shrugs. "Eloise, when are you going to come to terms with the idea that preserving this body of mine is not the end goal? If I fall, I fall. Either I can do something or I can't. If I can't, I'll ask for help. If I can, I'm going to do it because it might be my last hurrah. Today, I wanted to walk myself to the kitchen. Clearly I was strong enough because I'm here in one piece."

I open my mouth. Close it again. Open it again. I don't know how to respond to that. She's an adult after all. If she doesn't want my help, I won't force it on her. "Would you like some toast?"

"Just tea, thank you."

I move to the counter and fill the electric kettle.

"Did you see that man again last night? The same one as before?" She waggles her eyebrows at me.

I pick a yellow leaf off of the spider plant hanging next

to the sink and say a silent prayer that she didn't hear anything untoward. "I hope we didn't wake you."

"No." She laughs. "I didn't hear a thing, but the dark bags under your eyes don't match the sunny glow of your complexion. You look like a woman in love."

I scoff and trail my fingers through the air. "I'm not even divorced yet, Grams. Why would I want another man when I can't deal with the one I'm still married to on paper?"

"Aww, marriages are like pancakes. First one sometimes turns out bad."

"Grams!"

"I'm just saying you and Tony were never right for each other. No matter what the paperwork says, I cast no judgment if you have feelings for another man."

"Well, thank you, but it's nothing serious. I'm just having fun and enjoying how he makes me feel."

Grams grins. "And how is that? How does he make you feel?"

I only have to think on it for a second. "He makes me feel like I matter, like maybe I'm more powerful than I think I am. He makes me feel..." I search for the right word. "Seen. Seen and enough."

With a thump of her cane on the floor, Grams beams. "That is how a man is supposed to make a woman feel."

I pop two pieces of toast into the toaster, ignoring a tiny red flag that goes up in my brain. Damien is not technically a man. "It's been a long time since anyone made me feel that way. Tony sure didn't." I point at my chest, turning to face her. "I know that in the end, I'm responsible for my own self-esteem. I can't rely on any man to build me up day after day. But this... person makes me realize that maybe the problem is not the lack of building up but the constant tearing down."

Grams nods. "Wise beyond your years, Eloise. My cancer may be here to stay, but I'm happy you can remove yours with this divorce."

My heart swells for this woman and the unconditional love and support she has always doled out. "Thanks, Grams." The kettle clicks itself off and I pour the boiling water into a cup, adding her favorite tea bag. After buttering the toast I know she didn't ask for, I slide it and the tea in front of her and sit down with mine and the rest of my coffee.

"I saw Howard last night," she says softly, ignoring the toast but reaching for her tea. "He was outside my window with the fairies again. He's getting closer."

As much as I want to dismiss this fairy thing Grams keeps talking about as a dream or a hallucination, I now understand that shades, vampires, and witches are real, along with other dimensions. Why not fairies? "What do they look like, the fairies?"

"Small and bright. From my room, I see round lights bobbing among the trees, but I know what they are. Your great-grandpa wrote about them in his journals. It's why he decided to settle in Echo Mills way back when."

She's told me this story before, but I egg her on anyway. "Great-grandpa settled here when it was still a milling town, right?"

"He most certainly did. If you go to the old mill, you can find his initials carved in the tree growing on the property. H.H. Henry Harcourt. I was as close to him as my own father, you know. Dad died young, but Henry was with us into his old age. Howard's father was always good to me, just as Howard was. But Henry harbored a zest for the occult. He traveled the world photographing the strange and unusual. Boxes of pictures in the attic chronicle his escapades. His beloved Caroline, your great-grandmother, was the first to be buried in the family cemetery. Henry wanted her to rest where the fairies played. Told me there was magic on this land and all we had to do was tap into it.

"All the séances he held here and the conversations he had with the beyond aside though, it was Henry's belief that with magic in the land and love in these walls, his descendants would be truly blessed. And we have been. Love, magic, and family, that's the secret."

Behind her, the faded picture of Henry Harcourt takes on new meaning to me. I picture him coming here as a young man, settling in a place with no infrastructure aside from the mill, and building this house with his two hands, all because he felt something magical standing on these cliffs overlooking the Rappahannock River. My great-grandfather believed in something, and for over a century, my family has loved and protected it.

"When I'm gone, you will be the last living Harcourt, Eloise. I know young people don't stay in one place anymore, but this will be yours someday. You'll be tempted to sell it. I hope you'll consider staying."

"I'll never sell," I say with certainty. "My children are going to play on this land, and I'm going to be buried in that cemetery right beside you and my parents."

A smile warms her otherwise pale face. "I guess there is magic here."

The phone rings, and I furrow my brow. Who could be calling the landline? A chill runs through me at the timing, as if the ghost of my dead great-grandfather might be on the line. I lift the handset from its cradle and wrap my finger in the obscenely long coiled cord. "Hello?"

"Eloise? Ed Singer here. Can you sub today? Mrs. Adams had to go home sick."

I block the receiver and whisper to Grams, "The nurse is coming today, right?"

"Yes."

"Will you be okay if I work a shift?"

"Of course. Nurse or no nurse, I'll be fine." She nods.

I remove my hand. "Ed? I'd love to come in. I can be there in fifteen. See you soon."

We say our goodbyes and I hang up. Bouncing twice on my toes, I clap my hands together. "I have a job again."

"Go get 'em tiger." She laughs.

I speed off toward my room to get ready. Maybe this place *is* magic because I finally feel like my luck is turning around.

24

WRAPPED IN SHADOWS

ELOISE

Eight hours later, I arrive back at Harcourt Manor, utterly exhausted. I forgot how draining it is to teach art. From the sixth grader who was embarrassed when someone caught him painting his crush, to the twelfth grader who wanted my advice about majoring in graphic design, teaching proved once again to be about far more than the subject itself. I like working with kids, and I'm proud of what I've done today. But I'm also tired as hell, and a small but insistent niggle at the back of my brain wonders what it would feel like to paint again. Paint like I used to before my parents died. Create from the depths of my soul rather than because I'm teaching someone else to paint.

I push the thought aside as I park my Jeep, check on Grams, then sink into one of the rockers on the wrap-around porch out front with a hot cup of tea. October in

Virginia carries in the scent of change, the air threatening a chill that doesn't quite have teeth yet but will soon enough. As the sun sets, I appreciate it wrapped in a light but cozy blanket, sipping my chamomile. I think of nothing. Not the future. Not the past. Not when I have to go inside or what frozen casserole I'll eat for dinner. Blissfully fatigued, I watch the shadows of the trees stretch toward me as the day melts into the river, leaving behind a blank canvas of darkness.

The moment the shadows reach the porch, Damien appears in the empty rocker beside me. I almost drop my teacup. "Damn it, Damien. I'm going to tie a bell around your neck! You scared me half to death. Again! Didn't I tell you not to do that?"

He flashes a crooked grin. "You are far from half-dead, little bird. Your heart is fluttering as fast as always." His smile fades, and he turns his head toward the door, his nostrils flaring like he smells something coming from the house, something that makes him grow somber. "How is your grandmother?"

I don't like what I see pass behind his eyes. "She's dying," I say. "But she's here now. Resting. And I think she'll be here tomorrow."

"It won't be long now," he says softly.

I glare at him but only find empathy where there once was cruelty. What I ask next comes out shaky. "How do you know?"

"I can smell it." He looks toward the night sky. "It's not a bad thing, death. At least, my people don't believe it is. An honorable death brings comfort and freedom."

I wonder at his words. So many people avoid talking about death. Even Maeve. It's refreshing to have someone give it to me straight. I don't know if I agree with his notion. Death certainly doesn't bring comfort to those left behind. But I absolutely appreciate him not shying away from the topic.

"You haven't eaten." His brilliant silver eyes lock onto me again.

"I'm fine."

"I can smell your hunger." He frowns.

"I'll eat later."

"I won't share what news I have with you if you don't eat."

"Seriously?" I sigh. Damien looks resolved, and I want to know what he's come to tell me. I stand from the rocker and pick up the teacup, then lead him inside to the kitchen, where I pull out the fixings for a ham and cheese sandwich. "Okay. I'm making it. Tell me what you found."

He reaches into the inner pocket of his jacket and withdraws a folded magazine.

Dropping the knife I'm holding into the mayo, I snatch it from his grip. "Echo Mills Today! Oh my God, Damien. Where did you find this?" He takes over making my sandwich while I flip through the magazine.

"After I left you last night, I went back to the warehouse. Ran into our friend on the side of the road. Turns out he had a copy where he's sleeping. I traded him some shoes and a down blanket for it."

Heart brimming with new hope, I inspect the pages. Stock photography of a mom with a kid graces the cover, FREE in small caps in the upper right-hand corner. "Wait, I have seen this magazine before. I think they give it away at the doctor's office."

Damien finishes constructing my ham and cheese, cuts

it diagonally down the center, and places the plate in front of me. "Eat."

"Why would Tony publish a free magazine?" I ask him.

He sits down in the chair across from me, lifts a half sandwich between his fingers, and holds it out to me. I bite and chew. Mmmm. Food prepared by someone else always tastes better. And it doesn't hurt that my monster is watching me eat it with the type of care commonly reserved for someone you like and respect.

"Most of the time, these types of periodicals make their money selling advertising space," he says. "Look inside. It's all ads."

I open the magazine again and confirm as much. "This is weird. Don't they usually also have articles in them?" The pages are solid advertisements. I notice one for my grandmother's nail salon.

"That's my understanding," he concurs, feeding me another bite.

"So Tony is making money on the side selling ad space in a free magazine?" I swallow the bite in my mouth. "But where is the money going? Maeve has gone through all the accounts. There are no unaccounted-for deposits."

"What exactly does Denardi Enterprises do?" Damien pops the last corner of the sandwich half into my mouth. Damn, I'm already on the other half. I must have been hungrier than I thought.

"What doesn't it do? His family owns a string of car dealerships, a few restaurants, massage parlors, nail salons, mattress stores. He owns an entire strip mall in Richmond."

"All places that deal in a lot of cash."

I nod. "I guess, yeah."

"Maybe he's siphoning the ad sales through one of the cash-based businesses to hide the income and then pocketing the cash they take in."

"To evade taxes? Hmm, actually, that makes sense. He used to give me a weekly allowance in cash to buy groceries."

Damien sneers. "Your husband gave you an allowance?"

I release a beleaguered sigh. "There's a reason I'm not with him anymore." I rub the back of my neck. "He always gave me cash, though. That supports your theory. But how do we prove it?"

Damien drums his fingers on the table. "That's the problem. There's nothing linking the magazine or the warehouse to Tony. We have a company. You and I know he runs it. Unfortunately, aside from your memory of that invoice, we have nothing to prove he has any connection to it."

Damien holds the last bite of my sandwich between his fingers, and he's watching me with such care it makes my chest feel warm. I've been starved for this type of attention. Part of me suspects he's doing all this because of the candle. I don't care. I'm soaking it up like the last bit of gravy at the bottom of the plate.

"I'm full." I push his hand away.

He pops the remainder in his own mouth and chews.

"You eat regular food?"

"Often, although I prefer my meat rare."

I file that away into things I didn't know about shades and turn my attention back to the magazine in my hand. "So, without more proof, this doesn't help us at all."

"Unfortunately, no."

A heavy black tangle forms deep within me. I hate Tony. I hate the legal system and the fact I'm probably going to lose this house. I'm so angry and frustrated I can't think about it anymore. I fling Echo Mills Today across the kitchen.

Damien flashes me an empathetic look. "Little bird?"

"Are you ever going to call me by my real name?" I snap. His nickname for me hasn't bothered me before, but after last night, I want more.

He wipes his hands on a napkin. "Do you want me to? Names are... personal."

What an odd thing to think, but then I remember something. "Maeve told me they've always just called you the advocate."

His chin bobs once.

"But you told me your name."

"You asked, and I was obligated to respond to you as the bearer of the candle."

My heart clenches. "Oh. So, you'd rather I call you the advocate."

"No." His expression grows serious. "I like when you call me Damien. Just you."

I lean my elbows on the table. I want to hear him say my name, but I won't force him. "I don't want you to do anything you don't want to do anymore, okay?"

"Okay." His eyes tighten at the corners as if he finds this funny. I'm not trying to be funny.

"You have no choice, do you? Because of the curse."

"Correct."

"All right, then I command you to tell me if there's something I ask you to do that you don't want to do. That way, I can change what I ask you to do."

This time his laugh is robust enough to show fang. "There's no one like you, little bird."

"You can leave if you want to," I say. "Thank you for bringing me the magazine." I wait. The clock on the wall ticks loudly enough that it reminds me of our first meeting. "You're still here."

"I want to be here." His voice is so low and gritty I can barely make it out. His gaze drops to my throat, and I wonder if he's hungry for my blood.

"Why didn't you take my blood last night? You could have. I wouldn't have stopped you." I chuckle. "Honestly, you could have done anything to me last night, and I wouldn't have stopped you." My face heats at the admission.

He swallows, then reaches over to cup my chin in his big rough palm. "What I did with you last night was not part of our agreement. And I didn't take your blood because I didn't want you to think that what happened between us was... transactional. Understand? It wasn't related to your promise to allow the candle to burn. I wanted you. I wanted to taste you, and I loved giving you pleasure." He licks his bottom lip, his gaze settling on my mouth.

The air charges between us, and I feel his stare deep within me. I lick my lips. "Hold on to the sides of your chair and don't remove your hands unless I tell you."

His brow knits, but he does as I command. I stand, grip the back of his chair, and lean over him until our foreheads touch. His lips part, but when he moves to capture my mouth, I rock back and reach for his belt. Shadows flit behind his stormy gaze, then drift off him to swirl around me. Once the gathering darkness might have frightened me. Now, the cool brush against my hot skin stokes a deep ache in my core.

I make short work of the button and zipper of his fly. Underneath, he's hard and enormous. A hiss flows through his teeth as I palm his massive cock. He may be a different species, but his anatomy is warm, male, and weeping for me. I drop to my knees in front of him.

"What are you doing?" he grits out.

"Exactly what I want to do. Tell me to stop if you object."

He doesn't say a word. I tug his pants lower and admire the size of him. I'll have to unhinge my jaw like a snake to fit him in, but nothing is going to stop me from trying. I lean over and lick a drop of moisture from the tip, then circle my tongue along the ridge.

"*Fuck*," he growls, his knuckles turning white where he grips the chair. I lock eyes with him before running the flat of my tongue along his length. He mumbles something in another language that sounds like a prayer, but he doesn't tell me to stop. I suck him deep to the back of my throat.

His breath saws in and out of his lungs. I can hardly fit my lips around him and have to use my hand to accommodate his length, but I make up for it in enthusiasm. Swirling my tongue over the head of his cock, I revel in his moan and then take him deep again. I hollow my cheeks and pick up speed.

"Release my hands," he growls, his voice cracking.

"You can let go," I say between strokes.

He does, then grabs the back of my head and thrusts into my mouth again. I take him, all of him I can manage, my eyes starting to tear as he fucks my mouth in earnest, finding a tight, even rhythm. God, he tastes as good as he smells, his smoke and spice scent translating to a rich flavor I can't get enough of. I reach between his legs and stroke the heavy weights there, all the time watching him watch me. And what I see is the hottest thing I've ever experienced. The want, the need, it's raw and powerful.

His fangs are elongated, and he tugs on the back of my hair, but I only suck him deeper, scraping my teeth gently along his shaft. That's all it takes. With a low growl and a jerk of his hips, he empties himself down my throat. I love the way he looks in this moment, hunched and vulnerable. I may be the one on my knees, but he regards me like I'm a goddess, like I'm something to worship.

I sit back on my heels, and he reaches down to gather me off the floor and into his arms. "Gods, Eloise. Please be who I think you are."

I'm not sure what he means. I'm about to ask him when I realize what he's done. "You called me Eloise."

The kiss he gives me then makes me forget all about my questions. When he pulls back, I can tell he's hungry, but when I draw my hair to the side to offer my neck, he shakes his head.

"No." His expression is unreadable. "I need to go."

He stands, taking me with him and setting me gently on my feet. "Will I see you tomorrow?"

"I have some business to attend to, but I'll be back in a few days. If there's an emergency, use the candle to call me."

I nod.

"I won't give up, Eloise. I'll follow Tony every moment of the night if I have to." He flashes a wicked smile. "Or I could just kill him."

I sigh. That option is becoming more and more tempting as the clock ticks down to my court date. "Not just yet."

He kisses me again. The lights flicker. And then he's gone.

25
DREAMS

ELOISE

I dream of Damien that night. We're on the cliffs at the back of our property, having a picnic. His head rests in my lap as I run my fingers through his hair. Our children play around us. Faceless, laughing children who run too close to the edge. I'm not worried. My mother is watching over them, keeping them safe. She's calling to me again, saying something into the wind I can't hear.

When I wake, the happiness from that dream sticks with me, but then I realize it's impossible. A picnic in the sun would weaken Damien. Even if he'd do it for me, I wouldn't want him to. And we could never have children, could we? We're not even the same species.

Am I actually lying in bed thinking about having children with Damien? Yes, I am. Damn it. I'm falling in love with my monster. It's a terrible idea for many reasons, not the least of which is that I do intend to destroy the candle when we're done saving my house. Afterward, he'll disappear. Probably find his shade friends and a way home. He'll definitely steer clear of the Gowdies. Once he's liberated, I fully expect he won't waste his newfound freedom with a human in cashmere sweater sets and pearls.

I roll my eyes. I'm so sick of dressing like Tony's little Barbie doll. All my clothes are really his. How he wanted me to look. How he wanted me to act. Who he wanted me to be. If I wasn't on the verge of bankruptcy, I'd buy a new wardrobe.

I sit up in my childhood bed, my eyes widening as an idea ignites in me like I've tripped an explosive force in my brain. I'm an artist. I've worked with diverse media to produce creative work for most of my life, first at my mother's side and then to get my degree. I have talent, my mother's art studio, and fabric.

I don't need to buy new clothes. I can make them.

Popping out of bed, I dress in overpriced yoga gear, then run to check on Grams. Once she's settled, I visit my mother's studio.

The door is painted deep blue with stars and a moon, and my mother's favorite purple dragon curled and sleeping at the base. I think of my tattoo, how I always thought it was a key but Damien thought it was a dragon. How he said if I were ever to win this house, I'd have to wake my inner dragon. I understand now. I need to wake the part of me that fell asleep to please Tony. I need the girl who was reckless and wild. That was a girl who could get things done. And the tools I need are in this room.

Since the day I moved back in with Grams, I've walked past the door to my mother's studio but refused to go in. This is Mom's part of the house. Opening the door feels like tapping into her soul. Pressure builds in my torso, forcing my heart into my throat, as I turn the knob and the smell of stale air, oil paint, and dust hits me squarely in the face.

My mother made her money painting with oils. The Diana Harcourt brand paired fantasy creatures with ordinary settings. Two of her most popular paintings were titled Dragons in the Deli and Witches in the Waiting Room. But as I stride into the massive space that was once her studio, the central figure is a sculpture constructed of *knives*.

I've never seen this piece before. Kitchen knives, short daggers, curved blades, butter knives... even a rapier and a broadsword make up the sculpture. They're all arranged with sharp points facing out in a column running from floor to ceiling. I approach it cautiously and gently tap one of the points. Ouch! I suck my pricked finger. What the hell inspired this? I find my answer on a plaque mounted to the base: Motherhood by Diana Harcourt.

I bark a sharp laugh. My mom thought motherhood was a tower of deadly weapons. Wow. Was it because I was such a wild kid? I think back, tapping my chin. No, she'd loved that part of me. She always encouraged it. So then, what's the meaning? I pace around the sculpture. How is it possible I've never seen this one before? Admittedly she died when I was a teen, and I couldn't see more than two feet around myself back then, but still, I worked with her in this studio. This must've been a piece loaned out to a gallery. I pause when something caged inside the sculpture catches my eye. Squinting, I rise on my tiptoes for a better look at what's mounted there. A framed picture of me as a child is nestled within all those sharp points.

Now it makes sense. This is a sculpture about protective instincts. A mother becomes a whirlwind of weapons to safeguard her kid. This is how she felt about defending me. Memories of her wild blond curls and rambunctious smile flood me, followed by my father's taciturn strength. What would they think about the trials that I face now? What advice would they give me? I almost wish I could wedge myself into the middle of this sculpture and, for just a few moments, feel safe like I did when they were alive, when I was wrapped in my father's arms or tucked into my mother's side.

Do we ever again feel as safe as we did when we were children? Before we understood how evil the world could be?

I swallow around the lump in my throat, my vision blurring from tears I can't hold back any longer. It's time, I decide, to allow them to fall freely and to accept that this grief is a part of me now. I'm a survivor not a victim. I won't let it own me.

Through my tears, I find a few empty bins and start loading them with bottles of fabric dye, growing hopeful as I see that I have everything I need here. Minutes later, I'm back in my room, pulling all the clothes from my closet and drawers. I set up a system in my bathroom. Any fabric that is dyable goes into one of five vats, purple, black, red, orange, or lime green. Nothing is coming out of here remotely beige. All the pain, all the loss I've held at arm's length, I invite in. I grieve the end of my marriage right along with the loss of my parents and the preemptive loss of my grandmother.

I shove the last three years underwater and hold it there.

My fabric shears became a scalpel for what remains, extracting Tony from every piece. I grin at what he would think as I carve up a Brooks Brothers blazer he bought me for Christmas. Not even Grams would wear the ugly print, but it has lovely leather and brass detailing, and the lining is perfect. Once I'm buried in fabric scraps, I rev up the sewing machine and don't stop dyeing, cutting, or stitching for eighteen hours straight, aside from an occasional bathroom break and to check on Grams.

By the time I wrap things up, my hands look like Easter eggs, but I have a closet of original outfits I can't wait to wear. I don a pair of black cigarette pants and a green off-the-shoulder top that's fitted around my waist and descend the steps to grab something to eat for the first time that day.

"Eloise?" I hear Grams call. It's the middle of the night, so I race to her room. She's left the bedside lamp on and has propped her frail frame up in a foamy sea of white blankets. When she sees me in my new outfit, she gasps, a smile transforming her face. Her hand trembles as she raises it to her mouth. "Eloise," she says breathlessly. "There you are. You're back!"

I smile. "Do you like it?"

Her rheumy eyes swim with tears, her chin tucking into her chest. "Much better. You look lovely. Just lovely." Her gaze lingers on my still-blond hair.

"I'm dyeing it back to its natural shade tomorrow," I say with a laugh. "Ran out of time today."

She claps her hands together. "You're beautiful any way you wear it. But let it be how *you* want to wear it."

I nod, my eyes misting. "That's my plan. What are you doing up so late?"

She waves a hand like she's shooing the comment away. "When you spend so much time in bed, things like night and day don't have the meaning they once did. Anyway, I called you in here for a reason. Could you please open the drapes? I want to watch for Howard, and the nurse keeps closing them during the day. I told her I have no problem resting in the light of day. This body could sleep with a marching band going by. But she keeps closing them."

"I'll remind her next time." I walk through the room and open the drapes wide, allowing the moonlight in. Across the backyard and beyond a field of wildflowers, I see the marble crosses that mark my parents' graves. I haven't visited them since I've been back. Maybe it's time. God forbid, if I lose the house, it might be the last time.

Lights bounce beyond the graves, darting between the trees. My breath catches.

"You see them, don't you?" Grams says excitedly. "The fairies!"

"I see lights." I dart a glance at her. By the time I look back, the glowing orbs have vanished. Did I see what I thought I saw? I shake my head. "They're gone now."

"They come and go." She shrugs. "I've been seeing them for months now, always this time of night. I suppose the fae have things to do just like everybody else."

I have no explanation for the bobbing lights. Maybe they are fairies. Maybe balls of phosphorescent gas are rising up from the cavernous earth our property is built atop. Either way, it sure gave my heart a workout seeing that show. I cross to Grams and place a kiss on her cheek. "Now the shades are open. You won't miss them if they come back."

She squeezes my hand. "Thank you, Eloise."

"Have you been able to sleep at all?" I ask.

"Enough."

"Are you still up for your nail appointment tomorrow, I mean later today? I can ask Simone to come here instead."

She shakes her head. "Oh, I'm still getting around, and there's nothing I like better than listening to Simone spill the tea in that salon. It's not the same here."

It's Grams's last guilty pleasure. Even if I have to carry her into that nail salon, I'll do it to make sure she gets what she wants. "Great. It's not until one, so you can take your time getting up."

"I plan to." She smiles whimsically. "G'night, Eloise. I'm so glad you decided to become you again."

Me too. "G'night, Grams."

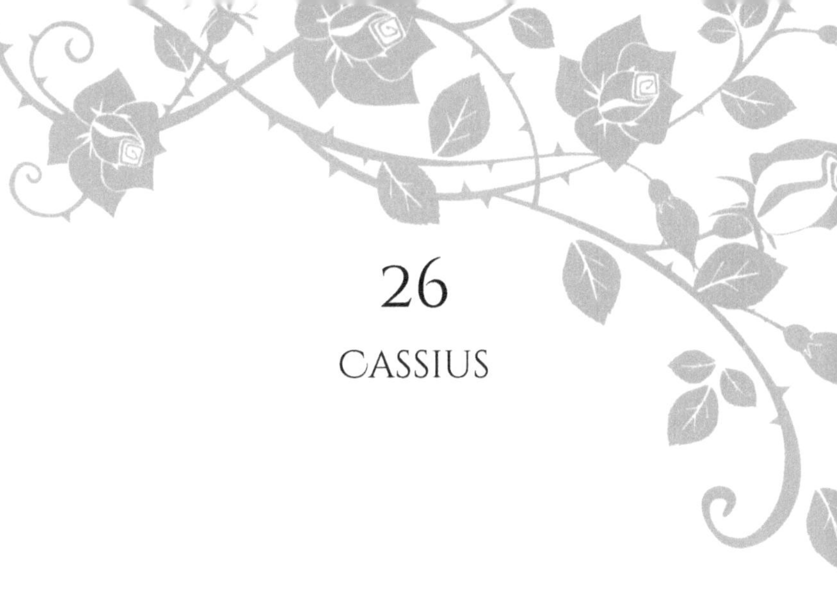

26

CASSIUS

DAMIEN

Business to attend to. It isn't a lie exactly, but also not the full truth. I need a break from Eloise, or I'm likely to consume her. Seeing her on her knees with my cock in her mouth made me feel like a god, and I, of all creatures, have no business feeling that way. I'm a monster cursed to serve other monsters, and unless something changes, that's all I'll ever be.

Problem is my feelings for her are as monstrous as I am, and I'm afraid they've outgrown their cage. What I need now more than anything is a confidant, and I know where to find one.

I manifest outside Cassius's Chicago brownstone, thankful my friend and fellow shade answered the call I sent him down our shadow bond. Cassius was once Stygarde's commander. Along with squad leader, Morpheus, we fought side by side in the battle for

Dimhollow, so closely that we were dragged through the rift together. I trust him with my life.

The door opens before I have a chance to knock, and the lithe figure of a dark-skinned man appears in the doorway, his smile reaching all the way to his equally dark eyes. "I felt you down the shadows. They ripple with your distress. Gods, Damien, your energy feels like a coming earthquake."

I sag in the doorway. "I'm afraid the disaster has already happened. I need your advice, old friend."

"Come in. I'm great with advice, just as long as I don't have to follow my own." He chuckles as he smooths a hand over his hair, longer on top and fading to bare scalp near his neck. He flips on the lights in the foyer even though neither of us needs them to see. Living topside requires certain accommodations to appear human. Lights are one of them.

"You look like you've been training," I say, noting the man's exceptionally lethal appearance.

"Thanks for noticing. Actually yes. I've accepted a position as commander of the Chicago vampire coven's guard. The master here is serious about defending her city. Even has a witch on her payroll." Cassius pauses inside a neatly arranged living room near the front of the house. "Can I get you a drink?"

"The stronger, the better."

"I have just the thing." He flows to a bar built into the far wall of the room, shadows clinging to him as he moves. "I think I know why you're here," he says as he tongs ice into two glasses and fills them with generous pours of Reyka vodka. "You've been tapped by the queen, haven't you?"

I snort. "Good guess. She did call me in, but, as you know, my curse prevents me from serving as her consort... thank the gods."

Cassius laughs and hands me my drink. We sink into leather chairs positioned perfectly around a glass coffee table in a rather austere room. Everything in its place. Just like Cassius. The shade is the most meticulous creature I've ever met.

"Use caution with Valeska, Damien. Even your curse may not be enough to dissuade her. She's hellbent on expanding the hive."

"Hive, yes, I noticed she used that terminology instead of coven."

"It started when her predecessor chose to use Queen instead of Master. That opened the door."

"Technically, Valeska is a queen. When Night Haven conquered the Blood Mark coven, she earned the royal title. Liberty coven followed. Between her predecessor and her, Night Haven has incorporated, what, at least ten—"

"A dozen covens at last count. Her lust for power is endless."

"I sense that too."

"You represent the ultimate opportunity to her. As a shade, not only could you provide her better protection than any vampire in existence, but also an alternative to feeding on humans. Imagine how useful that would be for her. Feeding is a source of vulnerability for any vampire."

"So, I gathered when she fed from me without my consent."

Cassius gives a disapproving hiss.

"I have no interest in serving as her blood bag, and I'm guessing you don't either, given that you're here."

"Insightful of you." He wags a finger. "I left before I could be invited to apply for the job and am now under the protection of the Chicago master. Morpheus left too."

"I'm aware. Ran into him at Bad Witches' Club, and he has no regrets about performing the triune bond or his newfound abilities to walk in the sun." I take a long sip of my drink, wishing it had a stronger effect on my constitution. My conversation with Morpheus had been enlightening. The shade accepted the bond immediately after receiving Valeska's invitation.

"Which means you are her last hope and her first choice." Cassius scowls.

"I am no choice." I lift my brows. "It's a moot point. If a Gowdie witch commands me to kill her, I'll be helpless but to comply. The Queen understands this."

"Don't put it past her to find a way to break the curse just to have you for herself."

I resist baring my teeth. "Good luck to her. I've spent centuries looking for an antidote. The Gowdies are the most powerful coven of animators on the planet. They'll be pulling her strings the moment she bares her fangs."

Cassius nods, turning serious. "Just be careful. There's something about Valeska. I don't trust her."

"Considering she likely murdered her predecessor..."

"More than that, Damien." He narrows his eyes, upper lip curling in disgust. "I sense she'd kill every last vampire in her own coven to reach her goals. She has no loyalty to our kind and values nothing beyond herself."

The shadows in the room shift and rearrange with our

shared tension. "I felt that in her presence too. I'll be careful."

"Excellent. If you want me to introduce you to the Chicago coven master—"

"No. Night Haven is home." *Plus, it's closer to Eloise.*

"Understood. Still, you're welcome to stay for a few days if you think it will help get you out of sight and out of mind. This city is brimming with nightlife."

"I will stay, but I'm not here because of the queen."

"No?"

I tell him about Eloise—everything from how she came to have the candle in her possession to the taste of her blood—and then I command the shadows to paint the tattoo on her back in the air between us.

"It's definitely a sigil. I recognize several of the arcane symbols."

"But not the figure itself. It's not a witch's bloodline. I know that much."

"Morpheus didn't have any insight?"

"No. Not exactly. Recently I've learned that Diana Harcourt was hired to paint Bad Witches' Club. She was a local artist, and several vampires suspected she was magical, but no one ever knew what she was. She claimed she was human but a friend to the supernatural."

"Maybe that's it then. You say, aside from the effect her blood has on you, Eloise seems human."

"Yes... but..." I scrub my face with my hands.

"What is it? You look tortured."

"I'm falling in love with her, Cassius, more deeply than I've ever loved anyone, in this world or the last."

"Fuck."

"Right, fuck." I stand and pace the room. "At first, I

assumed she was a witch, binding me with some new spell I hadn't yet encountered. But the more I'm with her, the more I'm convinced she's human. I'm not sure which terrifies me more. I need to know if it's real."

He sips his drink, delivering a thoughtful *hmmm* from his glass. "Tell me, Damien, what do you love about her?"

I rub my jaw, trying to put it into words. "The first time I saw her, I thought she looked like a typical human. The worst kind."

"Entitled? Wrapped up in her own little corner of eternity?" Cassius fills in.

"Exactly. But then I noticed more. She's young but living in this house that doesn't even have a television in the parlor. And I can smell death in the place. She's soaking in it. The more I learned about her situation, that she'd left her abuser and given up a wealthy lifestyle to help her grandmother die, the more I came to respect her. She's afraid. The scent of her fear burns in my nose often when we're together. But she fought for my help, desperate to save her home, not for herself but for her grandmother's sake, a woman who is dying anyway."

"You love her because she's selfless."

"No." I take a deep breath and blow it out slowly. "Selflessness and stupidity are too often bedfellows." I think back to my interactions with Eloise. "She smells human. Her heart flutters like a human's. The Gowdie witch confirms she is human. Aside from the sigil, which is in the wrong place to be a sigil, there is no reason for me to suspect she has magic. But that tattoo belied everything else about her. It's a sign that there's more inside her, a flame that can't be extinguished."

Cassius scratches the back of his head. "Why do I feel

like you're going to break into a stanza of 'Candle in the Wind?'"

A laugh bubbles from deep within me. I've come to the right place. "I'm not drawn to her because she's selfless. I love her, Cassius, because she's brave in the way of a warrior. That thing I saw in her that first day, she's shown it to me again and again. She's a fighter. She dauntlessly pursues what she feels is right. She's smart. Reckless perhaps at times but she knows her odds and overcomes her fears to protect the people she loves. In three hundred and eighty years, she is the only candle bearer who ever asked for my name, the only one who cared if I wanted to do as she commanded. She is one of a kind. To have a mate like that. To not be alone anymore."

"For the extent of her human life."

It's a shot to the gut and I pull up short in my pacing, lifting my glass from the end table and draining it dry. "It goes without saying, it would be worth it."

"Well, Damien, you asked me if what you are feeling is love or magic, and I have the answer."

"You do?"

"What you just said... everything you've told me about why you love her... you never mentioned her blood."

I close my eyes, suddenly hungry for her. "Her blood is incredible. I dream of it."

"But it's not why you love her." A statement. Not a question.

"No."

"Congratulations, you love her. It's not magic."

I circle my glass, listening to the ice clink against the sides. It's real. It is. "I'm not sure congratulations are in order."

"No?" Cassius's brow furrows.

"If I mate her, it changes everything. I can't truly be with her unless I break the Gowdie hold on me, and if I do that, what then? Do I give up on our quest to find a way home?"

Cassius drains the rest of his drink and rises to cross to the bar to pour himself another. "I'll tell you what I think. If she is the woman you say she is and she fights for what she holds dear, it won't be long until you know how she feels. She'll tell you. She'll show you. And if you choose to mate her, you'll know one thing for sure."

I hold out my empty glass to him and he refills it. "Oh? What's that?"

"When it comes to the rest of it, she'll only be a factor for her short human life. If you love her, Damien, enjoy it while it lasts."

27

NAILED IT

My mind drifts to Damien over and over as I drive Grams to Nails & Such. It's all I can do to focus and stay in the moment. But I refuse to allow myself to daydream about our last two nights together. Not today. Grams is feeling stronger, and I don't want to miss a minute of it. Of course, her excitement for our outing has something to do with it. Physically, she remains as feeble as ever, but she grins all the way to the salon, and although I have to help her out of the Jeep, she walks herself inside.

"Nora Harcourt, look at you strolling in here all gussied up." Simone Williams meets us at the door and takes Grams's elbow, helping her to her nail station. The heavyset woman has always looked out for her, especially since Grams's illness caused her skin to become as delicate as old newsprint.

"Hi, Simone," I say cheerfully.

"Love the hair, Eloise." She grins warmly.

"Thanks. It's as close as I could get to my natural color." I fluff my new red curls. I've been bleaching and straightening it since almost the moment I met Tony, and he made it known that he preferred it that way. He considered it more refined. This morning, I colored it back to red. The box dye I used took to my platinum hair like water to a sponge, and the color came out even brighter than my dark red roots. My head is bright enough to belong on a Marvel character and as curly and wild as Julia Roberts's in Pretty Woman. I love it. Along with the now purple dress I'm wearing, I feel free, like Tony is nothing but a speed bump in my life's roadmap instead of a permanent roadblock.

I take a seat in the waiting area while Grams picks out a color for her nails. She chooses an OPI shade called Suzi & the 7 Düsseldorfs, which is a sort of bright tulip purple. There's nothing old ladyish about it. We're cut from the same cloth, Grams and I.

While Simone starts removing Grams's old polish, I dig through a pile of magazines for something to read. I'm tempted to pull out my phone and scroll social media now that I'm somewhere with reliable Wi-Fi, but the truth is, I don't want to risk seeing pictures of Tony on his boat or leaning up against his newest car. I don't want to answer messages from acquaintances about what happened or how the divorce is going. The only friends I care about are Maeve and a few people I know from teaching, and all of them text me directly. So, I leave my phone in my purse and pick up a Cosmo, ready to read an article on how I can make my skin glow in three easy steps.

I cast the magazine aside, though, when I see what's underneath it.

The latest issue of Echo Mills Today stares up at me, a photo of a man walking his dog on the cover. I pick it up and start flipping through the pages. Same as before, it's filled with nothing but advertisements.

"Oh, you found another one." Simone glances over at me, shaking her head. "I thought I threw them all away. Don't waste your time, El."

"Why not?" I ask. "I thought I saw an ad for Nails & Such in here."

She concentrates as she slowly paints a line down Grams's thumbnail. "That's just it. We didn't pay for any ad. And the phone number's wrong. If someone wanted to gift us ad space, the least they could do is get the info right."

"Yeah, that is weird," I say in solidarity, my mind grinding on what that means in the context of Tony and the warehouse.

"I checked out some of the other ads," Simone continues. "Most of them are for businesses that don't exist."

"Huh?" That can't be right.

"Echo Mills is small, even for a small town. There ain't that many businesses that serve the folks around here. I started googling the names I didn't recognize. They don't exist. And the ones that do are listed with all the wrong information. I checked with a few folks, and they didn't pay for ad space either. We looked for a number to call, but there's not anything at all in that thing indicating who's responsible for it. It just shows up in my mailbox once a month. Something shady is going on there, mark my words." She redirects her attention back to Grams's nails.

"Something shady," I repeat. Why the hell would Tony print a magazine for free? If he's not getting advertising revenue, what is he getting? "I'll toss it for you."

"Thanks."

I move for the garbage, but when she isn't looking, I slip the magazine into my purse. I want to show it to Damien tomorrow night when he's back from his secret business and tell him what Simone said. This magazine is dated October, this month, which means that somewhere, Gold Weaver Inc is still operating, and I'm the only one who knows Tony is behind it. But the real mystery is why.

My gut tells me if I can figure that out, I'll have him.

"All right, Nora. You're good to go," Simone says some time later. She helps Grams up, and I meet her halfway.

"Oh, Eloise, can you help me get my credit card out of my purse?" Grams tries her best to move the bag hooked on her elbow closer to me, but she only manages to rock it in my direction. She looks tired and leans on me with most of her weight.

"Not today, Nora," Simone says with a smile. "Today's on me."

Grams grins. "No. You deserve to be paid! You shouldn't give away your services for free."

Simone pats Nora's back and looks her straight in the eye in a way that makes a lump form in my throat. "Please let me do this for you, Nora. You've been such a good customer over the years."

The shop grows conspicuously quiet as the three of us soak in the moment. And then my Grams hugs Simone with strength I know she doesn't have to spare. Afterward, I help her into my Jeep. She weighs nothing, which helps because I have to lift her into the seat. Once I have her buckled in, Grams places a hand on mine. "I should have given her a tip, at least."

I agree. "I got it, Grams." I close her door and head back inside.

Simone smiles warmly when she sees me, her eyes swimming with unshed tears. "Sorry if I made things uncomfortable. She's just so—"

"I know." Grams looks like someone who is dying now. There's no denying it. "Listen, she won't let me take her home unless I give you a tip, and you deserve one." I reach into my bag and pull out a ten.

Simone holds it up to the light briefly and then puts it in the register.

"Why do you do that?" I ask, remembering how Hank at the Mobil station had held up my hundred before he'd stolen it from me.

"Sorry. Just a habit. I'm checking for counterfeits. We take so much cash here, I have to be careful. It used to be a problem a few years ago."

"Oh? I saw a cashier at another store do it, and I was wondering what they were looking for. I had no idea it was a problem here."

Simone opens the register again and holds my ten up to the light once more. "Come around by me, and I'll show you." I sidle up next to her and look up at the bill. She points a beautifully manicured nail at it. "First thing I always check is that the president matches the denomination. One time I had George Washington on a ten-dollar bill!" We both laugh. "Those are the sloppy ones. Or, like the writing isn't exactly straight. But most of the time, what I'm looking for is the red and blue fibers in the material itself. See here and here?" I do see. My artist's eye picks it out immediately. "Also, sometimes counterfeits are faded at the edges or have fewer details in the art than a real bill. Sometimes it's hard to tell, honestly. Luckily, I have insurance in case one slips by me."

"You need insurance for that?"

"Oh, yeah. The bank has special machines that would catch it and take it out of circulation, but that means I have to eat the loss. The insurance covers the lost funds. I've had to use it a time or two."

"Even in tiny Echo Mills?"

"Sadly so."

"Thanks for satisfying my curiosity."

"You're welcome, El. Take care. And thank you." She holds up the ten.

I walk back out to the car, distracted as I try to put all the clues together. I climb behind the wheel knowing I'm missing something.

"Did she take the money?" Grams asks softly. She looks exhausted.

I wipe Tony from my mind, fixing a smile on my face. "She did after I insisted." That makes her smile. "Let's get you home."

28

HELLO, WITCH

ELOISE

After a long afternoon of chores, I grab a book from Grams's library and lay down in bed. But the more I try to read, the more my mind churns. I finally give up, put the book aside, and reach for the October issue of Echo Mills magazine. For the three hundredth time, I inspect each page.

The phone rings. Only one person would be calling me right now—Maeve.

"Hello?" I'm still a little miffed about what went down at Bad Witches' Club and all the secrets she's been keeping from me. A fracture has silently formed between us, a passive divide of things unsaid that could fester like a wound if left untreated.

"I thought I'd come by tonight. We're overdue for some girl time," Maeve says.

"You bring the wine. I'll make some snacks to go with

the tea we're going to spill." Her laugh heals something inside me. We'll get over this bump. I know we will.

"On my way," she sings.

I pop out of bed and run downstairs. As luck would have it, Grams has some cheese puffs in the deep freeze. I preheat the oven and spread them on a cookie sheet, making a mental note that I need to dig into my hidden stash and buy groceries or I'll be eating sympathy casseroles forever.

A soft knock comes on the front door, and there's Maeve, her black fringe drawing a stark line above heavy-rimmed glasses. Purple dragonflies decorate her casual black dress. A set of black moto boots completes her ensemble.

"Oh my gods, you look great, Eloise! You changed your—"

I lunge at her, hugging her hard like she's leaving for war. Pressure forms behind my eyes, and before I know what's happening, I'm sobbing into her shoulder.

"Whoa. Are... are you okay?"

Wrestling my emotions under control, I wipe beneath my eyes. "Sorry. I guess I didn't realize how much I needed a friend until I saw you there. This week has been... confusing."

She winces. "Then I'm sorry to tell you this, but I think my visit tonight might not make things easier."

I usher her toward the kitchen. "Start talking."

Twenty minutes later, we're two glasses and several cheese puffs in, and I'm more frustrated than ever. "Let me get this straight. You can see that Tony receives large sums of money via wire transfers from a shady foreign entity named Genesis Corp, but you can't prove it precisely because it's a shell company and the ownership of the account is locked down tighter than a nun's coochie."

"More or less." Maeve giggles. "I claim zero expertise in nun anatomy."

"But it's weird. Your forensic accountants see the red flags."

She massages the bridge of her nose like she's getting a headache. "Yes. We've even questioned Tony about it. He has paperwork saying that the company is paying him for consulting services. His phone records back that up. But *shit*, no consulting service is worth what they're paying him. It amounts to millions of dollars."

I show her the Echo Mills Today magazine and recap again everything we learned about the warehouse. "He's behind this. I know he is. I saw that invoice. And the operation is coincidentally torn down, right after? It's too fishy."

"And it's a free magazine with free ads. How would he make any money? It's not even a good free magazine." She rubs one of the pages between her fingers. "It feels like it's printed on recycled paper, and there isn't anything useful in here, unless you plan to wipe your ass with the pages."

"I know! It doesn't make any sense. Tony is an asshole, but he's genuinely good at business. He wouldn't invest in something that didn't pay off. And why the secrecy?"

Bending her fingers into claws, Maeve gives an angsty cry. "This stinks of tax evasion but without a direct link between him and Gold Weaver and Gold Weaver and Genesis, we've got nothing. As the goddess is my witness, I swear you married into the mob. Tony is up to some shady shit on a level on par with organized crime. We can see money coming in from Genesis but none going out from his companies, and definitely no outlays for a printing operation. When it comes to the courts, they're going to believe the simplest explanation." She slants me an empathetic look.

"That I didn't see what I thought I saw."

"Maybe he had an invoice, but it wasn't his. Who knows where that came from or why it made him angry? Maybe he has a friend who runs the magazine." She shakes her head. "I believe you but that's what his lawyers are going to tell the judge."

I lean my forehead against my fists, feeling deflated.

"Hey... " Maeve rubs my shoulder. "I'm going to keep trying. I just can't figure out what he's doing, and with less than two weeks until our court date, the chances that we figure it out before then are slight."

I bury my face in my hands. "You think I should prepare myself to lose the house?"

Gently, she guides my wrists apart and meets my gaze. "No, Eloise. I've never thought that. Call the fucking advocate and command him to kill Tony. As long as you are still married, you are the beneficiary of his estate. Not only does the prenup go out the window, but his claim to this property also becomes moot."

"But I'll be a murderer."

She blows out a deep breath. "I say this as your friend, not your attorney. You've got to defend yourself."

"This isn't self-defense. He's threatening my property, not my life."

Maeve groans in frustration. "There are more ways to kill a person than to stop their heart from beating. This house and everything in it *is* your life. It's the only life you've ever known outside of Tony. He's threatening to take that from you. Threatening to keep you from your inheritance, your ancestral bonds, and the heritage that makes you the beautiful person you are. If that's not threatening your life, I don't know what is."

I pour another glass of wine. She's right, about everything. "All right. If I can't figure out another way, I'll ask Damien to do it at the end of the week."

Maeve chews her lip. "Thank you."

I don't say anything more, afraid I'll talk myself out of it if I do.

"Still calling him Damien, huh?" She squints at me.

"You might as well know he ate me out and gave me the strongest orgasms I've ever experienced in my life."

Her brows shoot into her thick bangs. "Really?"

"Yeah."

"Goddess, Eloise. You come across all prim, proper, and gentle, and then you tell me you let a killer with fangs feast on your lady bits. I don't know what to do with that information."

"Be happy for me. I know that when I'm done with the candle, he'll be gone, but I need this. I need to feel wanted again, and he's done that for me."

"Okay. I guess that makes sense. And he can't hurt you as long as you have the candle."

I take another drink to keep from saying anything about how I plan to let the candle burn down the rest of the way the minute this is all over. I love Maeve, but keeping Damian a prisoner for several lifetimes is wrong.

I reach for the bottle and drain the remains of the wine into Maeve's empty glass. Her eyes are already glassy. A drunk Maeve is a forthcoming Maeve, and I still have questions. "So, uh, about my mom and Bad Witches' Club."

She frowns. "I was wondering when you'd get around to asking me about it again."

"How did she know about the supernatural world?"

Hesitating, she leans back in her chair. She seems to be deliberating on something, maybe trying to find the right words to break bad news. I make the gimme motion with my hand, but she just thrusts both arms toward me. "What do you see when you look at me?"

"My best friend, Maeve."

She narrows her eyes in annoyance.

"Okay, um, a beautiful woman." She circles her hand in the air, wanting more. "A beautiful goth woman."

"Closer. What do you notice about my tattoos?"

I shrug. "They're all skeletons. Skeleton mermaid, skeleton dragon, plain old skull." Maeve is covered in bones and skulls. It's her thing.

"Everyone in my family has tattoos like this, although maybe not so many as me. My father only has one, and it's right over his heart. Like this one." She moves the neck of her dress aside to reveal a tattoo of a skull and crossbones constructed of tiny symbols. "Can you guess why we all have this same tattoo?"

"Wait, Damien has one too! I saw it on his chest."

"Sort of. Damien's is different. It's the same shape, but the symbols that make it up are different. His is a mark of his service to us, but this—" She taps the tattoo "—is the Gowdie sigil."

Damien told me a few things about witches, sigils, and family spells, but I'm not sure he was supposed to share, and I don't want to get him in trouble, so I play ignorant.

"Does the tattoo have something to do with you being a witch?"

She nods. "Every witch bloodline has a sigil. It's a magical symbol that tells the world we belong to the bloodline and also imbues us with certain powers. Each family has a specialty, a keyspell that is handed down and perfected generation after generation."

"A keyspell?"

"Think of it like a keystone, a bedrock on which all the family's magic is built. All magical families have a unique keyspell. Only two other bloodlines have an animator keyspell, but theirs are different than ours. Animators can command anything." With a twist of her hand, one of the cocktail napkins folds itself into a bird and flaps its wings.

"Oh my God." I had the gist of what an animator could do, but nothing prepares you for seeing a napkin try to fly.

"The Gowdie specialty is animating the dead. Give us a cemetery, and we are something to be feared. Other animator families specialize in mechanical animation or animating plants or animals. We specialize in bones. It's how we were able to capture Damien. He's a shade, but when he manifests, he has bones like we do. My family was able to lock into those bones."

The implications send a shiver through me. "Can you control a living person, then?"

"It's possible, but the magic would require a lot of power and wouldn't last long. Living creatures with higher intelligence fight the magic. Vampires and shades though, are the exception. It works on a deeper level. They are supernatural creatures and our magic locks onto what animates them like...like...the teeth of a cog linking into another cog. It's possible for us to take control."

It sounds brutal. I redirect her back to our original conversation. "Maeve, what does any of this have to do with my mother?"

She wraps a hand around mine and squeezes. "Your mother and father both wore the tattoo that's on your back over their hearts."

"Yes. That's why I chose it. I wanted to feel close to them."

"Your mother was obsessed with fantasy creatures, so much so her work is dripping with them."

"Yeah? So?" Goosebumps march up my arms at the look in her dark eyes.

"You're going to make me say it, aren't you?" Maeve licks her lips. "I don't know for sure, okay? It wasn't like I knew your parents outside my friendship with you. But I believe the pattern on your back is a sigil. I believe your parents might come from a bloodline of witches, one that isn't registered with the Council of Witches, and I think you have witch blood in you, even if you can't do magic."

A sharp inhale lodges in my throat. Then I just laugh. "I think I'd know if my parents were witches."

"How?" she asks softly. "I didn't come into my power until I turned seventeen, and my parents gave me this tattoo." She taps the skull over her heart. "Only after did they start teaching me spells. Before that, my under-standing of magic was academic. It's possible your parents planned to teach you their magic eventually but never got a chance."

I can't breathe. My mind leaps between thinking this is a sick joke and thinking Maeve must be mistaken. But my mother painted those murals. She'd rubbed shoulders with the supernatural community. Then a question comes to me. "Did *your* parents know about any of this?"

"They suspected."

"Do they have any idea what the tattoo means? If my parents were witches, what's the Harcourt keyspell?"

She shakes her head. "They don't know. What I've told you about us, Eloise, is a tightly guarded secret. Other established families know, of course, but it's not something we broadcast. We gather with other magical families four times a year. Your parents never participated."

"So, what you're saying is, I have a magical symbol on my back that could mean I'm like you, or could mean nothing at all."

Maeve adjusts her glasses. "I'm afraid that's right."

29

THE PLAN

ELOISE

I flop onto my bed that night, my head pounding from too much wine and too much new information. Had my parents been witches? What did that mean anyway? Grams said the Harcourts were spiritualists. Were they the source or did the magic come from my mother's side? Her maiden name was Townsend. I know relatively little about the Townsends. Is it possible they dabbled in the supernatural?

Then again, does it really matter? I have no magical abilities and never will now that my parents are dead. I drift into a fitful sleep, mind reeling.

When I wake the next morning, I decide what I really need is some normalcy. I've been wanting to go grocery shopping for days, and there's no better time to treat myself to a freshly stocked fridge than now. Performing a simple errand is sure to clear my head of everything I've learned about Tony, the magazine, and the supernatural.

I open the bottom drawer of my dresser and lift the false bottom, revealing my small hoard of hundreds, fifties, twenties, and tens. I siphoned over two thousand dollars from Tony before I left him. It took time and patience, but I'm not sure how I would've survived without it. Sometimes I'd get extra cash back at the grocery store or tip a waitress or driver less than I told Tony I did. I'd take a few bills out of his wallet while he wasn't looking. I even lifted a couple hundred from his private safe one time when he'd left the room with it unlocked. For weeks, anytime I could secretly pocket cash, I did.

After he hit me the second time, I left, but I also understood there would be consequences. Almost immediately, he cut off my credit cards and filed for divorce, ensuring I had nothing and would get nothing. My parents didn't raise me to be a thief, but when I took this money, it was half mine. And I need it now, need it to see me through this divorce.

I slide two precious hundreds off the top of the pile and replace the false bottom of the drawer, moving my clothes back in place. Grabbing my purse, I dig out my wallet. It's as I'm sliding the bills into the slot where I keep my cash that I notice the two hundreds in my hand are a different color than the twenty already in my wallet. They appear slightly more gray than green. It's subtle. If I wasn't an artist I might not have noticed.

Intrigued, I hold one of the hundreds and the twenty up to the light, side by side, and check them as Simone taught me. President Jackson looks down on me from the twenty and Franklin from the hundred. The artwork is detailed on both. They look legitimate. But something is off. I concentrate on the hundred and run the bill between my fingers. Sure enough, it feels different. The twenty has raised print, the hundred does not. There's also the slightest variation in color at the edges. Both have the red and blue threads Simone told me about, although the patterns are different.

A prickle runs up the back of my neck. I set down the twenty and raise the two hundreds to the light. Same thread pattern. My heart starts to pound. I snatch the Echo Mills Today off my nightstand, open it with vigor, and tear a page from the front. Holding my breath, I lift it to the light, side by side with one of the hundreds. Holy fucking hell. Maeve thought Echo Mills was printed on recycled paper. No, it's printed on counterfeit money paper! All at once, I remember Hank at the Mobil station, how he'd been so sure I wouldn't call the police. Had he known the hundred I gave him was counterfeit?

Tony isn't earning money from Echo Mills Today. He's printing his own money and using the magazine as his cover! As soon as I think it, I know it's true.

"Holy shit. Gotcha, you bastard."

AT DUSK, INSIDE THE BUILDING ACROSS THE STREET FROM Tony's penthouse condominium, I light the candle to call Damien. Smoke curls against the dingy tile of the burnt-orange coffeehouse bathroom, growing from the shadows under the sink and behind the garbage can before coalescing into the shape of a demon—horns, wings, and a whip of a barbed tail. When the smoke settles, the monster is replaced by the man who's taken up residence in my mind the last few weeks.

He brushes his hands down the sleeves of his jacket, grimacing at me. "A bathroom, Eloise? Do you have any idea how filthy the shadows are in this place?"

"I'm sorry. I know you said you had business, and I probably interrupted you, but it's an emergency. I need you. It was faster to call you here directly than to travel here from my place."

He pauses his efforts at dusting himself off and gives me a long once over, his brilliant ice-colored eyes lingering on my curly red hair and then the neckline of my royal blue dress. He hasn't seen me since I changed my hair and wardrobe, and he looks speechless. After what feels like a full minute of his intense scrutiny, he whispers, "There you are."

"Here I am." I laugh and bite my bottom lip, smiling under his appreciative gaze.

He steps closer and brushes cool fingers over my heated cheeks. "I think that's the first time I've ever heard you genuinely laugh."

"It's the first time I've felt happy in a long time." I swallow and admit the truth. "The way you look at me makes me happy."

He surges forward, sweeping me into his arms and holding me against him. I'm breathless and entirely aware of every part of him as he says, "If I had my way, I'd spend the entire night staring at every part of you just to hear that incredible laugh. It's silver moonlight, that laugh. You are positively enchanting, Eloise." My name on his lips makes something heavy and low within me turn over, and my body hums with need. He brushes a hand over my curls, his gaze boring into mine. When he speaks again, he lowers his lips to my ear. "What do you need of me? Say the word so that I can do it quickly and then have you to myself."

My breath hitches at the feel of him hardening against me, and I rise on my tiptoes to kiss him. I moan when he moves his hands lower to cup my ass.

Dizzy, I give a breathy chuckle as I put space between us. "I want that too, but I really do need your help with Tony."

"Have you decided to let me kill him?" he asks hopefully.

"No, but I have a plan. All I need you to do is come with me to his penthouse and keep him from killing me while I say what I have to say to him."

He sets me on my feet and takes a step back, his lips peeling off his teeth. "How much am I allowed to hurt him to keep him from hurting you?"

I swallow, the memory of Hank's body slapping the side of the Mobil station moving front and center in my mind. "No permanent damage."

He returns a reluctant nod.

I snuff out the candle and put it in my purse. "Follow me."

Completely disregarding the gaping mouth of an old woman in the hallway as we exit the ladies' room together, I walk across the street to Tony's building with Damien trailing behind me. The pink Tory Burch tote tucked under my arm contains my last chance at ending this without resorting to using Damien in a way I know I'll regret.

It takes the doorman a second to recognize me. "Mrs. Denardi, I wasn't expecting you."

"Harcourt," I remind him. I kept my maiden name and he knows it. "Good evening, Ralph. I need to talk to Tony. Can you buzz me up?"

The elderly man adjusts his hat and shifts in his chair, overtly uncomfortable. He picks up the phone, his gray eyes darting away from me. "I'll call him and let him know you're here, sweetheart."

I reach across the small desk and depress the button on the old-fashioned landline phone he's using. I keep my finger there as I stare him straight in the eye. "Ralph, I'm not divorced yet, which means, until the judgment comes down, I have a right to access our penthouse. In fact, I still have the key." I'm not bluffing. I hold up my old key. No one has asked me for it. "All I need you to do is your job. Buzz me through to the elevators, and we'll be on our merry way, and I won't have to get lawyers or police involved." I hold up a finger. "And if you want to call Tony once I'm on that elevator and tell him I'm coming, go right ahead."

Slowly, I release the button, but I don't take my eyes off Ralph. His throat bobs, but he reaches down by his knee, and the door buzzes. I lunge for the handle and Damien and I board an open elevator.

"What exactly happened to you while I was gone?" Damien asks once the doors are closed, studying me in the small compartment in a way that sends fire jetting through my veins. Being in his presence is always so intense.

I lift an eyebrow. "I gave myself a makeover."

He licks his lips. "More than just the wardrobe."

Glancing at my manicure, I admit, "I was tired of playing the part he forced me into. I guess I just needed to remember who I was before him."

One of his big hands reaches out to rub a red curl between his fingers. "I find this side of you extremely interesting."

I arch a brow. "You found me interesting before... in my parlor and my kitchen." I slant him a wicked smile and he hisses through his teeth. As fast as a snake bite, his hand cups the back of my neck and pulls me close.

"Oh, I did. There are so many interesting things about you, my little bird. Your penchant for self-sacrifice. Your inability to be cruel. Your strength at the most inopportune times. And your bravery when you have little to back you up. I'm interested in all of it. I'm beginning to think I could spend a century discovering new ways to find you interesting. Not the least of which is this pretty mouth wrapped around my cock."

A small gasp sails across my parted lips, and he licks it away, flicking the tip of his tongue against mine. I fist his shirt, my inner thighs suddenly slick with heat.

His nostrils flare. "I hope this plan of yours works and quickly. The night is short."

He releases me at the sound of the doors opening, and I smooth my dress, feeling positively rattled. Stars above, I can't so much as look in his direction without the air crackling between us. Something has changed. A wall that was there only days ago is gone. But I can't think about that now. With a few cleansing breaths, I slow my pulse and get my head back in the game.

I try my key in the door to Tony's penthouse. It doesn't fit. Bastard changed the locks.

"Damien?"

He breaks into shadow and trails of darkness disappear under the door, leaving behind only a whiff of spice. A second later, the lock clicks, and the door opens. I walk into the foyer of a place where I used to live but was never home to me. It's sad really, how little I miss it. I close the door and turn the corner toward Tony's office, only to come face-to-face with the business end of a Glock.

30

HIT ME WITH YOUR BEST SHOT

ELOISE

"It's me!" I raise my hands, meeting Tony's eyes.

Tony glowers at me over his gun, his rumpled suit looking like he's just got home from the office. "What the fuck are you wearing, Eloise? You're lucky I didn't shoot you."

"Didn't Ralph call up?"

He juts his chin toward me. "Yeah, he called. But he didn't tell me you were dressed like a whore."

Fucking bastard. I refuse to let his insults shake me. I need to have a level head for this. "I just want to talk."

"How did you get in here anyway?"

I glance over my shoulder, but Damien isn't there. "I still have a key."

"I changed the locks."

"Guess it still works." Behind him, coils of darkness turn into a Damien-shaped cloud.

"Put the gun down, Tony. This will only take a second."

"Unless you came to tell me you're moving out of Harcourt Manor before our court date, we've got nothing to talk about." He circles his finger in the air. "Turn around and get the fuck out of my house."

"The hard way then," I mutter. I lift my gaze over Tony's shoulder and lock eyes with my monster. Damien forms in a flicker of darkness and pries the gun out of Tony's twitching fingers. I don't register how he does it. He moves so fast; he's nothing but a smudge of black. But when he settles into existence behind Tony, his arm is around my ex's neck like he means business.

"Settle in, Tony, and listen to what she has to say," Damien grits out. "And know this—I will kill you without hesitation if you try to hurt her again."

"You again? I'll have you disbarred!" Tony struggles against Damien's grip, and I realize he still thinks Damien is a lawyer from Maeve's practice.

Damien lands one giant hand on his shoulder and ushers him into the living room where he presses him down into the couch with enough force to pale Tony's face. "I'd like to see you try it from the grave."

I take more than a little satisfaction in the spark of fear I see in Tony's expression. Reaching into my bag, I pull out this month's copy of Echo Mills Today. Tony scowls. "I see you recognize this." I wave it a little in the air.

"So what?" he snarls. "It's a free magazine available all over the city."

"A magazine produced by Gold Weaver, Inc."

He shrugs. "Wouldn't know."

I stand straighter, tapping my chin. "In the two years we were married, you hit me twice."

He scoffs. "I never hit you. You're remembering it

wrong, Eloise. You always had your head up your ass or in the clouds. You probably imagined it."

"Gaslighting," I mumble, looking down at my toes. "I know it well, and I'm not buying it anymore. Here's what really happened. The first time you hit me was when I saw you signing a check to pay an invoice issued to Gold Weaver, Inc. You were signing someone else's name. I don't remember a lot about that night because you almost broke my jaw—"

Damien's growl makes my arms break out in goose-flesh. His hand closes around Tony's throat.

"Damien!"

His voice is pure monster as he says, "I won't break his neck. Just hurt him, the same as he hurt you."

"I need him to be able to talk." I spread my hands, pleading with him to back off.

His grip eases, and Tony takes a deep breath.

"I tracked down Gold Weaver's warehouse, Tony. And guess what we found there? Paper scraps and a man who said he worked for Gold Weaver printing this magazine." I wave Echo Mills Today again.

Tony grits his teeth. "Whatever you think you saw, it's got nothing to do with me."

I have to hand it to him. He almost sounds sincere. "I questioned whether there could be another explanation when I found nothing in that warehouse and couldn't link Gold Weaver back to you, until I recalled the second time you hit me. Do you remember?"

He shakes his head. "Never happened."

"It was the last time I slept under this roof. You caught me rummaging in your office safe. You'd left it unlocked, a mistake I have a feeling you regret. I slipped in and took a stack of bills. You didn't know that, though. I shoved them down my pants before you came back into the office. God knows you hadn't been interested in anything in my pants in a long time. You were much more turned on by controlling me."

"You took money from my safe?" His voice holds all the venom I expected.

"Oh yes. I stole thousands from you before I moved out. Had to provide for myself while I got back on my feet. Thanks for that."

Tony lunges for me. But Damien catches him by the shoulder and lifts his feet off the floor. His hand swipes harmlessly six inches from my face. "You fucking bitch."

I pull one of the hundreds from my bag and hold it up. "Weirdest thing. I always thought you kept a lot of cash around because you were sheltering it from the IRS. But then I tried to buy something with one of these hundreds, and the cashier had a strange reaction. I still didn't get it until another store owner told me what to look for." I brush my red curls from my eyes. "This bill is a very good, extremely sophisticated counterfeit, Tony. I bet that if I wasn't an artist myself, I would have missed the slight variation in color and the smudge in the scrollwork in the upper right corner. But I am an artist, and this *is* a counterfeit. It only took a second for me to figure out that the pattern of red and blue fibers in the material this bill is printed on matches the pattern in the pages of Echo Mills Today magazine."

Tony lowers his chin and bares his teeth but says nothing. I can almost hear the bones of his shoulder crunch under Damien's grip.

"Now, from there, it took me a little longer to put it all

together. When I first discovered Echo Mills today, I wondered why a man who'd built his career focusing on the bottom line print a free magazine? I thought at least you were making money off the ads. But I checked, and you're not. They're all phony. But once I saw the paper matched the counterfeit bill, it all came together. You use Echo Mills Today as a cover to bring in reams of paper specially crafted for printing money. You print the magazine, but you also print cash. Gold Weaver claims to have earned the money on the ads, but of course, that's all falsified. No one pays for the ads. But it justifies the income. Gold Weaver deposits the cash in a bank in the Cayman Islands, into an account owned by a second shell corporation called Genesis. Genesis wires it back to you in the form of business consulting fees, completely laundered. Oh, I'm not exactly sure how you get the printed cash to the Caymans, but I bet the FBI could figure it out."

"What do you want, Eloise?" Tony says through a sneer.

"What do I want to keep my mouth shut?"

He nods twice, slowly, and I'm relieved. Truth is, everything I've said has been theory and speculation. I don't know for sure how he's doing everything, only how I think he's doing it. But I'm right. He just confirmed I'm right. I have him.

"I want Harcourt Manor," I say. "Call off your lawyers. Sign an affidavit that you have no claim to my home, and everything here will remain our little secret."

Tony glares at me. "That's it? You're not going to try to get your hands on my fortune?"

"No."

"Why not?"

I take a step closer to him and look straight into his heartless, unfeeling eyes. "Because I never wanted the money or to hurt you. You came into my life during a painful time, and I'm not sure I would have survived those years without you."

"And don't you forget it," he mumbles under his breath. His voice is as harsh as ever, but his expression softens a little.

"What you do with your money is your business. But Harcourt Manor is mine, and it's going to stay that way."

"I want the money you took from my safe. If your offer is in earnest, you'll turn the bills over to me."

I reach into my purse and pull out the stack of counterfeits, tossing them on the coffee table. Damien loosens his grip and Tony grabs the stack, starts to count it. While he's occupied, I produce the affidavit I had Maeve draw up and a pen from my bag. "Sign this, and it's yours."

He slaps the cash against his palm. "Is this all of it?"

"I spent a hundred and kept one bill, for sentimental reasons." I give him a smug look. "That bill will never see its way out of my scrapbook as long as you're cooperative."

"How do I know you're not lying?"

Damien produces an atavistic rattle that sends a chill through me. It sounds like a diamondback snake, if the snake was as big as a T. rex. Tony grimaces, his lips drawing back as if he doesn't know quite what to make of Damien.

"You don't, Tony. You'll have to trust me. I have no reason to lie to you. Anything I want, I could ask you for right now."

He snorts, but with one last darted glance between

Damien and me, he picks up the pen and signs the affidavit. I sweep it off the table and check that it's his legal signature. "Thank you."

With a huff of disgust, he stands, planting his hands on his hips. I don't miss how Damien positions himself between us. "You've changed, Eloise."

I start backing toward the door, and Damien follows. "No. This is exactly who I always was. I just forgot for a while."

Nothing else is said. I leave the penthouse, and Tony, behind me.

31

BROKEN THINGS

ELOISE

My phone rings as I pull into the drive that leads to Harcourt Manor. The sight of the place causes my heart to swell. It's mine and will stay that way. Finally, I've awakened from the nightmare I thought would never end. It's over.

I tap the screen to answer on speaker.

"The advocate just delivered the paperwork," Maeve says. "Congratulations, El. You did it. The house is yours. I'm filing this first thing in the morning, and I've already faxed a copy to Tony's lawyers."

"Thank you. Oh God, thank you. I'm so happy it's over."

"Not completely. Not until our court date next Friday, but I doubt he'll give us any trouble, considering what you know. I'm curious, though, why you didn't take it to the authorities. You could have had him thrown in jail, had the prenup thrown out, and maybe got a better deal for yourself."

I sigh and hit the button to open the garage. "I just want it to be over. All of this has been such a distraction. I want to spend uninterrupted time with Grams without having to worry about Tony pulling the rug out from under us. I feel like I can finally breathe tonight."

"Understood. Honestly, I have to hand it to you. The advocate said you stood up to Tony with, and I quote, 'strength he's rarely seen in all his five hundred years.'"

"Damien said that? Really?"

"Yes, he did. Actually, he seems a little obsessed with you. Be careful, El. Keep the candle nearby just in case he tries something."

"Like what?" I ask playfully.

"You know damn well what I'm talking about. Remember, he's a monster. He's not a potential love interest. Got it?"

I've had about enough of the Damien bashing. "You know what? Damien isn't a monster. Tony's a monster. Believe me, I know. I still have the scars to remind me of the difference. Damien may be a creature, but he's a good person."

"But Eloise, you have to understand—"

"Goodbye, Maeve," I sing-song, then hang up the phone. As I enter the house, I silence the ringer so it won't wake Grams and toe off my shoes. I pad on stocking feet to the back of the house and check on her. She's fallen asleep propped up on pillows, facing the window to watch for her beloved Howard. For a few minutes, I follow her chest as it rises and falls in peaceful slumber, noticing that the drink and snack I've placed on the bedside table are still there, untouched. When was the last time she ate more than a few bites?

I close my eyes and whisper a prayer to anyone who is listening, then shuffle back to the parlor and use one of the long matches to light the fire. I'm still squatting, watching the kindling between the logs ignite, when a deliciously dark, spicy scent wafts past me and a pair of long, muscular arms wrap around my shoulders.

"Damien," I whisper, closing my eyes and taking a deep, cleansing breath. "We did it. Maeve just called. The house is as good as mine."

His fingers cup my jaw and turn my face to look at him. "*You* did it. I was wrong about you."

"Wrong, how?"

"All this time, I thought you were a little bird. But you're not. You're a dragon, just like your tattoo."

I laugh softly. "What about my fluttering heart?"

He shoots me a slow, crooked grin. "The sound you make before you breathe fire."

I laugh, even as my ears grow hot under his close scrutiny. "I couldn't have done it without you."

He tilts his head and shakes it once. "Yes, you could have. I came to be your advocate, little dragon, but I'm afraid I haven't served you well. I wanted to kill for you, but you solved the problem on your own, in your own way."

"No," I insist. "You helped me, but more importantly, you healed me. Tony had stripped me down to a shell of who I once was. He took me apart and tried to remake me into the robot he wanted, then left me in scraps when I didn't operate that way. I'd never have succeeded if I was still in pieces. Somehow, you put me back together. Do you know you did that for me?" I slide my hands up his chest. Our eyes catch and hold.

"Careful, you'll make me believe I'm no monster at all." He nuzzles my neck, pulling me closer, but I push him away.

"You did exactly what I asked you to do, and now it's done. And I promised you I'd do something in return." I cross the parlor to get the candle out of my purse and bring it back to the mantel, where I use one of the matches to light the wick. "Now we just let it burn, and when it burns out, you'll be free."

Damien looks between me and the candle, his expression wistful. His voice is all gravel when he says, "I admit, I was skeptical."

"About what?"

"That you'd truly attempt to free me. I thought you might forget your promise once you had what you wanted."

I rest a hand on his cheek. There are things I want, no need, to say to him. "What happened between us meant something to me." I watch him flinch as if I've surprised him but I carry on. "I don't expect anything from you. Please don't think that. I know as soon as the candle burns down, you'll be gone, and I'll never see you again. But while you're still here, I want to say thank you. Knowing you has helped me find myself again. For all the times you called me your little bird, you never infantilized me like Tony did. You challenged me to become stronger. You made me feel wanted and valuable. You made me understand I was broken but not ruined. So, yeah, all of this has meant something to me, and I'll miss you." My voice catches. I smile against the onslaught of tears I'm fighting back. "I hope wherever you go next that you're happy, and I hope by freeing you, I contributed to that happiness."

He closes his eyes. "You are the kindest soul, Eloise." My name on his lips does extraordinary things to my insides, but the agony I see in his eyes is sobering.

"Thank you," I say. "But why do you look like you're in pain?"

Shadows rise around him, and he takes me by the shoulders. "Because the candle will never burn out, no matter how long we wait, no matter your intention to free me."

"What are you talking about?" I dart a glance at the candle. "It's barely a stub. It shouldn't take long now."

"That candle has been the same size for a half century. The Gowdie curse ends when the candle does, and their magic keeps it from ever ending."

Flabbergasted, I take measure of the candle again. I assumed it's gotten shorter every time I've burned it, but it isn't noticeably different. "It's enchanted to never burn out?"

"The curse is designed to be forever."

Hot tears pool in my eyes. "But that's not fair. So... so... you're their slave for all eternity?"

He grabs my hand and places it over his heart. "Eloise, the fact that you tried to free me, that you intended to, even if the task is impossible, means every-thing to me. What happened between us meant some-thing to me too."

I shake my head vigorously. "This isn't okay." My monster, my advocate, my Damien... I won't let them do this to him. "That isn't our agreement. I'm supposed to get free of Tony, and you're supposed to get free of the candle."

"I wish it were possible."

A dark restlessness swirls inside me. As much as I love Maeve, I can't muster anything but rage toward her family. My skin burns with it. Bile rises in my throat.

"Eloise..." Damien's eyes rove over me.

I seethe at the candle, snatching it off the mantel. Hot wax drips down the back of my hand. "Shit! Fuck!" I toss the entire thing into the fire. The moment it hits the flames, a shower of sparks explodes from the logs. Suddenly, I'm across the room, protected in a cocoon of solid darkness. Damien forms from the shadows with his arms around me.

"Are you hurt?" He inspects my hand, rolling the wax from my skin.

"It's fine," I say. Truly it is. "I yelled because I expected it to burn, but it didn't."

He examines my skin. "Not even pink."

Together we walk back toward the fire. I'm relieved the shower of sparks didn't scorch the carpet. Thank God, there doesn't appear to be any damage. I search the flames for any remnant of the candle. With the poker from the rack, I move the logs around. Nothing remains. Not even a pool of wax.

"It's gone."

Beside me, Damien goes perfectly still, a preternatural stillness as if he's turned to stone. His chin jerks downward and his eyes rove to the space over his heart. Slowly, he unbuttons his shirt and moves the fabric aside. His brows knit and he looks between his chest and me in utter confusion.

The skull and crossbones tattoo that marked his servitude to the Gowdies has vanished.

"Holy shit," I whisper. Tentatively, I close the space between us and feather my touch over his smooth, unmarked skin. "It worked. You're free."

I've never seen Damien look like this. His expression turns frantic, and he grips my shoulders, giving me a light shake. "How? How did you do it? It shouldn't have been possible."

"Ow. You're hurting me!"

He releases me immediately. "I'm sorry. I—" Between us, his hands shake violently, and I take them in my own. "I didn't mean to hurt you."

"I know."

"But how. How is this possible?"

"You saw how I did it. The fire must have broken the spell. You're free." I smile up at him, ecstatic that both of us have managed what we wanted. But my smile fades when I realize what this means. He'll go now, maybe try to find his way home. He won't waste his time on me, on a human. I take a step back, dragging my touch from him. "Thank you, Damien."

In the silence that follows, our eyes lock, and in time, his hands stop shaking. Once he's composed himself, he asks, "Do you want me to go, little dragon?"

I press a hand to the ache in my chest. "No. I want you to stay with me. I want to... be with you." My cheeks heat from the admission. "But even more, I want you to do what you want to do. I think after centuries of being bound to someone else's will, you deserve it."

His lids sink to half-mast. "I want to be with you, too, but..."

I can see he's holding something back. "Whatever it is, just tell me."

"You should see what I truly am, Eloise." His voice is all leather and grit. "Before you invite me to stay, you need to understand the monster you're inviting into your bed."

32

PRINCE OF SHADOWS

ELOISE

Here's the thing about Damien's monsterhood. I know he's not like me. He's not even from this planet originally. But since the day I first called him, I've felt oddly safe in his presence. "I know what you are, Damien, and I want all of you."

He responds with a skeptical tilt of his head. "This man you see before you is an illusion. It's a form I take to put you at ease."

"Then show me what you look like without it. It won't change anything."

"You sound so sure."

"I am sure."

The lights flicker and then go out. Damien breaks into shadow as I've watched him do before, only this time, he holds the form I've only witnessed in passing. I blink my eyes to force them to adjust to the dim light. Before me stands the demon I glimpsed in the shadows. Black leathery skin spans a wide, heavily muscled chest. Two thick horns twist from either side of his head, tapering to sharp points that tower above me and almost scrape the ceiling. A dark mane of hair falls in waves to his shoulders. Massive wings, like a bat's, with a claw at their apex, span the length of his body from horns to hooves. *Cloven* hooves below shaggy black legs that meet at an intimidatingly large phallus.

He extends a hand to me. His fingers end in deadly black claws. Damien, in his shade form, is something out of my deepest nightmares, a monster in every sense of the word. I've noticed this form in passing when he's shifted into the shadows, but I've never had time to process it. Not like this. Not up close with time to truly absorb that this is the real him. He looks like a demon, a devil, a creature of the night. And although I know he's none of those things, the man I've known, whose lips have touched my flesh, is only an illusion.

His barbed tail flicks, twitching like a nervous cat's. Just like that, a smile tugs at the corner of my mouth. Damien may be a monster who can tear me to shreds as easy as breathing, but right now he's terrified of me, of my judgment. I study him with new eyes, like I might a work of art. While this form challenges my preconceptions, it is a window into his soul. Damien is made of shadow, and he is offering himself to me—all his darkness, his entire beastly nature.

Slowly, I wrap my fingers around his big, warm palm, careful of his talons, and run my hand up his torso. A deep rattle vibrates against my touch. A purr. My God, he's purring like a cat. His eyes glow silver and he smiles down at me with a mouth full of razor-sharp fangs. The effect is terrifying at first, but I focus on the way his skin wrinkles at the corners of his eyes. Definitely a smile. Slowly, my heart rate evens out. This is Damien. I'm safe.

Curious, I let my touch drift around his sides, stroking up the ridged skin of his back and massaging the place his wings attach to his body. The rough ridges of his flesh there are fascinating. I ease my fingertips along the edge of one wing. His eyes close on a sigh. Coasting my hand lower, to the base of his spine, I ring his tail with my thumb and forefinger and tug it gently. His skin is smooth and soft here. The purr I heard earlier turns into a gruff moan and his erection grows thick and long between us.

Massive, dark, and ridged around the head, it's the largest cock I've ever seen in my life. Releasing his tail, I skim my nails along his sides and wrap my hand around it. Well, I try. My fingers aren't long enough. I use my other hand and stroke from base to tip, running my thumb over the bead of moisture that forms on the head of it. His purr grows stronger, but reality sinks in. I haven't been with a man in years. This thing would wreck me.

"You're beautiful like this," I say, "but maybe... for our first time...."

A bark-like laugh rumbles from his chest and he digs his claws into my hair. A moment later he's transformed in my arms to his human shape. The lights flicker back on. "Is this better, little dragon?"

I shrug and flash him a coy smile. "I rather like the tail, but this will do." Trailing my nails up the back of his neck,

I dig them into his hair. "Is that the only thing you have to show me?"

"Yes," he says with a dose of relief in his voice.

"Then will you stay with me tonight?"

"You've been teasing me with that little blue dress all evening. Did you think you'd be rid of me so easily?"

The way he looks at me sends a rush of heat straight to my core. My heart springs to a gallop, and my inner muscles clench in anticipation. I want him. I've wanted him for weeks. Like always, he's waiting for me to make the first move. I may no longer have the candle, but he won't act without an agreement, without my consent.

I reach behind me and unzip my dress. His stare is a palpable thing as I brush the straps from my shoulders and let the dress fall in a heap around my pumps. All dark grace and lithe muscle, he wraps a hand around my waist and draws me hard against his chest, a hairsbreadth between our noses. My breath comes in pants, and my nipples strain against the black lace of my bra.

"Turn around," he commands. The low gravel of his voice does sinful things to my insides. My lids flutter. I turn in place and find I'm facing the oval mirror mounted to the wall. Self-conscious, I glance away from my reflection.

"Oh no." His arm slides around me and props up my chin. Gaze locked on my reflection, his lips brush my temple as he says, "Watch, Eloise." My name on his tongue is erotic as hell. "You've seen the real me. Now it's time for you to see the real you. Look how beautiful you are. How powerful."

My eyes lock on the reflection as he unhooks my bra and lets it drop to my toes. The dusky pink tips of my full breasts pearl, and when his hands smooth around my sides to pinch and roll them between his fingers, shivers travel down the very center of me, causing my body to twitch and my core to throb with need.

"You like that, little dragon?" His lips brush my neck, my hair, as he continues to cup and knead my breasts, plucking at my nipples. Arching, I grind my ass against him. He's hard, and I glory in the feel of his erection against the back of me, as well as the growl I elicit. I'm drawn flush against his body, held in place by one iron hand pressed into my sternum.

I gasp.

"Oh, Eloise, are you offering me this tight little ass?" His hand snakes between us, sliding between my cheeks and circling the puckered skin of my rear entrance.

I stiffen, my pulse ratcheting. "I want you, but not that way. Not the first time."

His lips trail kisses down the side of my neck as his fingers move from my backside to my belly, stroking up to brush under my breast and then down to just graze under my thong. I lean my head back against his shoulder, throbbing with need, wanting his fingers to ease the ache between my legs.

"How *do* you want me... the first time?" He licks behind my ear, sending heat surging through me.

Will there be more times than this? I don't know. But if this is our one and only time together, I'm determined to make it count.

"Face-to-face, so I can see you." My voice cracks. Have I ever felt safe enough to ask for what I want from a man? With Damien, I can. He's always done as I asked. Maybe that was because of the candle. Maybe now that he is free, he'll turn into the monster Maeve insists he is and fuck me any way he pleases. I'll let him. I'm so wet and needy that I'd probably go along with anything.

But he turns me gently in his arms and cradles my face in his hands, his eyes going soft in the firelight. "Face-to-face, then."

33
CONNECTIONS

DAMIEN

Everything I believed to be true is wrong, and I am shaken. I believed the candle's curse was eternal, and it wasn't. I believed the woman in my arms was only human, and based on the way she destroyed the candle, I now highly doubt that presumption. And I thought Eloise desired nothing more than pleasure tonight, but there is so much more in her eyes.

It's been centuries since a woman looked at me like this. Centuries since someone wanted me for me and nothing more. And the way she makes herself vulnerable, handing herself over to me—knowing my true form, knowing I can easily overpower her or drain her of her blood—shows a trust I never thought I'd experience. Not on Earth. Not on Tenebris. Never.

"Face-to-face," I whisper again, and then I bury my fingers in her red curls and kiss her. Gods, her mouth is as sweet as her scent. I breathe her in, savoring her bouquet like the finest wine, parsing out her fruity and floral notes —pomegranate and narcissus, layered over leather, bone, and a hint of smoke. Her scent has developed over the time I've known her, becoming more complex, more enticing. Every time I touch her, I notice something new.

Eloise Harcourt is no simple human, of that I'm certain.

As I explore her mouth, I have the fleeting thought that perhaps I died when the candle was destroyed. Died and gone to paradise hereafter.

I draw back and look into her wide green eyes, almost innocent in their clarity. How long since she's been with a man? It would have been a human man. Anyone else other than her husband? That derelict certainly never showed her any passion, any kindness. I can't ask her now. The answer would surely drive me insane with jealousy and come across poorly in the moment, as if I were weighing her past or judging her number of partners. But she might as well be a virgin for how much experience she's had with a monster like me. If I take her now, as I am tempted to take her, hard and rough, claiming her flesh with possessive violence, I can't guarantee I won't lose control and damage her fragile mortal body. I'd definitively terrify her. That's not how I want her to remember this.

"We have a problem, little dragon," I whisper. "Other than face-to-face, I'm not sure what you want. And as I'm a monster—"

"You're not a monster, Damien. Different. Not human. But not a monster. Just a shade."

I close my eyes against her sweet words. "Thank you for that, but I have little experience with humans. I don't wish to hurt you. You must show me how you want it." I step back and drop my hands to my sides. "Tell me what to do."

Eloise closes the space I've put between us and fists my shirt. "After centuries of bondage, the first thing you ask is for me to order you around?"

I slant her a wolfish grin and skim my hands down her sides. "This time, yes. Next time..." I allow some of the hunger I'm feeling to show.

"Oh... " Her brows peak, and something inside her takes hold. She stands taller, licks her full red lips. "Okay, then. Remove your shirt."

Fuck, the command in her voice travels straight to my cock, causing it to twitch in anticipation. Clawing at my buttons, I give up and tug the tails from my pants, then reach behind my head to pull it off and cast it aside. She shivers as her gaze traces my chest. The scent of her arousal makes my heart thump faster and my fangs throb.

"What now?" My voice sounds rusted out. My mouth has gone dry for want of her blood.

"Take off the rest of it. I want to see all of you." She points to my pants, a wicked gleam in her eye.

The truth is my clothing is as much an illusion as the rest of this form, and only moments ago, I stood before her entirely naked in my true form. I could make my pants disappear if I willed it. But I sense from the bloom of her arousal that she likes to watch me undress. And something else. I can feel heat coming off her flushed skin.

I toe off my shoes and unfasten my pants, sliding them off, along with everything underneath. Standing before her naked, I wonder how I got here, making myself vulnerable for a woman. Trusting her, after centuries of bitter hatred toward the ones who captured me, the ones who used me. Maybe it is precisely because of her fragility, her humanness, the idea that I could kill her with little effort that I do trust her. Even if she is somehow supernatural, Eloise has always exposed her vulnerabilities to me.

But deep down, I know it's more than that. She's owned me since the moment she called me. Since the moment I saw her bravery and conviction.

"Lie down on your back," she orders. Her gaze lingers on the erection jutting from between my thighs, and when she licks her lips, I feel the tip of my cock weep for her. I lower myself to the floor, easing onto my elbows in front of the fire.

"What now, little dragon?"

"It's settled, then. You are a monster," she says, staring at my cock. "I'm honestly not sure you'll fit, even in this form."

I shoot her a self-satisfied grin and allow myself to go smoky at the edges. "I'm made of shadows, little dragon. I'll fit anywhere you want me to."

Her eyes grow heated again and never leave mine as she strips off her thong and straddles my hips. With her towering above me in those spiky, black shoes of hers, I have a luscious view of her sweet pussy. A growl rumbles in my chest, the need to possess her almost unmanageable. I dig my nails, now hardened into pointed talons, into the carpet and the floor underneath me.

"Eloise, please," I beg her.

She bends over and places a finger over my lips, her lids narrowing. "Since you're having trouble staying quiet, I'll give you something to do with that mouth." She straightens, then presses my shoulder to the floor with the toe of her shoe. I lower myself until the back of my head touches the floor, then watch her, stunned by this magnificent creature who is no longer a terrified bird but a siren, a succubus. She squats over my mouth and the scent of her, the sweet glistening pink, is irresistible. I grab her hips, pull her down on my mouth, and lick up her slit, moaning at the taste of her.

She throws her head back in a silent scream. Blood rises in her cheeks, and I hold her in place, desperate to show her how much I enjoy this game. I settle in, sucking her clit, lapping at her folds, spearing her with my tongue. She writhes against me, and I summon the shadows to fill her, to caress her.

"Oh my God," she mutters under her breath. Her thighs tremble as if her legs might give out at any moment. I hold her up, hold her in place as I work her delicate flesh, grazing her clit with my fang. The orgasm rips through her like a wave of pure energy, and I can no longer control myself.

I flip her onto her back and push the head of my throbbing cock into her. My entire body shakes with the need to take her, but I hold myself back, not wanting to hurt her. Panting, she meets my eyes once more, grips my shoulders, and lifts her hips, sheathing me in her velvet heat. I sink into her in one powerful thrust. She bites her palm to keep from crying out.

Gods, I need this.

Her legs wrap around my hips, and she squeezes me deeper inside, her breath catching when I'm all the way in. I slant her a wicked smile. "Good little dragon. Show me how you take your pleasure when given the chance."

She drops one hip and rolls us both over until she's riding me. It's my turn to throw my head back and stifle a howl. I've never felt like this. Fiery tremors rush through me, tingling along my spine until I fear I might come apart into shadow. And when she starts to move, to ride me in a roiling, seductive rhythm, I have to concentrate to keep from filling her with my seed immediately. I grind my teeth and give her the ride of her life, matching her pace and thrusting upward until I feel the heat rising in her again. Her lips fall open as she gasps for breath. Her skin gleams with perspiration.

I sit up, holding her against me and trailing my fingers along her spine, driving myself deeper into her. The reflection of our joined bodies in the window tempts me, and I indulge myself, watching her rise and fall above me. And then I notice something else in the reflection. The symbols inside Eloise's tattoo spin and shuffle along her back like her sigil is alive. I blink, disbelieving what I'm seeing. Red light washes over the room and I smell ash in the air. The people in the pictures on the gallery wall begin to move. The silver mirror ripples like water. Nothing makes sense.

And then her mouth crashes down on mine. Her breasts press softly into my chest, and her inner walls tighten around my cock. I dismiss every thought, every feeling, except for her. I follow her over into oblivion.

Afterward, she clings to me. We're breathing as one, my heart pounding in time with hers. I thread my hand into her hair and press a kiss to her temple, enjoying the weight of her body on mine. Soft. Warm. Alive. So far beyond anything I've ever expected or experienced. That's when the memory of her tattoo comes back to me. But the room is no longer red. The ash is gone from the air. The photos are no longer animated. Everything is normal.

"You've turned cold." She draws back, sweeping her hair from her neck. "Do you need to feed?"

Her artery pulses. Gods, I am hungry, and her offer seems guileless enough, but I know what I saw. I glance at the window again, but the key tattoo is only a tattoo again. Nothing more. Still, I know I'm in deep. Eloise's bloodline is a mystery. *She* doesn't even comprehend what she is. I'm old enough to know better than to play with power I don't understand. "I do need to feed, but not on you. You're not food." I stand, bringing her with me, and set her on her feet. At my will, my clothes appear on my body again. "Only hours to hunt before sunrise. I must go."

She watches me for a moment, eventually pulling her dress back on and clutching her bra and panties to her chest. Her eyes are noticeably misty as she says, "Thank you, Damien, for everything."

It sounds a lot like goodbye. Fuck, maybe it is. I am free. Is there any reason for me to return to her aside from love? Cassius was right. I know that now. I am in love with her. But we're from different worlds, and she's a risk I can't take. Not now. Not now that I'm free.

Even love isn't enough to bridge a gap between worlds.

I give her a shallow bow and then leave.

34

GOODBYES

ELOISE

All along, even when he was arched in ecstasy under me, I suspected it would be the last time I ever saw Damien. He freed me from Tony, and I freed him from his eternal captivity. I'll never forget our time together. He was my advocate, *my* monster. That is all it was. Our attraction to each other, our bond, can never be anything more than temporary. He's not human, after all, and for all intents and purposes, immortal. A relationship with me would be a limitation he doesn't need. He'll always hold a place in my heart, but I understand that last night was goodbye.

I cried when he left, cried in the shower as I washed the remnants of our lovemaking from my thighs, cried as I dressed in my most cuddly PJs. Once I was under the covers, I cried myself to sleep. But this morning, with the sun sweeping across my face from my bedroom window, I feel good—at peace and whole again. The house is mine.

Damien has taught me I am still desirable. Still strong. Still *alive*. With his help, I've proven that I am capable of saving myself, even if I occasionally need some muscle to back me up.

My monster won't be the last man interested in me, of that I am sure. Although the mere thought of anyone else leaves me feeling empty. No man will ever measure up to him. Thankfully, I know now that I'm enough alone.

I sit up in bed and stretch my arms overhead, feeling the shattered pieces of my heart shift around inside my chest. I'm all out of tears. All that's left is numbness and the comforting monotony of breathing. I tell myself it will be okay, eventually. I have plenty to focus on besides Damien, first and foremost, Grams. Dressing quickly in jeans and a sweatshirt, I jog down the stairs, gathering all the positive energy I can muster to spare her from my personal problems.

"I hope you're in the mood for pancakes, Grams, because the sun is shining, the leaves are falling, and I want carbs!" I slide sideways on stockinged feet across the wood floor of the hallway and catch myself on her doorframe.

My smile and my world come to a screeching halt.

Grams is still propped on her pillows, but her eyes are wide open, her unblinking stare fixed on her window and the cemetery beyond. Her hands are clasped over her heart, and her thin lips curve into a smile. My throat constricts as if I've swallowed an invisible fist as I make my way across the room and raise my fingers to her neck to check for a pulse. Her skin is cold to the touch and it confirms what I already know. I can't feel her in the room anymore. Her body is there, but she isn't.

She's gone.

"Grandpa came for you, didn't he?" I choke back a sob. "I'm going to miss you. Grams... so much. But I'm glad you had the death you wanted, and I'm going to make damn sure the rest goes exactly as you wanted too." My gut clenches, and I shift into survival mode. I wipe under my burning eyes, but no tears have actually escaped. I'll let myself feel this once everything is taken care of.

Reaching for my phone, I dial the coroner.

ONE OF THE BLESSINGS OF GRAMS HAVING A LONG FIGHT with cancer is that she had plenty of time to document her final wishes. She wants to be buried in the family cemetery, that part was always a given, but she also made it clear she didn't wish to be embalmed. Not only did she feel it was a huge waste of money, she thought it was bad for the environment and, subsequently, the fairies she believed lived around the graveyard. Howard hadn't been embalmed, and neither had her mother or her father. On paper, it's a simple request. In practice, it means things have to happen fast.

The coroner comes within the hour to pronounce her dead. Then Chuck Harper, the local cemetery caretaker, shows up with equipment to dig the grave out back. Grams has already paid him for the service. Paul Walker, the mortician from Echo Mills funeral home, arrives next with a coffin she'd picked out. Aqua blue, her favorite color. They dress her in a gorgeous dress in a coordinating shade and arrange her in the satin lining. Paul does her makeup right there in the house.

Meanwhile, I message everyone who'd been close to Grams, which includes most of the town of Echo Mills and her cousins who live in Maryland. Those who don't respond within the hour, I call to deliver the news personally. Reverend Hollister from Echo Mills Non-denominational Church agrees to perform the service that afternoon, 4 p.m. sharp. I dress in a smart black wrap dress that has long sleeves and a hem below my knees. It's a cold day, so I add a long black wool coat and a tall pair of leather boots.

When I make the walk out to the cemetery that afternoon, I think Grams would have liked how it all came together. Rows of white chairs are set up beside the grave, with Grams lying in the coffin on a contraption that will lower her into the ground right next to Howard. Evelyn from Echo Mills Flowers and Gifts came through with a beautiful coffin spray made from a variety of Grams's favorite flowers: pink garden roses, scabiosa, wax flowers, and lisianthus. I imagine her ghost leaning over to smell them. A wreath of pink roses stands beside the coffin on a stand with a satin ribbon that reads Beloved Grandmother.

The turnout is disappointing, though. None of her cousins could make the distance before the event, and many of her Echo Mills friends are out of town. But Simone from the nail salon is here, as is Principal Singer, some members of her bridge club, and of course, Evelyn, Chuck, and Paul who helped make this event happen.

It's selfish, but I wish someone was here for me. I don't know many of these people well, having spent most of the last six years away at school and then living in Richmond. And although everyone hugs me and offers their condolences, it all feels impersonal. Until Maeve arrives. I release a huge breath of relief when she pulls me into her arms and hugs me so hard it almost hurts.

"I'm here," she repeats again and again in my ear. And it matters. It matters so much.

After that, I don't hear a word of the ceremony. Everything hurts. I don't know why. It's like every joint in my body has decided to ache for no reason. My throat is raw from an unyielding lump wedged in it. My stomach is empty and leaves the rest of me feeling hollowed out. Reverend Hollister reads from the Bible and then says a few words. When he's through, he introduces me. I'm supposed to give a speech. A eulogy. I stand and unfold the notes in my pocket.

"Nora Harcourt was my Grams, but she was so much more than that. She was born in a suburb of Chicago and met Howard Harcourt when they both attended the University of Illinois. Howard wasted no time marrying her, and they both moved back to Echo Mills after graduation. Grams never looked back. She took to this town like she was born here, and all of you know how much she loved you and was loved in return. From her volunteerism at St. Johns to her work at the Echo Mills community gardens, there isn't a single person in this town who hasn't been on the receiving end of Grams's good nature. Her casseroles were known throughout the county.

"She gave birth to my dad in this house, on the second floor, God rest his soul. When my parents died, she was so appreciative of all you did to help us get through that difficult time. And for all the meals you brought the last months while she was in hospice. But I need to tell you that Grams believed her beloved Howard was coming to take her home these last weeks. She told me she was ready to go, and when I found her this morning, she was smiling. I believe my grandfather did escort her to her final rest. And I believe that's where she is now. She's free of pain and happily tending her roses and peonies with Gramps on the other side."

Although my knees are shaking, I hobble over to the casket. "Goodbye, Grams. Give Mom and Dad and Gramps a big hug for me."

I return to my seat to the sound of sobs from the attendees, but I haven't shed a tear. Not yet. Reverend Hollister wraps things up and directs everyone into the house to share in the potluck supper the attendees have brought. When I stand again, I'm trembling so violently, I'm not sure I can make it back into the house. Maeve takes me by the waist and helps me inside, propping me in a cushy chair in the formal living room. She makes me a cup of tea that I'm sure has something witchy in it because once I drink it, the world takes on a hazy quality. People offer their condolences, and I respond politely. All their faces run together eventually. And then, like magic, my cup is empty and Maeve is showing the last guest out the front door.

"Do you want something to eat?" she offers kindly.

"No." I haven't eaten much all day but I'm not remotely hungry.

"Would a distraction help? We could stream a movie."

I stand. "I want to go back to the cemetery."

Maeve shakes her head. "I don't think that's a good idea, El. Everything is still so fresh for you. I don't think they've even cleaned up the grave yet."

I grab my coat and stick my arms into the sleeves. "I want to go. I want to wait for the fairies."

"The fairies?" Maeve follows me to the door, looking morose in her long black skirt and sweater. A giggle escapes me and it turns into a completely inappropriate laugh.

"Why are you laughing?"

"I just realized you wore your normal, everyday clothes today. You look totally and completely at home." I gesture toward her outfit as I walk toward the door at the back of the house.

"El? Come on. The sun's going down. It's getting cold out there." She holds out a hand to me.

I sigh. "Grams believed she saw fairies in the cemetery. She believed they'd come for her when she died. I want to see for myself. I need to see for myself. I need to know she's okay."

"You don't actually believe there are fairies in your backyard, do you?"

I whirl and glare at her. "My best friend is a witch, and a shade became my greatest advocate. So, yes, I believe my grandmother was telling the truth about this."

I turn the knob and stride toward the family plot. Tonight is going to be frigid. Already the cold bites at the tip of my nose and blows right through my coat, seeming to sink into my bones. Maeve's moto boots thump the grass behind me, but she doesn't say a word. And when I arrive at the heap of fresh dirt that is my grandmother's grave, my friend stands in silent vigil to my left, hands folded in front of her.

The sun has set, and darkness grips us in its icy fist. I watch the woods beyond the graves, hopeful for a sign. It doesn't have to be fairies. Anything to let me know she's okay.

"Your family raises the dead." I don't bother turning to face Maeve. It's too dark to see her anyway.

"My family animates the dead. The bodies of the dead. No souls are in there when we do."

"Right."

"I can't contact her, El. I'm not a medium or a necromancer. I'm sorry."

"But you know people who are?"

"Yes, but I don't recommend using them. Nothing good ever comes from disturbing a soul's rest."

I nod. I can see the wisdom in that. "But, I mean, you know for sure that there are souls, then. If there weren't, there would be nothing for them to talk to."

"Of course there are souls. Your grandmother has a soul, and she's in a good place, just like you said." Maeve's voice is sure and edged in anger at my doubt.

"You're right. I know you're right."

The wind blows, and I hear her teeth chatter. "Can we go in? Maybe we can watch from a window?"

I'm about to agree to that plan when I notice two small lights bouncing behind the trees to my right. Excitement lifts my spirits. "Look, here they come."

35
COLLISION

ELOISE

The lights grow closer until they're right in front of us, and that's when we both realize what we are actually seeing. The growl of a distant engine meets my ears, and the lights pass behind the trees bordering the graveyard, disappearing to our left.

"I think that was…" Maeve hesitates. "From the house, I bet—"

"It was a truck driving down the access road between us and the Anderson place," I say softly, my voice shaky with my trembling and hollow from my disappointment. "Grams wasn't seeing fairies. She saw cars. Someone must be staying in the old farmhouse again."

"I thought that place was condemned."

"It was. Maybe someone bought it to fix it up." I stare in the direction the truck has gone. And just like that, all the emotions I've bottled up all day rush through me like popped champagne. I choke on a sob, falling to my knees on the cold dirt. "It isn't real," I cry. "Oh my God, she waited for him, and it isn't real. Nothing is real!"

Maeve places a hand on my shoulder, but I can't take comfort in it. All the magic has drained from the world, and every bit of relief I've taken from religion, platitudes, and my grandmother's personal beliefs has been stripped away, replaced with only one reality. She is gone, forever. A body in a cold box in the ground. I am alone. So alone, even with Maeve right beside me.

The last Harcourt.

My grief is a living, voracious worm, eating my innards one bite at a time. All I can feel is pain and the emptiness it leaves in its wake.

Warm arms wrap around me—long arms that feel as though they could circle me twice—and I'm hauled against a broad chest that's definitely not Maeve's.

"No one called you, Advocate," Maeve hisses. "Why are you here?"

"Currently, it appears I'm saving a grieving grand-daughter from hypothermia. Why are you here, Maeve? To watch her catch pneumonia?"

"You came back." I sob, nestling into his chest. He cradles me like a child in his arms and strides toward the house.

"I'm taking you inside." Warmth from his body perme-ates my own, and I can hear his strange heartbeat, a steady thump-thump against my cheek. The smell of him eases me. I release a sigh.

"Thank you," I say softly. For coming back. For carrying me. For keeping me safe. I don't say those things out loud, but he must understand because he presses a kiss to my temple. I allow myself to drift to sleep, the trails of my tears drying on my face.

DAMIEN

Eloise feels far too vulnerable in my arms. Far too delicate. I need to warm her. Feed her. Guard her. I should have never left her side.

"Advocate, I'm speaking to you!" Maeve snaps from behind me. At least she's attempting to keep her voice down. Fuck, I don't need a Gowdie witch riding my ass at the moment. Not when I need to care for my *mate*.

I grit my teeth at the word. Despite my best efforts, I've bound myself to this little dragon, already thinking of her as mine. I want to deny it. But here I am. With no candle to blame, I felt her torment through the darkness and hastened to her side. I am free. I could leave. But I am here solely because I want to be. Solely because I love this tiny force of a woman in my arms and can't bear to leave her in her grief.

Which means I am already hers.

Once we're inside the foyer of Harcourt Manor, I cast daggers at Maeve over my shoulder. "Later. Let me put her to bed. She's not well."

The witch winces as if the thought disgusts her but nods once. "Fine. I'll be in the kitchen. Come talk to me when you've... *put her to bed.*"

Taking the stairs two at a time, I carry Eloise to her

bedroom, then carefully set her on her feet. She yawns and rubs her eyes. "I think I fell asleep."

"You passed out. Have you eaten anything today? You're shivering." I shuffle her into the bathroom and start the water.

"No, but I'm not hungry. Damien, my Grams, she's..." Her voice cracks.

"I know." I start undressing her, slipping her dark wool coat off her shoulders.

"What are you doing?"

"You're freezing. You need to warm up. A shower will help." The black dress she wears hangs on her like a sack and makes her skin look sallow. She's lost weight these last few weeks. She isn't eating enough.

"Stop looking at me like that."

"Like what?"

"Like you're two seconds away from carting me off to the emergency room."

I stroke her hair back, studying the graceful lines and angles of her face. "I owe you my freedom. The least I can do is look out for you on the day you lose your grandmother. Let me take care of you, Eloise. Do it my way, just this once."

A tear slips from the corner of her eye, and I wipe it away. "You know I can't say no to you when you use my actual name." The corner of her mouth turns up, and my heart swells. Does she realize the power she has over me?

"Do you want me to assist you?" I jerk my head toward the shower.

Her eyes grow heated. "Sure."

I slice my head to the left. "That's not what I meant."

"Why not?"

I cup her chin and bare my fangs. "There is nothing I'd like more than to be inside you right now, little dragon, but not like this. Not when you're so distracted with grief you can't think straight. You need rest and to eat. I will not take what you don't have to give."

She slides her hands up my chest. Gently I take her wrists and press her palms together inside my own. "Shower," I say again, and this time it's a command. "There's something I have to do. I'll be back to watch over you soon."

Her face changes, growing suspicious. "What?"

"Maeve is downstairs. She wants to... talk."

"I should—" She moves for the door, but I stop her.

"Please." I place a kiss on her forehead. "Get ready for bed. I will return to you."

This time she nods, although I can see the conversation isn't over. My little dragon will not give up so easily, which means I have only a few minutes to deal with the witch downstairs. I back through the door, meld into the shadows in the corner of the room, and manifest in the kitchen across the table from the Gowdie witch.

Maeve glares at me over a cup of something steaming and dark, the only sound that of the shower running above us on the second floor. When she speaks, she gets straight to the point. "Why are you here, Advocate? You've served your purpose and met the terms of your agreement with Eloise. She did not light the candle to call you again."

"No. She didn't light the candle, but anyone could have heard her cries. Why did you allow her on her knees in the cold and dark? Why didn't you care for her?"

Her cup clanks onto her saucer. "I don't have to answer to you."

I unbutton the top button of my shirt and pull it aside to reveal the space over my heart, now free of the Gowdie tattoo. "Nor I to you."

Terror flashes through her expression, and she darts up and around the back of her chair, ready to bolt. Her hands fly up in what I can only assume is the start of a defensive spell. Shadowing through the table, I form beside her, restraining her wrists before she can finish. I hold them in my grip and bring my face close to hers.

"Oh, *please.*" I roll my eyes. "If I meant to kill you, the table would be a minor inconvenience. And I would have done so before you knew I was free from the candle's hold."

Her eyes grow wide. "How did you do it?"

"The candle burned out," I say simply. After all, wasn't that the promise she and her ancestors had always made me?

Her jaw clenches. "How did that happen, Advocate?"

I extend my fangs in a growl. "My name is Damien Hymir, prince of the Kingdom of Stygarde, and I am no advocate of yours, Maeve Gowdie. The only reason your life isn't in danger is Eloise. She loves you, and I won't give her one more thing to grieve tonight. I'd prefer we move forward civilly."

Her expression softens, but not with empathy. It's pity I see in those dark depths that serve as eyes. "You love her."

"My feelings for her are none of your concern." Roughly, I release her wrists and back against the yellow counter, studying the spider plant that hangs from a crocheted sling beside the sink.

"None of my concern? I can practically smell the mating scent coming off you. You've had her blood, multiple times I bet. You're not a vampire, but you're enough like one for me to draw some conclusions. You've bound yourself to her."

I rejoice in my ability not to answer her. I don't owe the witch an explanation.

"You're playing with fire." She shakes her head, her words coming through gritted teeth. "You've known about the tattoo from the beginning. If there's any vestige of magic in her blood—"

I narrow my eyes. "Wasn't it you who led me to believe she was human?"

"As far as I know, she is," Maeve snaps defensively. "But then who destroyed the candle? And don't give me any bullshit about it burning down. You and I both know it was enchanted so the flame could never reach the end of its wick."

The creak of floorboards draws our attention to the hallway. Eloise stands there, dressed in nothing but her pink bathrobe, hair soaking wet. I've been so wrapped up in this thing with Maeve, I didn't hear the water shut off. I can feel her presence now, though. Her grip on the doorframe and the tension in her jaw communicate only one thing—*FURY*.

36

JUST SEX THEN

DAMIEN

"How could you?" Maeve's eyes flare with her anger.

"You admit it," Eloise shouts. "The candle was spelled to keep him a prisoner forever!"

The table rattles as Maeve's power rises in the room. "He murdered a witch, Eloise! My ancestor. He deserved what he got."

A growl tears from my throat and I position myself between them, my shadows crawling the walls and pointing dark and razor sharp in Maeve's direction. "Mind your power, Gowdie."

The table settles, but the witch's hands remain balled into fists.

Eloise points at me, her ears growing red with her anger. "Only because your family conjured him from his home. He's served the Gowdies for multiple lifetimes. Any debt he owed you is paid."

Maeve slashes a hand through the air. "How did you break the spell?"

"I tossed the candle into the fire."

She scoffs. "That shouldn't have worked. The wax is enchanted never to fully melt. It's laced with his own blood."

"It didn't melt," Eloise says through her teeth. "It exploded into a shower of sparks."

Maeve grips the back of a chair until her knuckles turn white. "Goddess, El. Don't you see what that means? It's like I told you, your tattoo *does* mean something. The vibes I get in this house... the fact the Wi-Fi never works... there's something magical here. Something magical in you. You may not be a witch like me, but you have power."

What Maeve says is true. I've sensed it for a while now. But hearing her say it sends a frisson of fear through me. If I wasn't such a fool, I'd run from Eloise immediately, because whatever this power is, it's sinking its teeth into my soul. I don't move and I realize maybe it already has.

Eloise runs a hand down her face. "I think I'd know if I had any power. But that's not what's important here. What's important is that Damien is finally free, and I want you to promise me you'll let him go."

I dart a glance between the two women. Do the Gowdies still have my blood? If they've preserved a vial, they could attempt to recapture me, but I would not come easily. Once again Eloise has surprised me. To leverage her friendship with Maeve to secure my freedom is a gift I do not take for granted.

"I can't do that. It's not my decision to make. This won't go over well with my family. It will weaken our position."

Eloise grips the collar of her robe, her jaw clenching. "Promise me, Maeve. As your best friend."

Maeve groans, her eyes rolling toward the ceiling before she tosses up her hands. "You don't understand."

"I do. I'm asking you, if you ever truly were my friend, to promise me you'll do everything you can to keep Damien free."

"You'd end our friendship over him? Over this monster!"

"He's not a monster!" Eloise bellows. "And I love him."

"Goddess help me." Maeve stares at the floor, gripping the chair and shaking her head. "Fine! I'll do what I can."

"Thank you."

Maeve scowls. "Don't thank me. I'm doing this for you, for the sake of a friendship that used to be precious to me."

"Used to be?"

"This isn't okay, El. Freeing him without my permission, isn't okay." For a moment, the two women just stare at each other, the room thick with shadows and charged with barely contained magic.

Eloise sighs. "I think you should go."

A strangled sound comes from Maeve's throat. "No. We need to talk. If you have power, you and Damien have to be careful. If you're a witch, it could explain why he's enchanted by you. Don't you see? That's why he's here. You're binding him, and if you continue, he'll claim you as his mate. There's no candle to stop him now."

I growl low and deep, baring my fangs. A small part of me acknowledges the possibility that what she says could be true. Eloise hasn't forced me to take her blood, and she doesn't command me now. I am here because I desperately want to be, and I can leave anytime I choose. But I don't want to leave. Not now. Not ever. And that is frighteningly close to the enchantment she describes.

A tense silence spreads across the kitchen, punctuated by the way Eloise is looking at me, almost as if she *wants* me to confirm she is my mate. The urge to possess her twitches along my spine and pulses in my fangs. "We should both leave," I say to Maeve. "Eloise needs rest and a chance to mourn in private. This conversation can be had another day."

I'm a coward not to address the mating instinct I'm battling head-on, but if I don't leave Eloise's presence now, I will take her and I will claim her as mine. Already everything in me feels it. She is mine.

"Fine," Maeve says, sweeping her coat from the chair and throwing it over her shoulders. "We'll both go."

Maeve shoves past Eloise toward the foyer. I follow. I refuse to leave until I know Maeve is on the other side of the door.

"No," Eloise says firmly. I stop. Maeve does the same. "Maeve, I'll call you tomorrow." Her piercing gaze locks on her friend and then shifts to me. "Damien, I want you to stay. Please."

"Eloise, you don't know what you're doing," Maeve protests.

"I know well enough!" Eloise's crossed arms hold a marked tension. For the first time, I'm gripped with despair and truly sorry I've caused her the pain I see in her eyes.

Maeve shakes her head one last time. "Never say I didn't warn you."

"I won't."

The witch exits the house without another word. Eloise locks the door behind her, then whirls to face me.

"She's right, you know. You have power. It's possible this attraction between us is magical... metaphysical." I hate admitting the truth and my voice comes out gritty, the words forced.

"Are you suggesting you only love me for my power?" The corner of her mouth twitches with her jest. I can't find the same humor in the situation.

"No," I say with certainty. I should stop talking. I'm revealing too much. "But I will not deceive you. Your magic is strong enough to bind me. I sensed it last night. Maeve was telling the truth."

"But my power isn't why you're here."

"No." I swallow. "I fell for you long before I thought you had any magic. My feelings for you are true, but your feelings for me might not be. Magical creatures create magical bonds. You'd do well to fear what is happening between us."

"I don't believe that for a second. Nothing I feel for you is because of some magical spell between us," she hisses through her teeth and takes another step toward me. "Is it true you want to mate with me?"

Her words burn through my blood, and my cock grows hard instantly. "Yes."

"What's that mean? Sex?"

"More than sex." My voice is a rusted-out scrap heap, nothing but grit and growl.

"Then what does it mean to mate with a shade?" Her lids droop, her gaze drifting to my mouth.

The short leash I've kept myself on all evening slips from my hands, and I sweep into her like a dark storm, only stopping when her back is against the wall. Spreading her robe open, my hands grip her waist, and I press myself against her, my lips lowering to her ear.

"Careful, little dragon," I growl. "When you speak about becoming my mate, it does something to me." I hoist her up my body until we're face-to-face. Her legs wrap around my hips. "To be a shade's mate is to be *his*. To belong to him in every way. To be claimed by him. Once you are mine, you will always be mine. Do not tease a commitment you're not willing to bear."

"Do you want that?" she asks softly. "Do you want me to be yours?"

"More than you know." Running my thumbs along her bottom ribs, I grind against her.

"I want that too," she says. "I want to be yours."

It's almost more than I can resist. With her pinned against the wall, I wrap one hand around her throat in a loose grip, and lick along her jugular, barely keeping my instincts in check. But it's wrong to do this when her grandmother has just passed. She's vulnerable. It's too soon. "Then you will be mine. But not yet. Not now, when your wings are clipped by loss and heartache. When I claim you, it will be at your strongest."

Her breath hitches. "Not tonight?"

I swallow hard. "No."

Her arms wrap around my neck, and her voice is all breath as she says, "Just sex then."

37

CHANGE OF HEART

ELOISE

Death is a train you see coming from a great distance and think will never reach you until it knocks you out of your shoes. The grief it leaves in its wake is bone-rattling and soul-deep. After everything that has happened, my grandmother's death, her funeral, and the confrontation with Maeve about the candle, I suppose most people would want to wallow in it, to crawl under their blankets and sleep for three days. But Damien is a light in the darkness tonight, a balm for my pain. He may be made of shadows, but he's the only warmth I can feel through the cold sadness inside me.

As my lips crash down on his, all I think about is that he returned to me. He is free, but he came back... *for me.* He's right about it not being the time to make any permanent decisions. I'm not even officially divorced from Tony, and this thing with Damien is more intense than anything I've ever experienced. But as I deepen our kiss, every fiber of my being screams that I *must* have him. I cling to him like he's a rock in a turbulent sea. Everything hurts, and then I touch him, and it doesn't hurt as much. Maybe I'm delaying the inevitable weight of grief. I don't care. I want to lose myself in this passion. I want to forget everything and feel good, just for a little while.

I break the kiss. "Please, Damien, I need you. I need to feel good. Make me feel good."

The rumble in his chest is somewhere between a purr and a growl, but I know the second there is no turning back for him. He carries me up the stairs to my bedroom so fast the hallway is nothing but a blur. Then he spins me around and removes my robe, throwing it across the chair. When I attempt to undress him, his hands cinch around my waist again and toss me easily onto the bed. I land on my hands and knees, panting as my heart sprints to keep up with the action. Damien grips my ass and spreads my cheeks.

"What are you—" I gasp as his tongue licks up my center from behind. My inner muscles clench, and I fist the comforter. Another lick, this time lifting me to tease my clit with the tip of his tongue before spearing me with it. My thighs tremble. I try to push back against him, but he hoists me higher, gripping my thighs. My chest collapses on the bed, my nerve endings flickering to life as he licks and sucks, spreading me wider.

I moan.

Abruptly, he sets me down and backs away, leaving me cold. When I look over my shoulder at him, he says, "Last night, I did as you commanded. Tonight, you obey me."

I nod. God, how does he always know exactly what I need? "Then tell me what to do."

"Eyes on me," he commands.

I flip over and sit on the edge of the bed, aching and slick with need. He removes his shirt, then his pants and briefs. His long, thick erection juts toward me, and I lick my lips, thinking about what it felt like when he was inside me, surging beneath me. He palms his cock, staring at me as he strokes himself from root to tip.

"Spread your legs," he growls.

I do, my nipples tightening as his gaze settles between them.

"Are you wet for me, little dragon? Reach between your legs and check."

I slide my palm down my stomach and then over my soaking wet core. "Yes." My throat's so tight it comes out like a croak.

"Better be sure. Play with yourself. Make yourself feel good."

I tip my head back and rub my clit in tight, quick circles the way I like it. My blood heats, and the gathering storm of an orgasm coils tight at the base of my spine with the building pressure between my legs. Damien's hand lands on the back of my head. He's moved to stand in front of me, the head of his cock pressed to my lips. I open for him, and he slides himself to the back of my greedy mouth, his fingers digging into my hair. The erotic feel of it pushes me over the edge.

I suck him hard, heat and pure sensation filling out every cell under my skin.

I'm just coming down from the orgasm when he pulls his dick from my mouth and pushes me down on the bed. And then he's over me, surging into me, spreading me wide and entering me so hard and quick that I cry out.

My inner walls contract, my orgasm doubling down with the intrusion. I close my eyes against the intense fullness as he settles into me, waiting for me to accommodate his size.

"Look at me, Eloise."

I obey, relieved to think of nothing but him in that moment. My mind is otherwise blissfully blank. Our eyes lock, and the intensity I see in his gaze steals my breath. "Good girl."

Holding my stare, he starts to move, draws back, almost to the tip, then slams into me. He's so deep I can feel his thrusts in my throat. He doesn't slow down, and he doesn't ease up. Like a wave, he crashes against me and I meet him stroke for stroke. He supports my back to keep me from sliding up the bed from the force of our collision. All I can do is absorb the power of it. There is nothing slow or gentle about this coupling.

We fuck as if the end of the world is coming and all we have is each other.

I cling to him as he lets loose, pinioning faster and harder until I can't hold back. White light and showering stars accompany my scream of ecstasy. His orgasm comes on the heels of mine, his cock growing longer and thicker inside me, our bodies truly becoming one.

It's perfection. All I want is more.

And then his lips are on my neck, brushing over my vein. I tip my head to the side, offering my blood. He strikes. I'm just coming down from the strongest orgasm of my life, and the effect of his bite sends me over the edge again. Everything I am, everything I feel, narrows to the places we connect, where my body milks his and he drinks me in. My eyes roll back. I'm drowning in pure, intense pleasure.

Let me drown. I don't care to breathe.

When we finally come down to earth, I'm exhausted, and he's lapping my neck to close the wound. Still inside me, he meets my stare again. "Gods damn the consequences, I won't give you up."

"You don't have to." I stroke my hand along his face.

"You are *mine*, Eloise Harcourt. No other man will touch this body." He runs a hand up my side, growling and squeezing my breast. "Or kiss these lips." He kisses me, hard. "Do you understand me? I claim you as my mate."

My breath catches. *Mate.* The significance of the word settles over me like a shroud. He explained it to me earlier, but it's different to experience it. I feel my soul binding to his, like someone has sown our shadows together. It's more than we agreed to. How do I feel about this? I search my soul and find only peace. I feel wanted. I feel safe. I feel content. "Yes," I say, pressing my lips to his. "I'm yours."

He smiles wide enough to show his fangs. Some time later, he lifts off me and returns with a towel. Once I'm cleaned up, he climbs in beside me, covering us with the plush comforter. I fall asleep, my back to his front, sharing a pillow with my monster.

38

EVERYONE STOPS WHEN THEY'RE DEAD

ELOISE

Something—I'm not sure what—drags me out of a deep sleep. My clock reads 4:30 a.m. I reach behind me for Damien, but he's gone. He must've left for the day. That's probably what woke me. Restless, I roll over onto my back. A creek from the floorboards in the hall perks my ears.

"Damien?"

A figure moves toward me in the darkness. Smiling, I sit up to turn on the light. I realize it's not Damien, when the cold edge of a knife presses against my throat. I scream, but I cut myself off when the blade bites into my skin. A hand fists my hair and yanks my head back. Rank breath hits me in the face, and when the stranger speaks, he has the wheeze of a long-term smoker. "Hold still and shut up, or I'll make this slow and very, very painful."

I'm not sure how I can hold any more still. If I flinch, he'll pull my hair out by the roots. "What do you want?"

"Let me have a look at you." The lamp on the bedside table clicks on, and I glare into the face of a soulless killer. Empty pits watch me, his pockmarked skin and gap-toothed smile much too close. He's balding. Late fifties. I have the instant, ominous feeling I will not leave this room alive.

"Hmmm." His oily gaze slides over my chest, and I'm overcome with dread. I'm still naked from being with Damien. I try to draw the blankets higher to cover myself, but the man yanks them back down again.

"Please—" A warm, wet bead of what I can only assume is blood drips down my neck and slides between my breasts from where he must have cut me.

"Shhh. Close those lips, girly, or I'll have to put something between them, and you won't like it." He chuckles. "Or maybe you will. A woman like you probably likes a lot of things."

Icicles of fear form in my blood, and my limbs tremble. *Think. Think. Think, Eloise.* I assess my situation. I have only one thing going for me. My body is under the blanket, pinned down by his knee. Although my chest is exposed, he'll have to stand up to get at the rest of me, and when he does, I'll be ready. I'll shove the knife away and sprint for the door.

As I expected, he grips the edge of the blanket and shifts onto his feet to expose me. I shove at his wrist with both hands, lean my head back, and roll toward the window. He lunges across the bed, but my feet are already under me. I dash for the door, throwing myself into the hall.

I'm faster than he is, but when my foot hits the old runner carpet in the hall, it slips and I go flying. I slide across the wood floor, my body slamming into the far wall, *hard*.

Before I can right myself, the stranger is on me, pinning my back against the wall with his portly body, and this time, when the blade presses to my throat, it stings. I grab his wrist with both hands but the sharp edge digs in. Tears dribble from the corners of my eyes as he positions his feet for leverage to overpower me. "Could've been fun. Now I'll just have to kill you."

"Why," I ask, hoping to distract him as a murky shadow in the corner thickens and broadens behind him. "At least tell me why!"

The man bares his teeth... just as a horned, barbed-tail demon forms behind him—Damien in his monster form. My mate releases that strange atavistic rattle I've heard before when he's angry, draws his clawed hand back, and swipes. My attacker has one second to spot the threat behind him before razor sharp talons rip through his lower half.

I gasp in relief as the blade drops from my throat and the stranger crumples to the floor in a heap of blood and entrails. I have to look away. I squeeze my eyes shut against the horror as Damien's growl fills the space behind me and echoes down the dimly lit hall.

"Never. Touch. What's. Mine," he says in a voice so low and gritty it sends goosebumps marching up my arms. I doubt the man can hear him though. He has to be dead. No one could live through that.

"Fuck you," comes a gurgling rasp. I peek over my shoulder at the man, thankful that Damien's enormous body blocks everything but the intruder's face. Blood dribbles from the corner of the stranger's mouth but he's alive, those dark eyes filled with a medley of pain, rage, and malice. Damien brings his fangs closer, locking eyes with the creep. The man goes limp, his pupils widening into dark disks.

"Why did you come here?" Damien demands.

"To kill Eloise Harcourt." Venom oozes into his voice as he adds, "Shoulda done it quick."

He came to kill *me*. A ball of hot lead forms in my stomach. His malicious intentions were obvious, but hearing him say he'd *planned* to murder *me* specifically chills me to the bone. Not to rob a rural home. Not to rape a woman who happened to be in it. This man I've never met before wanted to kill *me*.

"Why? Who sent you?" Damien snarls.

"Denardi." The man's tone is weak and robotic. "Wants her dead."

I stumble back toward my room, my hand reaching out to grip the doorjamb as my knees turn to gelatin. What the hell? Tony is behind this? I have to let that sink in. I can't fathom it. Why would he do something like this? Because of the house? He's rich enough to buy any home he wants. Fuck, he could have a dozen! I always knew he was an asshole, but this is pure *evil*.

Images of my wedding day flash through my mind... our honeymoon... our years together. Tony had once been kind to me. He'd been affectionate. True, it didn't last, but he must've felt *something* for me once. Now he wants to murder me? I have nothing... nothing aside from this house. It's just so cruel.

"Supposed to... make it... look like a break-in," the man adds, gurgling. He gasps, lips working like a beached fish.

"Why does Denardi want her dead?" Damien's voice is comprised of two parts fury and one part sandpaper.

"Don't... know."

Damien searches the man's eyes as if sifting through his thoughts. With a deep sigh, he grabs the man's head and twists. A sharp snap resonates in the hallway.

I squeak, sliding down the wall as my trembling legs finally give out. Damien rushes to me, gripping my shoulders and moving in close so he's all I can see. In the time it takes me to draw my next breath, he's in his human form again. "Don't tell me you expected me to show that man mercy," he murmurs.

I swallow. "No." Tears roll freely down my cheeks. Damien has saved my life by killing an evil man. Seeing it has shaken me, but I don't think it was the wrong thing to do. "I've just never seen anything like that before."

Damien shoots me an empathetic look. I want him to hold me, to pull me into his arms and comfort me. But when I reach for him, he keeps me at a distance. "Hold still," he says. Gripping my jaw, he tips my head back and licks across my neck. *Oh*, I forgot about my knife wounds. Once he eases back, I can see my front is covered in rivulets of blood. The damage the knife has done to my throat must have been worse than I thought.

"Thank you."

A muscle in his jaw twitches. "I shouldn't have left you."

"Why did you?"

"To hunt." When my brows rise, he clarifies, "Animals. I heard you scream and came as fast as I could. Listen to me carefully, little dragon. I have to go now. I must dispose of this body before sunrise forces me underground. But I need you to do something for me. The man broke a sidelight window on your front door to get in. Call the police. Tell them you saw this man but that he ran off when you turned on the light."

I rub my eyes, feeling absolutely exhausted, too exhausted to ask what he plans to do with the body. "Okay."

His gaze scrapes down my blood-soaked skin. "Shower and dress first." He pulls me into his arms, kissing me softly.

His tenderness draws a sob from my throat. "Tony will never stop, will he?"

"Everyone stops when they're dead," Damien says in a tone that is soft but matter-of-fact, patient but unyielding. "I tried to tell you before, a man like him won't be told no. He wants this house, and he's willing to kill you for it. He cares for nothing but himself and his fortune. He won't hesitate to try again."

My heart rises until I can feel it pounding in my throat, and my voice comes out barely a whisper. "Damien, will you help me kill him?" I can't believe what I'm asking. I squeeze my eyes closed against it, even as cool air tells me that Damien has drawn back to look at me.

"Open your eyes, Eloise."

I obey, drawn out by the rare sound of my name on his lips.

"Are you sure about this?"

"Tony wants me dead. It's undeniable." As painful as it is to grieve what I thought we'd once had, I have to face the truth. "It's like you once said in your story about Isobel Gowdie. This is kill or be killed. I won't be killed."

He sighs, smoothing my hair back from my face. "When the sun sets tonight, I'll take care of Tony." It's a promise. "Now, the night grows thin."

I look away as he rolls the intruder in the hall carpet, then lifts the bundle into his arms. With one last goodbye, he leaves in a blur of speed, racing down my steps and out the front door. Alone again, I pad back into my bedroom, take the world's fastest shower, and shove my body into a pair of jeans and a T-shirt. Hugging myself against a chill that has nothing to do with the temperature in the room, I trudge downstairs, view the damage, and call the police.

39

LIFE IS FULL OF SURPRISES

ELOISE

It takes all morning for the tiny Echo Mills PD to investigate my break-in. I describe the killer in detail, although I lie as Damien suggested and say he ran off once I turned on the lights. I've never enjoyed lying, and lying to the police, considering I went to elementary school with the officer assigned, is completely against my nature. But what choice do I have?

The officer takes all my information and promises to patrol the area for the next few days. He also reminds me that insurance should cover the damage.

Once he's gone, I clean up the broken glass and cover the sidelight with plastic wrap and duct tape. Then I call Grams's old insurance agent, Marilyn Maples. She says she'll send someone out to fix the window as soon as possible.

"You know, I was going to call you," Marilyn says.

"Nora had a life insurance policy, Eloise. You are the sole beneficiary."

"Oh?" Grams had mentioned something about that, but I forgot all about it.

"Is it okay if I stop by with the paperwork sometime in the next few days? It's not something we can do over the phone."

"Sure," I say. "Maybe tomorrow? It's been a busy day, as you can imagine."

"Sounds good, hon. And I am sorry to hear about Nora. She was one of a kind."

"Thanks. I thought so too." I end the call and have a good cry.

I've experienced plenty of loss in my life. My grandfather first when I was barely ten, my parents at seventeen, and now my Grams. Even my divorce is a type of death, although that one brought me more relief than anything. But sitting in this empty house, surrounded by things from the past, fading pictures and furniture from another time, is like being surrounded by ghosts.

I try to nap but can't sleep. TV is impossible. The reception is worse than ever, and the Wi-Fi is out again. Finally, I decide if I don't give my grief somewhere to go, it will ruin me.

In one word, I feel raw, like a layer of flesh has been stripped away and everything that touches me hurts, physically and mentally. I love Damien, entirely and irrevocably. But I wrestle with what that means. Have we doomed each other to something we didn't entirely think through? I trust him more than anyone but maybe Maeve, and even that relationship is now on shaky ground. I sigh when I think of her. I owe her a call. What happened between the three of us is morally complex. I believe I've done the right thing freeing Damien, but I owe her a conversation to clear the air.

Not today, though. Today, I'm going to paint.

I pad down the first-floor hallway to my mother's studio, noting the purple dragon curled at the base of the door. I reach for the doorknob and then stop, studying the mural again. The dragon's eyes are open. The two-dimensional creature was asleep before. I'm sure of it. But that's impossible. Either I imagined its eyes closed before, or someone's been in my house and painted the eyes open. I run my fingers over the dragon's face. Dry and of similar texture to the paint around it. I have to have been mistaken about its previously sleeping state. Either that or I'm losing my mind. I give my head a good shake.

Entering, I walk around the tower of knives, giving the sculpture a wide berth. At the rear of the studio, I find a small, blank canvas and set it up on an easel near the window overlooking the side garden. Autumn is here. Leaves have started to fall. Half bare trees stand like skeletons over browning peonies. Oddly, though, the yard looks freshly raked. Grams must have hired someone. I'll have to track down who and for how much. If I can afford them, I'd love to keep them on. With the grounds being so extensive, I doubt I can do all the maintenance myself and I fully intend to stay here. This is my home.

As I place dollops of paint on my pallet and select a brush, I sense Grams and my mother beside me. And then, for the first time in years, I bring brush to canvas and begin. Hours pass like minutes while the shape of my family takes form before me. Grams and Gramps stand at the center of the canvas, grinning. Grams winks at me, her face round and hair thick as I remember it from before she developed cancer. Mom stands beside her, wearing a royal blue halter dress. I paint my dad next to Gramps, arms folded comfortably as he watches me with that proud expression I remember so well. I've painted them all in the backyard, surrounded by the bobbing lights of a family of fairies.

"There," I whisper. Grams wanted fairies, so I gave her some.

I stand back and admire my family. All gone now. The crushing realization that I'm alone in the world opens a black hole in my chest that absorbs everything and leaves me empty. But as I continue to admire my painting through teary eyes, eventually, another emotion moves in. The faintest whisper of hope courses through me. My family has moved beyond this plane of existence, but somehow they are still with me, in me, around me.

A long time passes as I ponder that thought and my own mortality. I focus on my Grams again and remember the truck's bobbing lights. Where the hell were all those trucks going? The Anderson's farmhouse was condemned right after Tony and his family moved out. There's nothing else back there. The road behind my family's cemetery is a dead end, only designed to give access to the Anderson's farmland. I quickly debunk the theory that the truck took a wrong turn. Grams had been seeing lights every night for who knows how long. She'd talked about it for months.

Possessed with a need to know the truth, I quickly soak my brushes and trudge to the back door, grabbing my Barbour jacket off the hook and pulling on my tall rubber boots. It's a cool, wet afternoon, and I walk out into a cloud of gray mist, my red hair curling tighter, until pieces come loose from my ponytail and coil around my face. I try not to think too hard about Grams as I walk past her grave. Crying again won't help anything. I've cried myself out already. Today, I want answers.

The access road is nothing but two ruts in stone-packed earth. Beyond it, the Anderson farmhouse looms in the distance, dead stalks that were once soybeans peppering the field between us. Its unkept exterior gives the house a haunted appearance against the overcast sky. I start in the direction the trucks traveled. Something is off about the dirt road, but exactly what remains irritatingly out of mind. Until I reach a very odd metal grate that does not belong there and put together what's missing.

Weeds. There are none growing through or around the grate. A quick inspection confirms that this road is being maintained in a way the Anderson farm is not, down to its neatly trimmed shoulders. And as it is technically on my property and I am not keeping it up, someone else has to be. It's possible Grams hired someone to do it, perhaps the same person caring for the yard, but why? No one should be back here.

I approach the grate and then stand on it. The only thing visible through the holes is more metal. Turning in place, I search for any clue to its purpose. A glint to my right draws me toward an overgrown yew. When I push the branches aside, I find a keypad on a metal pole. The three, six, and nine are abnormally worn, and my inner Nancy Drew kicks in. I try different combinations of the three numbers in four and six-digit combinations. Nothing works, and I think about walking back to the house. But then I remember something—the code for the penthouse's security system. The numbers were similar.

"No..." A dark foreboding feeling comes over me. Swallowing hard, I type 693369 into the pad, the same code we'd used to disarm our residential system. The metal-on-metal grind of something large and automated causes me to whirl around from the keypad. One end of the grate has lowered into the earth, revealing the gaping maw of an underground passageway.

Part of me thinks I should turn around right now, return to the house and call the police. This is weird. What is this doing on my property? The code can't be a coincidence. Whatever is down there, Tony thought it was worth killing for.

But if I call the police, I can't tell them about Tony trying to kill me without also reneging on my story that the intruder ran. Damien did something with the man's body. Changing my story sounds like a good way to be charged with murder.

I could wait until nightfall and come back with Damien. But Grams only saw the lights at night. Now, during the light of day, might be my only opportunity to investigate without being seen. I listen for voices. When all is quiet, cautiously, I descend into a well-lit, concrete-floored room that looks a bit like the entry to a parking garage. With only one way to go, I follow the ramp around the corner and stop short.

"Holy, fucking hell. Shit, shit, shit." My mouth keeps muttering random curses as my legs carry me forward of their own volition. I'm in a massive, underground cavern with a dock at one end that extends into a deep, murky inlet. Buoys are tied to its posts as if boats dock there regularly. Between me and the dock, stacked on pallets, ready for transport, are cubes of plastic-wrapped cash..

My palms start to sweat as I shuffle to the closest cube and rise on my tiptoes to inspect the faces of the bills. Damn, there has to be millions here. My arms break out in gooseflesh as I smooth the plastic with my hands to get a better look. A tiny smudge winks up at me from the upper right corner of the bill.

My mind spins out like a car on ice. This is Tony's counterfeit money, waiting to get loaded onto a boat in a sea cave under my property. I can't see where the water leads, but I can guess—the Rappahannock River. Tony is floating his fake cash down to the Chesapeake, the same way old mill workers floated logs. That's as far as I get piecing things together, though, because the low hum of a boat's motor rings through the cave. I run for the cover of a metal shed, flattening myself against the side, my chest rising and falling in ragged pants.

The boat engine grows louder, then cuts out, the sound of voices taking its place. "We're behind schedule. Get these loaded and to the ship. I don't want any surprises today."

I gulp. That's Tony's voice! I peek around the corner and confirm it's him, along with two other men who start loading the cubes of cash onto a medium-size trawler.

"It's still early. Are you okay with us risking the river in daylight?" one of the men asks.

"Do it," Tony says. "No one's going to question it."

"What about the girl?" The other man points skyward at what I can only assume is my house.

"I'll take care of the girl."

I flatten myself against the shed again. I'm the girl in

this equation. How exactly is Tony going to "take care" of me? But then I know, don't I? He sent that man to kill me last night. Does he mean to finish the job? By the way he answered, he must know the man he sent was unsuccessful.

Pulse pounding, I glance toward the exit. I have to get out of here before someone hears my increasingly shaky breaths. I wait until all three men are inside the boat's cabin, then sprint on my toes in the direction I came from. I pause around the bend that leads to the ramp and listen. Did they see me?

I can hear Tony and the other men continuing to load the money. No, I'm safe. Silently, I return the way I came. But panic sets in when I find the ramp is gone. Until I notice another keypad on the wall. I plug in the code. The ramp engages, lowering with a screech.

Fuck! I shoot a panicked glance over my shoulder. There is no way those men didn't hear that. As soon as the ramp is low enough, I jump on, climb the grate, and bolt for home. I don't stop until I'm inside Harcourt Manor with the door locked behind me.

40

THE KEY

ELOISE

Seconds later, a heavy knock comes on the back door and the knob jiggles. "Eloise, open up!" Tony yells. "We need to talk about what you saw. Let me explain."

Heart threatening to explode out my ribcage, I race to the other end of the house, initially rounding the newel post to head upstairs. I stop short when I hear a noise like a key slipping into the back lock. Fuck! As far as I know, Tony doesn't have a key, but I wouldn't put it past him to have made one when he had access to the house. I've left my phone upstairs, but my bedroom will be the first place he'll check. I spin around and slip back into the art studio. My eyes lock on the window behind the easel where I've been painting. If I slip out, maybe I can get to my car.

Fiddling with the latch, I brace my hands on the edge of the panel and push. It doesn't budge. A cursory inspection shows me why. Painted shut. *Shit.*

"I always suspected your mother was a freak, but I

wasn't sure until now." I spin around to find Tony smiling at me from beside my mother's knife sculpture, a bottle of rosé in one hand and a pair of glasses in the other. I recognize both as coming from my kitchen.

"What are you doing here?" My blood runs cold. He looks congenial enough, but I know better. I brace myself as I would if I awakened a sleeping rattlesnake.

"I followed you. I thought we should celebrate our new partnership in the operation you witnessed." He points at the floor. "It's long past time we shared a drink and talked. I heard Grams passed. We can start by sharing a toast to her." He holds up the wine. "I always liked the old broad."

I watch him easily uncork the bottle with his teeth and fill two glasses. *What the fuck are you up to, Tony?* That bottle of wine is from my kitchen. It wasn't open. Which means he opened it there, recorked it, and opened it again here.

My eyes dart toward the window. The sun is sinking but not fast enough. I glance at my watch. At least an hour until sunset. Damien will come. He promised to kill Tony. He'll protect me. All I have to do is survive until dark.

I hold up one hand. "I don't drink anymore. Health reasons."

"You'll make an exception this time. I insist." His dark gaze rakes over me, and his voice is eerily soft as he adds. "Take your coat off. Stay awhile."

Instantly, I know three things: one, Tony tried to kill me last night; two, he knows I've seen his secret operation under my home; and three: he wants me to drink the wine. Conclusion, the wine is drugged or poisoned. I'd have to be stupid to think anything else.

I glance at the window again and the sun beyond. If I can just delay him.

"Take your coat off, Eloise," Tony commands again. "Let's share a drink. You owe me that much for giving you this place."

Owe him? I bite my tongue and slide my jacket off.

His smile fades. He sets the bottle down on the large, paint-splattered table at the center of the room and moves toward me with the two full glasses in his hands. He thrusts one my way. "Drink the wine."

I take the glass but don't drink. "Why are you really here, Tony?" I ask, adding a flirtatious smile. "You're not second-guessing the divorce, are you? It'll all be over in a matter of days. Like ripping off a Band-Aid."

He rolls his eyes toward the ceiling and shakes his head. "You are one giant pain in the ass, you know that? Just drink the fucking wine, and this will all be over."

"What will be over?"

Darkness passes through his expression, turning his gaze as cold and dead as a shark's. I've seen that look before, last night in the eyes of the man who tried to kill me. Tony has come to finish the job. "You didn't think I'd let you keep it, did you?"

The words send a shiver through me, and I look down into my glass. "I'm not strong enough to fight you."

"No, you're not." He snort-laughs at the thought.

Keep him talking. "We both know how this is going to end, but first, tell me what I saw down there. It's been driving me crazy. Is that why you wanted this place so badly?"

He smirks. "You fucking Harcourts never did understand what you have in this place."

I bristle but keep my face completely impassive. "What do we have?"

"Your estate is on the Rappahannock River, sweetheart—the only privately owned land that ends at the cliffs. The rest is tribal property. The real secret of this place is the caverns."

"Is that what I saw?" As if there were any other explanation.

"Caves in the side of your cliff lead from the river to an underground network of caverns perfect for conducting delicate business. Oh, and these are special caves. Unbelievably unique. They make the bat cave look common. Unless you know what you're looking for, you might not even see the opening from the river. But you better believe that you can drive a boat right into the cliff and park it safely in a space the size of a warehouse. My family invested a lot of money to make it work like a warehouse too."

My stomach twists as I put two and two together. "The sinkhole."

"Nothing gets past you." He chuckles wickedly. "Yeah, there was no sinkhole. While we were renting the Anderson's, we ran everything from the farmhouse, and the series of caverns under it. But when the Andersons canceled our lease, we needed to move more of the operation underground. I put the crack in your foundation while you two were getting your grandmother's nails done, then paid the inspector to tell her it was a sinkhole. All those workers we paid for? They fixed more than the foundation. The operation we have down there now is state of the art."

"We?"

"The Denardi family."

Organized crime. Just as Maeve had suspected. I don't stop to beat myself up over not realizing the obvious. No time for that. I swallow. *Keep him talking. Tony loves to talk about himself.* "I have to give you props. It's brilliant. You ship the counterfeit money in on trucks via the access road. Was it you who got the old Anderson place condemned?"

"We couldn't have the Andersons moving back in. There are woods between this house and the road. Not so on their side of things. We were too exposed. I greased a few wheels and made sure no one else would be living there."

I glance again at the sinking sun. "There's something I don't understand, though. Once you put the money on the boat, what then?"

"Down the river, out the Chesapeake Bay, to a cargo vessel in the Atlantic where it's disguised among other cargo and shipped to the Caymans."

I nod. I can see it all now, the piece I was missing. "You deposit it in the offshore account of Genesis Corp before wiring it back to yourself as consulting fees."

He preens. "There are a few other transfers before it makes it back to me. By the time it does, it's completely clean."

Hell, if the fucker isn't a miserable, egotistical narcissist with self-aggrandizing tendencies. He tricked my grandmother, all so he could—I gasp, realization dawning as the timeline falls into place. "Was that why you married me?"

Snorting, he offers a dismissive shrug. "Why I dated you. Why I married you. Why I was even there on the side of your fucking cliff to keep you from jumping that day. It always made me laugh how you never questioned why I was just wandering around your property."

"Wow." I wish I could say it doesn't hurt, but it does.

"Did you think I had a crush on you, Eloise?" He laughs harder. "Following you around like a puppy? No, sugar. I was there making a plan for how to scale the operation. Why do you think I encouraged you to go away to college, only to insist you quit your teaching job only months after we were married?"

I've wondered about that. I always thought it had to do with control, the hallmark of an abuser, but the hostility in Tony's eyes tells me it's something more. "Why?" I can't keep the pain from soaking the word.

"I needed to keep you away from home. Your grandmother was easy. She rarely left the house and never at night. But if you were here, you were a liability. You, Eloise, liked to take long walks to the cemetery or the cliffs. And then, when you took the job at the local high school and would pop in to check on your grandmother at any given moment, you became a liability again."

"So... everything I thought you did for me wasn't because you cared for me at all. It was to keep me away from the property so I wouldn't discover what you were doing." I swallow down the urge to be sick, my stomach tightening like he's punched me. If there is anything more painful than learning he wants me dead, it's learning that he never loved me. All my memories are false. I've been used in the most cruel and intimate way.

"Now you're getting it." He gives me a pitying look. "Don't take it personally, doll. This started way before you." A wicked glint sparks in his eye.

All the breath leaves my lungs. Oh my God. Is he suggesting what I think he is? My eyes narrow, and my next words come in fits and starts. "Tony, are you responsible for the deaths of my parents?"

He places a hand on his chest. "Not me, personally. My dad handled that one. They asked a lot of questions, your parents. Always nosing around. If it makes you feel better, Pop said they weren't easy targets."

Everything in me sparks into a burning rage, and I hurl the glass in my hands at Tony with all my strength. He raises his forearm and blocks it from hitting his face, but the glass shatters, slicing into the meat near his elbow. Never taking his eyes off me, he reaches around, plucks the shard from his flesh, and tosses it aside. I wouldn't have thought it possible for his gaze to turn more murderous, but it does.

As quick as I can move, I reach for my palette knife, but he's on me in an instant, punching my head and clutching at my throat. I desperately block his blows, screaming for him to stop and then losing all the air from my lungs when his knee connects with my gut. I double over, but he drags me up by the throat. Black dots circle in my vision. I need air. I pound on his arms to no avail.

"Fine. You don't want to go to sleep peacefully. I'll put you to sleep with my own two hands, you fucking cunt."

No air. My blows to his arms grow weaker and weaker. The black circles in my vision expand in size until the darkness overcomes me completely. And then it's all there is.

4I

A MOTHER'S LOVE

ELOISE

When I can see again, I'm no longer in the studio but standing on the side of the cliff behind our house, the river raging below me. Not the river I know though. This one flows with liquid fire, the stone dark and porous as lava rock. Ash rains from the sky like snow. Have I died and gone to hell?

"Oh, Eloise, this isn't how we'd hoped to tell you." My mother appears beside me.

"Mom?"

"Your father is here too." She gestures behind her and I see Dad heading toward us, Max at his side. The dog's tail wags and his gait is a light, happy jog. Despite the ash and the hellscape behind us, when I turn to face him, it's paradise. The sun is shining. Narcissus blooms in the yard between us and my house, which rises in perfect splendor before me. When I look to the porch, Grams and Gramps wave to me from their rockers.

"Am I dead?"

"Oh no, sweetheart. Not yet. But if you're going to beat that bastard, you need to connect to what is rightfully yours. I'm afraid we waited too long to show you how." Her oversized blue eyes spark with magic.

My back starts to itch and I squirm.

Her arms wrap around me, pulling me into a hug. "You hold the keyspell, Eloise," she whispers into my ear. "There's magic in this land. Magic in your blood. It's time you used both."

"What keyspell?"

She pulls back. "It's already in you. You've already tapped into it. You simply didn't know what you were doing."

"I don't understand." I have no idea what she's talking about but the itch between my shoulder blades has turned into a burn. I reach to scratch it and realize it's my tattoo.

"The thing about the underworld is it links to everywhere. Every dimension. Every source of magic. Every soul. You hold the key, the ultimate key, just as we once did. We created it, your father and I, fueled by dragon's blood and Harcourt magic." She cups my face in her hands. "You share a sigil with the rest of the order, but the Harcourt keyspell is yours and yours alone. Find our grimoire. It will tell you everything you need to know."

"Your grimoire? What grimoire?"

My father reaches us and places a hand on my shoulder, and I gasp as pure energy flows into me. I've never tried drugs, but I have to believe this is what they feel like. It's like I've ingested ten cups of coffee. I have lightning in my veins.

"It's time, Eloise," my father says. "Deal with him quickly. What we've given you won't last. We'll help you."

"But... but... What should I do? How do I stop Tony from killing me?"

"Everything you need to know is in the attic," Dad says. "You'll learn with time."

"I don't have time," I protest.

"Wake up," Mom yells. "Wake up, now! We're with you. We're always with you."

"Wait!"

No explanation is forthcoming. The world fades from light into drowning darkness and then light again. I rejoin my airless body. The pain is instant and excruciating. My lids flip open to find Tony's psychotic face leering as he squeezes the life out of me. Again, I stretch for the palette knife, but it remains frustratingly out of reach by a matter of inches. *Come on. Come on.* I try to force my joints to grow longer and pull against his merciless grip with all my strength.

Suddenly, the cup rocks on its base, then tips over, sending the knife flying directly into my grip. Without hesitation, I plunge it, hard and fast, into Tony's side, up and under his bottom rib.

The look of surprise on his face is priceless. He releases my throat and stumbles backward, confusion warping his features as he glances first at the knife in his side and then at my mother's sculpture. A metal-on-metal whir fills the room as the blades shift and rotate. Tony's dark eyes widen to the size of saucers .

With air burning down my raw throat, I push myself off the wall, take three running steps, and kick him right in the chest. I'm weaker than him, starved for oxygen, and barely hanging on. But Tony, distracted by the sculpture's eerie whine, stumbles. Swords and daggers slice through his back like he's made of butter, scooping and lifting him off the floor.

Only then does the sculpture screech to a halt. Arms spread wide and pierced through, Tony gurgles, a scarecrow on a stake. Blood dribbles from a dozen open wounds. He mouths something foul, his expression stained by disbelief, but there's no air in his lungs to fuel the words.

He struggles, kicking his legs and flailing his hands, but the blades hold him. Slowly, the light fades from his eyes. I wipe his blood from my face with the back of my hand.

"You will never, ever have my home, you filthy, evil bastard. Enjoy hell."

His head lolls forward on his neck, and his muscles go limp. Tony is dead.

Stumbling back, I catch myself on the wooden table and try my best just to breathe. Every sip of air feels like fire. My arms are covered in red marks that I'm sure will turn to bruises, and the skin of my face feels tight from dried tears and blood and probably more bruises too. I flash back to Tony beating my head. I'm hurt, and the longer I stand there, the adrenaline draining from my body, the more I feel it.

My knees decide they can't hold me any longer, and I sink to the floor with my back to the table leg, staring up at Tony, impaled on my mother's sculpture. The knives actually moved. My mother is here. Somehow, she protected me.

I take refuge in that thought as Tony's blood pools closer to my toes. I hug my knees to my chest so I won't get blood on my shoes. Then I rest my head on my folded arms and return to the darkness.

42

BLOOD LEGACY

DAMIEN

I wake before twilight, opening my eyes with one thing on my mind: killing Tony and bringing Eloise his head on a platter—metaphorically. In reality, I'll spare her any details of the man's death. Although she understands now what must be done, her heart is too soft to enjoy it, and I don't want her to feel any guilt about what I plan to do. As far as she and the rest of the world are concerned, Tony will simply disappear. But I will know. My heart is not soft, and I plan to make him suffer. I'd kill a legion of men to protect my mate.

Closing my eyes, I take a deep breath and remember the source of that particular impulse. I mated Eloise. Despite all my promises to myself not to, despite knowing it's a terrible idea, despite not asking her explicitly if she wanted to be mated, I claimed her as my own, irrevocably.

Gods, I'm well and truly fucked.

I'm free of the Gowdie curse, which means I can go

home if I find the magic to open a portal to Tenebris. But I must be careful in that quest. No one can know I'm free or I might again attract the attention of the queen who wants me as her consort. Only, even if I find a way home, I won't leave this planet without Eloise. Not now that she's my mate. But if she won't leave, what kind of life can I make for her here where the sun drains me?

I jolt when a knock comes on my door. Not the Queen's Guard again? "One moment," I call. I dress quickly, ensuring the location on my chest where my tattoo once was is completely covered before answering it. But when I open the door, it's Lazarus on my doorstep.

"Old friend, to what do I owe the pleasure?" I'm surprised to see the scribe outside the library. He rarely leaves the stacks.

The ancient vampire grins up at me with wide, excited eyes. "I hope you don't mind me stopping by at the twilight hour, but I have sensational news."

He's cradling an ancient tome in his arms. "Oh?" I try to keep my voice calm, but only three things would motivate Lazarus to seek me out. His visit is either about my curse, my way home, or Eloise's sigil. My skin prickles with excitement. "What do you have there?"

"The sigil you brought me—the tattoo—I found it, Damien. I know what power the bearer wields!"

Looking both ways to confirm the hall outside my dwelling is empty, I open my door wider and usher the scribe inside, locking it behind him. Lazarus hobbles to my table and drops the book with a dust-producing thump. "Judging by the coat of grime on that thing, I'd say you scoured every corner of the stacks to find this."

"Oh, I did." His crusty chuckle reveals all of his yellowing teeth. "It became a bit of an obsession, I admit."

"But it's definitely a sigil? A witch, then?"

He holds up one gnarled finger. "One would assume a witch, given the design. But I researched every witch family in history, Damien, and none use the collection of symbols that appear in this sigil."

"What then?"

Lazarus opens the book in the middle and turns delicate vellum pages until Eloise's tattoo stares back at me from a two-page spread written in a language I don't recognize. The scribe taps the page with his nail. "Here it is. This sigil was used exclusively by a small magical coven in England called the Order of the Dragon. There have reportedly been less than two hundred members over the centuries."

My lip curls. "I thought you said this wasn't a witch family's sigil?"

"It's not." His eyes widen. "Practitioners of this order gain their magic not from their ancestry or the elements. They use dragon's blood." His voice holds a sense of wonder.

"Dragon's blood? As in, there's a real dragon living in England."

He huffs. "Not anymore, unfortunately. If any still existed, I assure you our queen would be interested. Dragons were extremely powerful beasts."

"But, you say there once was a dragon."

He nods. "A shifter, mind you. He appeared human. I did some research. He disappeared a few years ago, and the order was abandoned. But he'd led the Order of the Dragon for some three hundred years before then. Our texts suggest that the members of the order were initiated by drinking the dragon's blood, which imbued them with a variety of powers, powers they could then refine using traditional magics. Some mimicked witchcraft, others were psychic in nature, but all were completely unique because…" He lowered his voice. "Their power is both magical *and* therianthropic by nature."

"Witch and shifter combined?" The insides of my veins frost over as I begin to ponder the implications.

"Yes," the scribe says excitedly. "Not to mention, according to this text, the runes in this sigil denote a keyspell with the power to break curses. This sigil could *free* you."

I already know this to be true. Eloise did break my curse. But I act surprised. I want to know more, anything to help her understand her power.

Lazarus grins. "Queen Valeska will be amused to learn of this. Do you think you can capture the creature you saw bearing this sigil? I believe all of us could benefit from studying it."

My talons dig into the tabletop, and my jaw clenches with the sudden desire to tear Lazarus to shreds I force my expression to remain static. "I thought you said each recipient of dragon's blood has a unique power. Why do you think this one can break my curse?"

"Ah, because the coven that developed the magic inside this version of the sigil perfected a keyspell with very specific powers. These archaic symbols refer to dissolving, breaking, and unlocking. I believe the wearer of this sigil can undo any curse. And, Damien, it is possible the bearer can unlock portals as well. Walk between worlds as easily as walking from one room to the next! The person with this tattoo could send you home to your world."

I stiffen. Eloise did break my curse, and this is her tattoo. How appropriate I've been calling her my little dragon, when it is dragon's blood coursing through her veins. But Eloise doesn't know any of this or how to control it. Her parents died before they could teach her.

"Do you think you can find the wearer again?" Lazarus asks excitedly. "The magic is very rare."

No one can ever know about Eloise. If Night Haven discovers what she is, they'll want to capture her. To own her. Even I won't be able to protect her. "No," I say flatly. "Lazarus, I thought I made it clear. I saw the symbol on a man's chest in the train station in Richmond while on assignment for the Gowdies. I have no idea who he is or where he was going. I was simply intrigued because I've never seen the sigil before."

The scribe taps his chin. "I could have sworn you said it was on a woman."

"You misunderstood. I was with a woman when I saw it. A Gowdie witch."

Lazarus hisses. "How you tolerate the company of those animators is beyond me. You bear your curse with such grace."

"Over the centuries, I've learned to survive. But even now, the candle calls to me." I draw my phone from my pocket and snap a picture of the pages. I want to show them to Eloise.

Lazarus laughs. "You won't be able to read that, my friend. That language hasn't been spoken in a century."

I shrug. "I hope you don't mind. I want to take a closer look. Indulge my curiosity."

The scribe waves a hand. "Feel free, although you know what they say about curiosity and cats." The vampire snorts, closes the book, and scoops it back into his arms.

"Thank you, Lazarus."

The vampire presses a hand to his chest and bows. "It is my sincere honor to be useful. I will be sad to give up this project. Truly intriguing."

I flash a charming smile. "I'll try my best to find something else to keep you busy."

"There's always the chance you'll see the man again and capture him for study," Lazarus adds hopefully.

"Always the chance," I repeat.

The moment Lazarus is out of my apartment, I lock the door and dematerialize, traveling by shadow, anxious to complete my mission to kill Tony and again be in the presence of my little dragon.

43

SO AM I

DAMIEN

Something is wrong. The moment I leave Night Haven and enter the network of shadows, I sense Eloise's pain down our bond. Not like before. This isn't emotional pain. It's physical. She's injured. *Fuck*, if Tony has hurt her, I'll flay his skin from his body.

The rank smell of blood reaches me the moment I manifest in her parlor. I follow the scent to an art studio at the back of the house.

"Eloise!" I find her curled in a ball, at the base of a tower of blades. Tony dangles from the structure, staring at her through dead eyes. Blood pools beneath him, spreading, threatening her even in death. Commanding the shadows, I sweep her out of its reach and carry her away from the scene of death and violence. When I feel her chest rise and fall against mine, I'm so relieved I almost weep. But any comfort I take that she's alive fades quickly when I'm unable to rouse her.

In the parlor, I gently lay her down on the green velvet sofa and carefully assess her injuries. Every inch of her is covered in bruises, even beneath her clothing. Rage kindles deep within me, a spark growing into a blaze. I feel cheated knowing Tony is dead in the next room. I almost wish the Gowdies owed me a favor so that I could reanimate his corpse and kill him again. "That fucking bastard."

Mercifully, Eloise's eyes blink open and meet mine, but they're glazed, and motherfucker, the pattern of bruises on her neck suggests she's been strangled. Her injuries are serious. More than shade saliva can heal or what little magic I wield can fix.

"You need a doctor," I say, pulling out her phone. "I'm calling 911."

She shakes her head. "No hospital."

"Eloise, you're hurt. I can't fix this." Panic rises to fill every part of me. Doing nothing is unthinkable. So much can go wrong with her fragile human body. What if there's internal bleeding? Losing her now would be the single worst moment in my existence. I'd rather have my heart torn from my chest in full sunlight.

"They'll ask questions, Damien. I'll be blamed for Tony's murder." She takes a deep, rattling breath.

A vampire could turn her, make her immortal. I'd do it, if I could, but shades have live young. It's one of the ways we differ from vampires, along with our heartbeat. Vampires turn humans.

No. I wipe the option from my mind. Becoming a vampire involves suffering death, and it doesn't always work. Cursing her to that fate is unthinkable. Not if there is another way.

"Fine." I swallow, knowing what I must do. "No doctors. But there's someone else I can call."

"Who?"

"You know who." Maeve is a powerful witch, and even amateur elementals have healing spells.

"She may not come." She swallows and winces like it's painful. "Hates me... the candle."

I grind my teeth. I'm prepared to do whatever it takes to save Eloise. Maeve is her friend but I don't trust the witch not to use the circumstances to her advantage. If I call her, it will not be beyond reason for her to expect restitution. But I don't hesitate. I will allow myself to be bound again if that's what it takes to save Eloise. Resigned, I rise and walk to the kitchen so that Eloise can't hear if I have to bargain for her life. I place the call, and Maeve answers on the second ring.

"Did not have this on my bingo card today," she says by way of hello. "Why the hell are you calling me, Advocate?"

"He hurt her," I grit out, unable to suppress a growl. "I think she's dying."

Maeve doesn't ask me to elaborate. "Where are you?"

"Harcourt."

"Where is Tony?"

"Dead."

"I'll be right there."

I end the call and rush back to Eloise's side. She's worse. When I touch her, she shivers but will not open her eyes. I tuck a blanket around her body and start a fire in the fireplace. The room warms quickly but her shivering doesn't stop. Desperate to help her, I gather her into my arms, rocking her like a child.

A frustratingly long hour later, Maeve arrives and lets

herself in the front door, pulling up short when she sees Eloise. "By the goddess."

"Thank you for coming," I say, bracing myself for the worst. What will the witch make me do to save my mate? "We need your help. Please."

"Shut up. You did the right thing calling me. I'm going to fix her. I brought my Aunt Hildegard's tea. It's never been known to fail." Maeve's voice holds a slight tremor, and I wonder how sure she is she can fix this. I'm not familiar enough with human anatomy to know how damaged Eloise is, but I sense her injuries are severe. I'm doing my best not to notice the smell of death that surrounds her.

Maeve pads off toward the kitchen and I hear her lift the kettle from the counter and start the water. She returns later with tea, and together, we sit Eloise up and rouse her enough to get a few sips down her throat. After a few more, her eyes are clearer, and the swelling is down.

"I'm so tired," she says. I release a relieved breath to hear her speak again.

"It's okay. Rest. I'll watch over you," I promise her.

"I'll stay too. At least until you've had another cup." Maeve takes a seat in the lion's head rocker near the grandfather clock.

Eloise frowns, her gaze shifting toward the fire. "Tony admitted to murdering my parents."

Maeve hisses, leaning forward to brace her elbows on her knees. "I thought they were killed in a robbery."

Eloise repositions herself in my arms. "They were, but Tony told me tonight the murder was orchestrated by the Denardi family. You were right, Maeve. They're mobsters. Everything he did, even marrying me, was to get his hands on this property and the caverns beneath it." She goes on, telling us about how Tony has been using the caves to smuggle counterfeit bills. I listen, but by the end, I can barely hear her through the roaring in my ears. I will kill every one of the Denardis to make sure she remains safe. I will bathe in their blood.

"The man was pure evil." Maeve rubs her eyes with both hands.

"I killed him," Eloise says, squeezing her eyes shut. "He's dead because of me."

I hate how much guilt I hear in her voice. Doesn't she realize she had no choice? After everything Tony had done to her, the hell he'd put her through, the fact that she can still think him worthy of life both endears me to her and turns my stomach. "How very human of you," I say, unable to keep the cynicism from my voice.

"Hmm?"

"Little dragon, you have more bruises than skin. Tony admitted to killing your parents, then tried to kill you. You didn't murder him; you defended yourself." I bare my teeth. "I only wish I could have done it for you."

"I agree with the advoc—Damien," Maeve corrects herself, forcing out my name. I tamp down vocalizing my satisfaction with the change, for Eloise's sake. "Tony's had it coming for a while now. If you hadn't killed him, you'd definitely be dead."

Hearing that makes me feel like I want to shred Tony's body just to have somewhere to direct my rage. I force my protective instincts into a box at the back of my mind. It doesn't help Eloise for me to lose my shit right now, and I'm close.

"I think he succeeded in killing me, actually." Eloise's

brows pinch over her nose. "I mean, it felt like I died... for a while. I saw my parents."

Maeve stops rocking. "What happened in your vision when you saw your parents?"

"They said I had the blood of a dragon in me. We were on the edge of our cliff. They told me I was in the underworld and that my tattoo means I can travel between dimensions. It was such a weird dream. My entire family was there."

I exchange a nervous glance with Maeve. "Your sigil contains a keyspell to open portals and you spoke with the dead?"

Eloise tips her head back to look at me. "Yes. I didn't know, Damien. I swear I didn't. Maeve suspected and I broke the candle but...I never thought my family was like hers. I never noticed any... magic before."

I kiss her head. "Shhh. It's okay. You didn't do anything wrong."

"The dragon on the door to my mother's studio, the eyes were closed and now they're open." She continues, looking back toward Maeve. "And when I reached for my palette knife to fight Tony, the cup fell over and it was almost like it flew into my hand. At the same time, my mother's sculpture started to whir."

"Whir?" Maeve chews her lip.

"The knives moved. They repositioned themselves. I kicked Tony and set him off balance, but the sculpture... the blades sliced right through him. Scooped him up into the air."

"That's definitely magic, El," Maeve says softly.

Eloise stares at the gallery wall. "I... I think there's a connection between the house and my family, my ancestors. Like they're here, helping me. Like the house is... alive somehow."

She shifts in my arms. She's agitated. Thanks to Lazarus, I know what she is and where her power comes from, but I sense she's not ready for the details. Not tonight. I pull her closer and exchange an uneasy glance with Maeve. "I have you now. You're safe."

Maeve takes a deep breath and sighs. "About that. She said there were others in the cavern. They'll come looking for Tony. Something has to be done with the body, Damien."

I nod. "I'll go."

Eloise twists in my arms. "What are you going to do? They're dangerous."

I lower my forehead to hers. "So am I, and I will do what is necessary to keep you safe. Stay with Maeve. Drink your tea. I'm going to make this go away, little dragon. Trust me."

44

THE MAGIC IN YOUR VEINS

ELOISE

"If I drink any more tea, I'm going to float away," I tell Maeve. I've slept on and off on the sofa all night, with Maeve filling my cup every time I came to. "I think I've drank an entire pot of the stuff by now. It tastes like ass, by the way."

Maeve shrugs. "Yeah, but it's working. Look at your arms."

I do and my breath hitches. The once bright red bruises are barely discernible anymore. I gently prod the skin around my eye, and that feels better too. "Your aunt Hildie is a genius!"

"Yeah. I'm pretty sure she saved your life last night. You were in bad shape."

I heave a sigh. "I can't thank you or her enough. You must know that. And after everything with the candle, I wouldn't have blamed you for not coming at all."

She brushes her thick fringe of bangs to the side, her

eyes lined with red behind her glasses. "I did take some heat from my family about that. Honestly, I was worried Aunt Hildie wouldn't agree to give me the tea. They're all so angry about losing the Advocate—I mean, Damien. But everyone agreed to give you grace because you're new."

"New?"

She looks down at her fingers. "I know you've been through a lot, and your mind is fighting the truth about this. It's a self-protection mechanism. But denial is not just a river in Egypt."

I huff. "I'm not in denial. I realize there's got to be something magical going on here, I'm just not sure what it is, exactly."

She nods, gripping the arms of the rocker. "Only a powerful witch could have broken Damien's curse. You may not have known what you were doing when you threw the candle into the fire, but your magic knew. Your magic wanted Damien for itself."

It's a sore subject that we've never fully addressed. "I... I just... I thought he'd served his time."

She waves a hand dismissively. "It's done... and a moot point. I forgive you. But this is bigger than that. It's like I said before. That pattern on your back isn't just a tattoo. It's a sigil containing your family's keyspell."

"Right." I narrow my eyes on her. "But what does it all mean. You said I wasn't a witch. You checked. Damien would have known if I was, right?"

"You're not a witch. But you're magical, just like your parents. Damien—"

"Where is Damien?" As much as I want to know what Maeve is going to say about my family, I'm worried about him. It must have been hard for him to call Maeve. He did that for me.

"He had to go back to Night Haven because the sun is rising, but while you were asleep tonight, he told me something. He didn't want me to pass it on until you were stronger. He didn't want you to worry about it."

"As you pointed out, I'm practically healed, so tell me."

"Damien's friend found your sigil in a book in the Night Haven palace library. An ancient book, Eloise, written hundreds of years ago."

"How is that possible? My mother was thirty-nine when she died. The key was her creation."

"No, it wasn't." Maeve sighs. "The key shape is a sigil developed by a secret society of witches and wizards with very rare magic fueled by dragon's blood. There have only been a few hundred members of the Order of the Dragon throughout history. Your parents were two of them. Your mother came from a family of witches, the Townsends —I found them in the book once I researched her maiden name and discovered her birthplace. She joined the Order of the Dragon as an adult. They practiced outside of London until she met your father.

"He wasn't a witch but came from a family of spiritualists, the Harcourts. I used to think your grandmother was exaggerating about the stories, but now I wonder if there really are ghosts in this house, El. The Harcourts were mediums. They could talk to the dead. Your mom initiated your father into the order and when he drank dragon's blood he gained powers. Afterward they both adopted that sigil on your back and developed the spell inside of it. The Harcourt family keyspell. They both drank dragon's blood, Eloise, before they conceived you.

Their blood is your blood. And you initiated yourself into the coven the day you tattooed that key with those runes on your back."

"So, I am part witch?"

"You have witch blood, and dragon blood, and Harcourt blood. You're magical." Her gaze drops to her tangled fingers, and she rests her elbows on her knees. "There's no one like you. There's nothing like you."

"How is this all possible?" I believe her, but I can't wrap my head around it all.

After drawing a slow, deep breath, she says, "Usually, when it comes to sigils, another witch has to be present to ignite the magic once it's in your skin, basically prime the spell until it can start drawing from its host. I, uh, I was with you the night you got your tattoo. Do you remember how much it hurt?"

I do remember. "We were both drunk, and I asked you to use your witchy powers to numb the pain."

"You were always joking about my witchy powers. We both pretended they weren't real."

"But they were," I say breathlessly. "They are. And when you touched the tattoo, the pain stopped."

"I've never been any good at healing. The pain went away because the sigil was primed with my magic. It became part of you."

I push myself up to a seated position just as silver light cascades through the window and the blood-colored leaves of the mighty red oak tree in the front yard become visible. I can't help but think of Damien, how he'd stood there, watching me through the window the first night we met. I try to picture him in his underground room in

Night Haven. I wonder if he's thinking of me. "So the keyspell... ?"

"I think it's exactly what your mother said it was."

Fuck. The idea that what I experienced was real sends goosebumps marching across my skin. "She told me that everything I need to know is in the attic." My voice trembles.

Maeve stands and walks over to me, taking my hand. "This is a lot. Try not to worry about it. I'll help you when you're better. We'll practice your magic, together."

"You'd do that for me? Still?"

"Of course. You're the only best friend I've ever had. I'd like to keep you." Maeve winks.

"I should've told you how I felt about Damien and that I planned to free him. I should've trusted that you'd do the right thing." A stray tear leaks from the corner of my eye, and I wipe it away.

"Yeah, you should have. But honestly, I'm not sure we would've agreed on what constituted the right thing." She frowns.

I rub my face. "I love him, Maeve. Like I never loved Tony. Love like you read about."

She doesn't smile. Her face becomes as expressionless as a stone.

"Maeve, say something. I know you think he's a monster, but—"

"No, Eloise, I don't *think* he's a monster. He *is* a monster. He's a shade, a rare and powerful relation to vampires, which is, by definition, a monster. But even monsters fall in love. Your feelings are real, and based on what I saw tonight, he loves you too. I want to be happy for you. I do. But you must know this relationship will be... complicated."

"Isn't every relationship?"

"He'll never have breakfast with you. No picnics in the park. No church on Sunday morning. Your life is spent in the sun. He's a creature of shadow."

"We'll figure it out."

Maeve sighs. "There's one more thing. A big thing. Something I tried to tell you before, but you wouldn't listen. When a vampire drinks a witch's blood, it has a bonding effect on the vampire. It's how triunes are usually made. The witch bonds the vampire with her blood and lures the shifter with her promise of helping him control his curse. Shades are like vampires. They're possible to bind by blood."

"I haven't bound him. I love him. This is real," I say adamantly.

"I believe you. But—"

"But?"

Before you give your heart away, just make sure it's *you* he loves and not the magic in your veins."

45
INHERITANCE

ELOISE

Maeve leaves just as the sun breaks the horizon. After a stiff cup of coffee and a slice of toast, I shuffle down to the art studio to see if I have any cleaning to do. Maeve told me that Damien disposed of Tony's body, but I am pleasantly surprised to find he's done more than that. There isn't a trace of blood left behind, not even on my mother's sculpture, which has returned to its original shape and position. The entire studio is spotless and smells faintly of bleach. "Thank you, Damien," I mutter. I'm not sure what I'd do if I had to clean it up myself. Just the thought gives me chills.

Hesitantly, I stride to the picture I painted of my family, then examine my brushes. He's cleaned those, too, and returned them to the cup I keep them in. My palette knife is gone, though, the one I stabbed Tony with. I'm thankful for that too. No way would I have used it again after what happened, not to mention, it might carry

Tony's DNA. Shit, that's two men dead in as many days in this house. A shiver runs through me.

Satisfied that there's nothing left to do, I find myself standing at the foot of the narrow back stairway that leads to the attic. I've never been up there before. My stomach flutters with nerves to think of what I might find. Another part of me fears I won't find anything. That would be the worst. It would mean my dream about my family wasn't real. I desperately want it to be real.

The old wood creaks as I climb by the light of a single bare bulb above my head. The door isn't locked, and I step through it expecting a dusty, neglected space crammed with the cast aside relics of my ancestors. What I find is a tidy room with sloping walls lined with shelves of books and baskets of trinkets and herbs. The floor is strange, painted matte black, like a chalkboard. At the room's center is a worktable, and in the corner sits a plush red velvet chair next to a side table bearing a small reading lamp.

After a cursory inspection of the shelves, I find an entire wall of journals. Some bound in leather worn soft from use, others simple composition notebooks. My mother told me in my dream I could find what I need to know about my tattoo up here, but where do I start?

I run my finger along the spines until a dull thud calls my attention toward the chair. A large, purple bound book the size of the Oxford dictionary has appeared on the side table. I'm sure that wasn't there before. I creep toward it, the hair on the back of my neck starting to rise. My breath catches when I see the cover. My tattoo is embossed in the leather, the gold foil key shape winking at me. Slowly, I reach for the book.

I jump when the sound of the doorbell ringing comes through the floorboards. Who could that be? I leave the book where it is and jog down two flights of steps to the main floor. A quick peek out my kitchen window gives me my answer. A man in a gray uniform stands on my stoop, with a truck with an A+ Windows and Siding logo parked in my driveway behind him. I hurry to the foyer and open the door.

"I'm Bob. Mrs. Maples sent me to fix your sidelight window." He glances disapprovingly at my plastic wrap and duct tape situation.

"Thanks for coming so quickly. As you can see, this is not an ideal solution."

"Nope. But I'll get you fixed up."

He hasn't even made it to his truck for supplies when Marilyn Maples herself pulls up in her Lexus SUV, dressed in a sharp gray suit and carrying a briefcase. She waves at me from the drive and yells, "I hope this is a good time, Ms. Harcourt."

I nod. Grams's life insurance policy. She told me she'd left me something to help maintain the property, and Lord knows I'll need it. It's going to take me a while to get on full-time with the district, and although I'm painting again and have some ideas for commercial work, it will take at least a few years to build an arts business, even leveraging my mother's name.

"Come on in. Would you like something to drink?"

Marilyn smooths her hair. "No, that's all right. This shouldn't take long. I have your check. I just need you to sign a few forms."

We set up in the kitchen, and she hands me a stack of papers, rattling off what they are so quickly I barely glean that they are my legal acceptance of the payout of Grams's life policy.

"We normally do this type of thing electronically these days, but your grandmother specifically requested I pay you by check. She told me you're going through a messy divorce. I've been there myself. This way, you can decide exactly where you want to deposit this and when. Maybe wait until all your banking mess is straightened out."

Will everything be straightened out now that Tony is dead? Does it even matter what I do with the check anymore? I try to look as normal as possible as I say, "Our court date is Friday. Everything should be finalized then."

"Glad to hear it. Love can be better the second time around. Trust me on this." She holds up her left hand and thumbs the massive diamond ring she's wearing. "You'll be okay. Your grandmother made sure of that."

Grams *had* made sure of it. All the life lessons she taught me have made me who I am. "Right. Of course."

"So, here you go. This should help you make a fresh start." She pulls a check from a business-sized envelope and slides it across the table to me.

I read the amount and choke on my tongue. Through a fit of coughing, I try to wrap my head around what I'm seeing. "This is for a million dollars!"

Marilyn nods. "Nora loved you so much, Eloise. She took this out right after your parents died. Wanted to make sure you were taken care of. Again, I'm so sorry. She was one of my favorite people."

She puts all the papers back in her attaché case and stands, holding out a hand to me. I shake it, still dazed by the amount of money in my hands. I had no idea Grams was leaving me this much. I wipe under my eyes as I picture her smile and know she's laughing on that porch in the next world. She would have loved seeing me speechless.

I rise from the table and follow Marilyn to the door where Bob is just finishing up with my sidelight window. But before she leaves, she turns to me and holds up a finger. "Oh, Eloise, if I can make a suggestion, you may want to spend some of that money on a security system for this place, given recent events."

"I'm sure it was an isolated incident." I gesture toward the new window. "Grams never had any problems with crime here."

Marilyn places a hand on her throat. "I'm not talking about the window, dear. Haven't you heard? There was a massacre just up the river from you last night." She lowers her voice. "Three people dead in what appeared to be mob-related violence. The FBI is investigating, but whoever did the deed burned the bodies. They're bringing in forensic scientists to determine the identities of the victims."

I gulp. "Maybe I will invest in a security system."

She nods. "I would if I were you, living out here all alone. A girl can't be too careful."

We say our goodbyes, I sign for the new window, and then they're both gone. Overwhelmed with gratitude, I carry the check to my Grams's office, where I've been putting all the bills and things, and sit down at her desk, breathing in the fading scent of her rosewater perfume. After staring at the check for a good long time, I leave it on the desk and move to the kitchen to heat up one of the many funeral casseroles for dinner.

I'm standing in front of the stove, staring at the

striking blood-red leaves drifting like fallen feathers from the tree out front, when the ugly yellow wall phone rings.

"Eloise, thank the goddess." Maeve's voice crackles down the land line. "Why aren't you answering your cell?"

"What?" I draw the phone from my pocket, noticing the ringer is off and there are six missed calls from her. "Shit, sorry. Ringer was off, probably since the funeral."

"Well, at least I have you now."

"What's up?"

"There's been an incident. I've learned that Tony's body was found dead and burned on a boat with two other men who have mob ties. The police think foul play was involved. Probably also mob-related."

Maeve reports this as if she doesn't know exactly what happened to Tony last night, and I go along because who knows who else is in the room with her, listening. We both know Damien took Tony's body. What happened next isn't too hard to imagine. "That's terrible!" I say disbelievingly. "I wouldn't have expected that of Tony."

"No one would. But, since he has been pronounced dead, the divorce is no longer necessary. I'm calling because your court date has been canceled."

"What?"

"You're effectively widowed, Eloise. I'm still investigating what that means for you with regard to Tony's estate."

"I see." I don't know what else to say. A storm of emotions wars within me. Relief that the divorce is over, guilt that I'm responsible for Tony's death, and anxiety that somehow the FBI's investigation might lead back to me. "Thanks for everything, Maeve."

"I'll be in touch once we know more."

With an uncharacteristically professional goodbye (there is definitely someone in the room with her), the line disconnects, and I reposition the phone in its cradle. I take a few deep breaths, trying to wrap my head around it all, then look out toward the setting sun.

Damien will be here soon, and I have a book waiting for me in the attic.

46

THE RIGHT THING

DAMIEN

I return to Eloise the moment the darkness will carry me, anxious to touch her again, to remind myself that she's safe, to hear her tell me she's mine. Tony is dead, as are the only other two men who saw her in the cavern. Eloise will have heard about the fire by now. Learned that Tony and his two allies were onboard. She'll know I was the one who came down on them like the night itself, who torched the evidence.

For centuries, I've been bound to another's will. Is it any surprise then, that when given the freedom to do as I pleased I opted for the dramatic? Last night, after I left Eloise, I carried Tony's limp body down into that cavern and sent a text from the phone in his pocket to the number he'd last contacted about "taking care of the issue". The issue was Eloise seeing his operation. I would have loved to be the one to kill Tony for intending to eradicate my mate, but since Eloise exacted her own vengeance, I had to settle for all that was left, namely sending a message to anyone or anything that would dare consider harming her.

When I heard the hum of the boat's engine in the sea cave, I punched through the back of Tony's skull and held him next to me like a puppet. His brain matter was sliding down my sleeve by the time his two cronies exited the trawler, one blond and one with some kind of bird tattooed on his face.

"Thanks for coming." I worked Tony's mouth like I was the ventriloquist and he was the dummy, clacking his teeth together as I added, "Tony and I would like to have a few words with you."

A clump of something dark and wet sluiced from Tony's head, glopping onto the sand somewhere near my toes and eliciting a dark laugh from me. True terror registered on their faces then.

Welcome to your darkest nightmare, assholes.

The answering barrage of bullets slammed into me and what remained of Tony, riddling us both with enough lead to kill any human a hundred times over. I laughed. If bullets could kill me, I'd have been dead a long time ago. I let them believe they hurt though. I let them believe they'd killed me. I let them completely empty their weapons into me before tossing Tony's leftovers onto the sand and flopping onto the ground.

And then I waited. Waited for those two lowlifes to creep up on me and lean over, nice and close, to make sure I was dead. With a cross and flick of two fingers, I sent a needle thin shadow to pierce the blond one's throat, while I sent a second to puncture the lung of face tattoo. The two men crumpled, dropping their empty weapons.

They needed both hands to staunch where they'd sprung a leak.

"I could kill you instantly," I said, as one crawled toward the boat while the other squirmed on the ground, reloading his gun. As if the magazine of bullets they'd already emptied into me wasn't proof enough that that plan wasn't going to work. "All it would take would be a shadow to burrow through your brain. Unfortunately for you, I'm enjoying this. Your friend Tony attacked my mate tonight. I warned him that if he touched her, I'd kill him. He's already dead, though. And I don't feel any better about what happened. Yet."

I sent another arrow of shadow though the blond's ribs, narrowly missing his heart, and then through face tattoo's liver. Then his stomach and his thighs. Their cries were wasted on me. I share none of Eloise's softness or compassion. Blood smeared across the sand as they dragged themselves away from me, and I reveled in their suffering, until I could no longer ignore the pull of sunrise. "Alas, play time is over."

Grabbing the blond one by the back of the neck, I dragged him up and bit through his jugular. His blood flowed down my throat. It wasn't particularly satisfying, but it would have to do. I needed my strength.

I released the man's throat and tossed his lifeless body onto the boat, then did the same with Tony and tattoo face, whose neck I snapped when he still showed signs of life. Then I drove the trawler out onto the river.

Conveniently, I found a red plastic container of gasoline onboard and a lighter in tattoo face's pocket. I doused the entire vessel, then lit the fucker on fire. Oh, how I reveled in that blaze, until the first rays of sunlight broke the horizon and I surfed the last shadows of the morning back to my apartment, back to Night Haven.

Eloise may never know exactly what I did to those two humans, how I cruelly prolonged their suffering, but she knows enough. All I pray is that she accepts that what I did was necessary, and that her soft heart doesn't cause her guilt or shame for it.

As usual, I manifest in the parlor beside the grandfather clock and sniff the air for Eloise's scent. It's there, but faint. I prowl the rooms of the old house, flitting from shadow to shadow until I hear her voice from above.

"Damien, I'm in the attic."

I shoot through the web of darkness and form on the landing at the top of the stairs. I can't get any closer to her. When I try to enter, the room is... locked. Inaccessible to me, even in my shadow form. "Eloise?"

The knob turns and the door swings open, power washing over me like a swarm of bees buzzing against my skin. Before I can even greet her, she's throwing her arms around me. Her lips crash into mine the moment I lean down to her height. When she breaks away, her eyes are wild with excitement.

"Come in. Wait until you see. I have so much to tell you." She takes my hand and pulls me over the threshold.

All my cells come to attention. This room is enchanted. The walls, the ceiling, the floor. Gods, what is this place?

"Is that the keyspell?" I ask breathlessly. The symbols from her tattoo are sketched on the floor, but not in the shape of the key. They're drawn in chalk along the border of a wide rimmed circle, and the power oozing off it rattles my fangs.

"It is." Her voice is soft, laden with a note of sadness. "I know what it does now."

I can't take my eyes off the symbol. I step deeper into the room and the tingling along my skin intensifies. I'm shifting into shadow along the outside of my arms and legs as if the symbol is coaxing me to change into my true form.

"It's tampering with my illusion."

Her fingers thread into mine, tears in her eyes pooling along her lower lashes. "It's your way home."

Now I do break apart, circle her in my shadow form and come together with her in my arms. My mind is everywhere, remembering what Lazarus told me, the page from the book. I shouldn't be surprised, time and time again my mate has proven herself to be more than anyone around her expects, but still, I fight against the implications. "How can you be so sure?"

Her smile falters. "It's in my parents' spellbook. My family's keyspell unlocks curses but also portals between worlds. That's how I was able to speak with my parents when I... when Tony..." Her gaze drops. "When he was strangling me and I might have died."

A growl rumbles in my chest. "He's dead. They're all dead. He'll never hurt you again."

She places her palms on my cheeks. "I know. I know. Thank you for that. The boat, the fire."

I'm relieved she understands and accepts what I had to do. Taking her hands between my own, I say, "We'll have to be careful. There could be others in the Denardi family. If they suspect you were behind his death, they'll come for you."

Her gaze falls to our coupled fingers, and although her

brow creases, she doesn't respond to my warning. "The keyspell will carry you home to Tenebris, Damien. This was my parents' specialty. They developed it after drinking dragon's blood when they were members of a coven called the Order of the Dragon. According to the spell, all it needs is your blood. If I've drawn it correctly, and it works as the book instructed, the symbol will open a gate to take you home."

Instantly, I know everything she says is true. I can feel the pull of the symbol, practically smell the warm scent of the crimson fields of my world. A pulse in the air around us beckons me to activate the magic. The idea that I'm so close to going home, to potentially seeing my parents and siblings again, to righting centuries of wrongs, is almost overwhelming. The draw of the symbol tugs an invisible cord in me, tying it into a knot that clogs my throat and makes it hard to breathe.

"What about you?" I squeeze her hand tighter. "What about us?"

"What about me?" Her tone is light, but her eyes tell a different story.

"You're my mate, Eloise. I will not leave without you." I pull her closer, until we are nose to nose. "Come with me," I say quickly. "I will make you a princess of Stygarde. My people will adore you. My family will be your family. We will not be separated by night and day."

She opens her mouth, closes it again. "I want to, but I can't. Not yet. Not now. I just found this place." She sweeps a hand toward all the books and baubles on the shelves lining the walls. "I need to learn my family's magic. Maeve is going to help me. I have to know who I am before I become someone else."

I stare down at our coupled hands. "Then I will remain here."

"But you can't stay because of me," she grits out. I can smell the salt in her tears, and the scent burns in my throat. I hate that scent. I never want her to cry, especially not because of me.

"I can and I will." My voice is trashed and comes out more as a growl than human words, but she hears me and understands.

"No, Damien. I can't keep you from your home, your family, your people. What the Gowdies did to you was wrong, and this is the way to make things right."

My muscles tense like I'm being torn in two. I do want to go home, but every instinct tells me I can't leave her behind.

She's sobbing in earnest now. I've longed for home, but I know she'll always regret it if she doesn't uncover the secrets this room holds.

I take her face in my hands, my mind made up. "Then I will stay for as long as it takes for you to read every word and practice every spell in this room, and when you are through, and only then, I will return home with my mate on my arm."

She wipes under her eyes. "Are you sure?"

"Beyond certain."

Her lips draw into a smile. "Damn it, Damien, I love you. With everything I am."

"I love you too, my mate."

The emotions I'm feeling for her are too strong to contain. My lips crash down on hers and my form slips. Before I know what's happening, I'm looking down on her from a greater height, my hands larger and taloned, my skin darker. Her eyes widen as I spread my wings, my tail flicking behind me. "The magic in this room is powerful," I say softly. "It's hard for me to hold my illusion here when my instinct to claim you owns me. We'll have to go downstairs for me to change back."

She runs her hands up my chest, then around my sides. My cock throbs at the feel of her touch. "No. Let's stay here," she says softly. "I think I like you just as you are."

"Little dragon, are you sure?"

Her hands wrap around my shaft, their color pale against my shadowy skin. Gods, it feels good as she starts to work me from base to tip. I lean down to kiss her carefully around my fangs, as I stroke along her spine, careful not to tear her skin with my talons. She pulls back just enough to get her shirt over her head and the rest of her clothes off as the rumbling purr of my excitement fills the room.

I take her by the shoulders and pull her against me again, so small, so soft. Smoothing my hands down her back, I cup her ass and drag her up my chest so we're face-to-face.

"Oh, yeah. I like this side of you," she says, in a heady voice, course with heat. She spreads her legs wide to wrap around my hips.Her fingers explore my mane, my horns, my wings. She trembles.

"I won't hurt you," I rumble, wishing I could control myself and appear more human for her.

"I know." She kisses me again, but when I draw in her scent, I can tell she's not ready. Not yet.

I lift her higher. I will give my mate what she needs.

"What are you—? Oh!"

Resting her thighs on my shoulders, I brace her back

against the wall and lap up her folds, holding her in place, tasting her, pleasing her. My shadows rise to caress her skin, circle her breasts, brush along the arch of her foot, the back of her knee, the space behind her ear. She sighs as I tease her most intimate flesh. Her fingers dig deeper into my mane, encouraging me. Another lap up her center and I delve inside, spearing her.

"Oh, God, your tongue—Oh my God. Oh my God." My little dragon is learning the joy of a shade's tongue, its texture rougher, its length longer than in my other form.

I lick along her inner walls, then graze the side of her clit in the way I know she enjoys. In time, her body loosens, her scent telling me she's close to finding her release. Hands braced on my horns, her thighs tremble against my cheeks. I work her tender flesh until her body spasms against me, the room echoing with the sounds of her pleasure.

Now she's ready.

"I never knew it could be like that," she says, as I slide her body down mine until the crown of my weeping cock is at her entrance. "It's like you know exactly how to please me."

I kiss her softly, then run my nose through her hair, breathing in her scent. "Always. You're my mate," I explain, although I wonder if the bond is the same for her. Ever so slowly, I enter her inch by inch. She's small and tight, and I don't want to hurt her. But she wraps her calves around my back and squeezes, drawing me deep, hard, and fast. I hold her there as she gasps and pants.

"Yes. Oh, Damien, yes!" She writhes against me.

I lift her almost off of me and then thrust into her, hard.

She cries out. "More! Oh fuck, more." She clings to my neck as I spread my wings and give myself over to the monster I am. The walls rattle. My entire world is her ragged breath. She thrashes her head back and forth, her eyes rolling skyward. "Yes! Yes."

When her inner muscles contract around me, it's all I can take. I fill her with my seed and sink my fangs into her throat. Her blood and her body are pure ecstasy and the tiny, satisfied mews she makes fill me with pride. I've pleased her. There's nothing a shade values more.

I'm still holding her close when I begin to shift, morphing into my human-like form. Gently, I lower her to her feet.

She strokes her hands over my shoulders and blinks up at me through full lashes. "You're back."

I offer her a lazy smile. "You've appeased my inner beast."

She laughs through a lopsided grin. "He appeased me as well. More than once." Her legs shake and I move to help her into the red velvet chair, but she shakes her head.

"Wait, I'm covered in you." Her fingers trail down my chest and gesture to her lower half. Her thighs are slick with the results of our mating. I love it. My scent covers her, exactly as it should. But she points to her shirt. "Can you?"

Of course I can. I'll do anything for her. As I cross the room to retrieve it, I smile at her over my shoulder. I want to carry her downstairs, put her into a hot bath.

The moment I lift the shirt from the floor, I know something's wrong. A sound like the buzz of cicadas in late summer has me on high alert. Light flares around me, locking me in before I can take another step. I try to leap through the beams but I bounce off the magic, skin burning.

"Damien!" Eloise rushes toward me. "What's happening?"

She looks toward the symbol she'd readied, but it isn't *her* magic encircling me. I know all too well what this is. My hair blows back in the mounting power. "It's another trap. One that requires my blood. *The Gowdies!*" I growl my fury that they'd dare recapture me.

"No. She promised!"

The light herds me backward toward a whirling vortex of nothingness. It's dark but there are no shadows in those depths. Nothing to cling to. I shift into my native form again and dig my talons into the floorboards, but it's no use. Inch by horrifying inch, the wood gives way as my claws tear through and I draw closer to the inevitable. I can't escape this.

I meet my mate's eyes. I have no words.

Wild eyed, Eloise thrusts her hand through the light, and grabs on to me. "What do I do? How do I stop it?" She squeezes my arm, but her grip slips to my wrist, then my fingers.

Over my shoulder, the glimpse I get of the widening portal tells me all I need to know. She can't stop this. No one can. My feet are already gone. I lock eyes with her again and shake my head.

"Damien!"

My fingers slip from hers.

[Read on to enjoy an excerpt from Battle for the Shadow Prince—>]

EXCERPT: BATTLE FOR THE SHADOW PRINCE

Chapter 1
Blood and Binding

DAMIEN

I lose my grip on Eloise's fingers, and dread consumes me. Not again. The Gowdies captured me once with their dark magic. To do it again now, after everything, after Eloise, it's too cruel to fathom. I will kill them. I will kill them all.

As a shade, I'm usually soothed by the darkness, but the shadows I command are gone, magically stripped away to leave nothing but a void. I fall and fall and fall. Eloise's expression of anguish grows smaller, more distant, as the black throat of the portal constricts, swallowing me. I roar as it closes completely, cutting off the channel between us. All that's left is nothingness and pain and loss. Until I drop into a blinding ring of conjured sunlight. My wings flare and my talons itch to tear through as many Gowdie witches as possible. I won't allow them to bleed and bind me this time. Not again.

"Welcome back to the palace of Night Haven, Damien. It's been far too long."

That's not a Gowdie voice that pierces the blinding light but one from my nightmares. *Fuck*. How... how did she find out so quickly?

"Valeska." The vampire queen's name leaves my mouth on a hiss. My wings spread defensively until the tips singe against the bright circle containing me. I retract them with a wince. That's pure sunlight. We're underground in Night Haven, but this is the real thing. No vampire can wield this kind of magic. She has help. Powerful help.

"Damien." The slight tip of her head conveys the greeting. "Allow me to introduce you to my new friends." She gestures toward two humans to our right, twins. The exceptionally tall and narrow Korean men have spiky, blond-tipped hair and high-collared dusters embroidered with a sun sigil over the left breast. "This is Tae and Lang of the Kim family of witches. I'm sure you've already guessed that their family's keyspell is sun wielding."

Shit. Powerful help indeed. Sun wielding is rare. The Gowdies needed a coven of witches and a full ritual to summon me from Tenebris. These two did it without breaking a sweat.

"I thought witches were forbidden in Night Haven?" I say dryly.

Valeska's tall, shiny boots clack on the stone just outside the reach of the light. Although sunlight weakens me, it can kill her. At least there is that. She can't touch me without breaking the magic that binds me, and if she breaks the spell for any reason, for any length of time, my shadows will slaughter every being in this room, including her.

"I make the law here, Damien. You'd do well not to forget that." Her words snap like a whip. "I have to admit I hesitated to employ their help, given our general distrust of each other as a species, but when Lazarus explained how the Gowdies captured you, I realized the beings who could bind you would also be the only ones strong enough to free you, and as it so happens, the Kim family owes me a favor."

I clench my jaw as she paces around the walls of light, studying me as her blood-red fingertips drum on her biceps. She knows. Somehow she's learned I'm free of the Gowdie curse. A low growl percolates in my chest, and I search the boundary for vulnerabilities. Even though the light keeps me from using my shadows, if I can charge through the beams, escape is possible.

"Don't try it," she snarls, presuming what I plan to do. "I promise you the Kims will not allow you to leave this room without my permission."

"And when will that be?" I grit out. I position myself at the exact center of the symbol, where the light is only a mild irritation.

Her nostrils flare. A vampire's sense of smell is unparalleled. There's no doubt what she's picking up in this enclosed space. Eloise. We had sex not ten minutes ago. I am covered in her. I dig my talons into my palms as my protective instincts rage.

"Imagine my surprise when I engaged the Kims to break your Gowdie curse only for them to discover via their private network that someone had already broken it!" She bares her teeth. "What luck. I'm sure it would've been only a matter of time before you shared the happy news with me. I've made it known to you twice now that I need a consort and you are my first choice."

"Let me out and we can discuss it," I say calmly. One shadow is all I need.

She huffs. "Oh, Damien, don't take me for a fool. The stench of human sex coming off you carries the unmistakable musk of bonding. You've already mated someone. Didn't take you long to find a willing partner. Not surprising considering your power, although I am shocked you chose a human." Her gaze hollows, turning impossibly darker and even more soulless. "They are so incredibly breakable."

Every part of me longs to knock Valeska's head off her body. Mentioning the vulnerability of my mate is meant to be a threat, and it takes all I have in me to suppress my murderous response. But I must suppress it. Valeska is deadly in her own right but weakened by sunlight—my only chance at freedom is convincing her to release me. That won't happen if she suspects I intend to kill her.

"Why have you brought me here, Valeska? What do you want from me?"

"You know what I want."

"I won't be your consort." Even vampires have rules and limitations. I will never voluntarily agree to be Valeska's consort. If she tries to force me, I'll either escape or kill her the second she frees me from this cage. She wants to use me as both protection and a weapon, but as long as I have free will, she can't let me out of this cage. I'm useless to her in here. The only way she can take my free will away is to bind me. If she forced a mating bond, my instincts would compel me to protect her. Not only could

I not kill her, but no matter how much I wanted to, it would be almost impossible for me to avoid executing her commands. Mated shades, like mated vampires, serve their mates.

Vampire tradition, though, forbids taking a mate without their consent. Mating is more than sex; it's bonding by blood and old magic. As queen, Valeska could ignore that prohibition and force a mating bond on me. She'd likely even escape any reproach for it. But she can't ignore that I am already mated. A vessel can only hold so much, and mine is full. My biology will not allow me to have sex, let alone mate another as long as Eloise is alive.

The last thing I want is for Valeska to target Eloise. The queen absolutely cannot know my mate's identity. The second she does, she'll send the finest soldiers from her army to kill her. I can't let that happen. Maybe I can distract her. "I'll be returning to my homeworld as soon as I find a witch who can open the rift. I'm the wrong choice for you."

"That would be counterproductive, Damien. You're needed here. I find your specific talents to be exactly what I'm looking for in a mate and consort."

Yeah, the ability to serve as her combination blood bag and watchdog makes me the ideal companion. Only problem is I hate the bitch, and the idea of spending a single night in her bed, let alone hundreds, turns my stomach. I'd rather fall on my blade. "Not interested."

"Maybe you just need the proper motivation. Who is it I smell on you Damien? Who is this human woman you've mated?"

I say nothing. I'll die before I offer a single thing about her.

"Who is she?" Her shrill voice echoes off stone.

I glare at her from my prison of light.

Our eyes lock, and I don't mask my hatred for her.

She releases a frustrated hiss. "Conjure the woman!" she commands the Kims.

Tae exchanges a worried glance with his brother. "If you have a vial of her blood, we can attempt it once we've rested."

"Of course I don't have her blood. Use his. He must have drunk from her."

Lang swallows hard, then bows. "Your Majesty, it isn't possible. While he is surrounded by light, he is mortal. If her blood remains in his system, its magical properties are, unfortunately, destroyed and therefore useless to us."

The way Valeska's lips peel off her teeth removes any pretense of humanity from her visage. She's an animal. An unholy demon.

"Bring the scribe!" the queen commands.

The sound of footsteps heralds Lazarus's arrival. Armed guards escort my friend and confidant into the room. His conformation is even worse than normal, his skin ashen and papery, as if he's underfed. The guards thrust him forward, his oversized nocturnal eyes blinking against the bright light that surrounds me. "My queen?"

"Is there a spell in that vast pile of books you keep that the Kims can use to conjure Damien's mate? Something in the lost-or-forgotten-magic section, perhaps?"

Lazarus frowns, his bulbous eyes seeking mine for a fraction of a second before he rushes forth an answer. "No, my queen. It is impossible without her blood."

I grimace. In all my years of friendship with the scribe,

he's never called something impossible. There's always more research to do. Finding lost magic is his specialty.

Valeska's scowl turns murderous. She knows he's lying. "How can you be sure, scribe, unless you check every book?" She bares her fangs. "Guards, escort Lazarus back to the stacks and keep him there until he finds a way to be more… helpful."

"Yes, my queen." One guard bows, then takes Lazarus roughly by the arm and drags him from the room.

Valeska redirects her rage-filled glare at me. "Who. Is. She? Tell me now and I will show you mercy."

Mercy, my ass. Eloise poses a problem for Valeska, and she knows it.

"Who is the woman?" she demands again.

I flash a wicked, taunting grin. "Come to me through the sunlight, Valeska, and I'll whisper her name in your ear."

The vampire queen paces around my cell, wringing her hands. She's frustrated. This plan of hers won't work and she knows it.

"Tell me her name."

"Free me and I will." *Right before I slice your head from your shoulders.*

Valeska laughs, and the sound is like shattering icicles. Frigid. Brittle. Heartless. "I'm afraid that won't be possible, Damien. You see, I may not be able to mate you or take you as my consort under the circumstances, but I am within my power to keep you as my political prisoner for as long as necessary."

"Political prisoner?"

"Yes. You've admitted to me you herald from a different world, a different kingdom. How do I know you haven't been spying on Night Haven the entire time you've been living among my vampires, taking advantage of our hospitality?"

"That's bullshit and you know it."

She shakes her head. "One way or another, you'll remain at my side. Give me your mate's name and your living conditions will be far more comfortable."

"I will never give up her name." I growl, baring my teeth.

She turns toward the Kims. "Please escort our guest to the cell we've prepared."

Tae lowers himself into a crouch and circles his forearms at the elbow, hands clutching invisible spheres. I'm temporarily blinded by a flash of light that stings my skin. Weakness and fatigue settle on me like a disease, and I stagger forward just as the symbol dissipates.

Immediately I attempt to escape through the network of shadows, but my power fizzles, and it doesn't take long for me to understand why. My wrists are bound in front of me in cuffs of pure sunlight. All my energy drains into those cuffs. My knees wobble with the effort to remain standing.

Valeska flashes an evil grin. I cringe when she crosses to me and brings her blood-red lips close to my ear. "In time you'll be begging to be my mate."

My teeth grind even as my bones ache where the light shines through my skin. My voice holds every ounce of hatred I feel for her as I respond. "Don't. Bet. On. It."

Thank you for reading A Bargain With The Shadow Prince, A Bargain with the Shadow Prince, book 1. If you enjoyed this title, please leave a review wherever you buy books!

Damien is captured, but this time, he won't accept his servitude so easily. He'll do anything to reach his mate or die trying. Eloise has the power to free him again, if she can find him and tap into the magic of her house and sigil to face a ruthless enemy. It will take both their powers, working together, to survive what is to come. Continue their story with BATTLE FOR THE SHADOW PRINCE!

MEET GENEVIEVE JACK

USA Today bestselling and multi-award winning author Genevieve Jack writes wild, witty, and wicked-hot paranormal romance and romantic fantasy. She believes there's magic in every breath we take and probably something supernatural living in most dark basements. You can summon her with coffee, wine, and books, but she sticks around for dogs and chocolate. Her novels feature badass heroines, fiercely loyal heroes, and fantasy elements that will fill you with wonder. Learn more at GenevieveJack.com.

Do you know Jack? Keep in touch to stay in the know about new releases, sales, and giveaways.

facebook.com/AuthorGenevieveJack
instagram.com/authorgenevievejack
bookbub.com/authors/genevieve-jack
tiktok.com/@Genevievejackbooks

MORE FROM GENEVIEVE JACK!

A Bargain With the Shadow Prince Series

A Bargain With The Shadow Prince

Battle for the Shadow Prince

Bartered by the Shadow Prince

Bride of the Shadow King

The Treasure of Paragon

The Dragon of New Orleans, Book 1

Windy City Dragon, Book 2,

Manhattan Dragon, Book 3

The Dragon of Sedona, Book 4

The Dragon of Cecil Court, Book 5

Highland Dragon, Book 6

Hidden Dragon, Book 7

The Dragons of Paragon, Book 8

The Last Dragon, Book 9

The Angel of Paragon, Book 10

The Three Sisters Trilogy

The Tanglewood Witches

Tanglewood Magic

Tanglewood Legacy

His Dark Charms Duet

Lucky Me

Lucky Us

Knight Games

The Ghost and The Graveyard, Book 1

Kick the Candle, Book 2

Queen of the Hill, Book 3

Mother May I, Book 4

Logan (companion novel)

The Wolves of Fireborn Pack Trilogy

Fated Bonds

Feral Instincts

Forever Mated